THE TALE OF THE MILLER'S HANDMAIDEN

BY JIM IZATT

ISBN: 10:1477594647
ISBN: 13:978-1477594643

Dan had finished his last full day of work, before retirement. As he wandered out of the office, he was struck on the head by a rock, falling from the sky. He yelled, "OWW!", and looked up. He saw nothing, except for a couple of ravens flying by. He looked around, and found a stone, about two inches across, with a note, carefully tied to, and protected, on the rock. As Dan reached down to pick up the rock, he muttered, "What the Hell……?" He untied, and unwrapped, the mysterious message, and thought to himself, "Why would anybody want to do this?" The message read:

16 MARCH

"Good Evening, Sir Daniel! Congratulations on having reached this momentous occasion. I will now extend to you the opportunity to come and join me, as you prepare for the next phase of your life. Should you make the right decisions, tonight, your journey will begin."

Sir Percival the Great.

Dan thought, "What the Hell are you talking about? Is this a joke?" However, he had the presence of mind to pick up the offending rock, and put it in his coat pocket, along with the note, which went into his shirt pocket. He continued walking on his route to the appointed bar, designated by his friend, Bill. Dan, upon reaching Shenannigan's Pub, walked inside, spotted Bill seated at a booth, and went over, to sit down and join him.

Bill said, "Congratulations, you have survived your time in servitude, in the place of filth and excrement! In honor of this special occasion, I have persuaded the Barkeep to bend the rules, just a little bit, with the help of my friend, Andrew Jackson, to make a slightly oversized Grasshopper, for you, also in honor of St. Patty, who will help us with this party."

Bill shoved a freshly made Grasshopper, appropriately very green in color, at Dan, while explaining that this particular Grasshopper is a full liter in size, and double strength. Bill clinked his shot glass on Dan's full liter, knowing that the Grasshopper could not be readily lifted, without slopping it, and said, "Bottom's up!" Dan took a hit off of the green drink, decided he liked it, and then took a real slug, and said, "Nice drink. Thank You!" They chatted a couple of minutes, and then motioned for an appropriately dressed serving wench to come over, and then they ordered some munchies, and Bill said, "Whiskey, straight, and make it a double, with a slice of lemon." Dan was still working on the green liter.

Deciding that this was as good of a time as any, Dan told Bill about what had happened to him, on his way to the pub, and showed the note to Bill, while saying, "What do you make of this?" Bill read the note, and then studied it several more times, before saying, "Well, right now, I haven't a clue. I would have to refer you to this little town in Idaho, which specializes in such things : I was born there. It's called: 'Hellifino.'"

The food arrived, and Dan, having finished the Great Green Liter, got himself a, "Bourbon and water, with a twist of lemon, and please make it a double, with another one for Bill, here." They ate the food, and continued to discuss other matters of interest, but little importance, before returning to the mysterious note from the sky.

Bill said, "Well, even if it was a joke, it is a Hell of a good one! For one thing, how is anyone going to know who to hire, to get them to train a raven, to happen to fly by at the right time, to drop a rock onto your head, with a note attached? I might add, to have successfully beaned you, with a direct hit, to boot!? Who do you know, or have ever heard of, who could pull off a stunt like this one? Besides, why would they care, and how much money would they have to pay for this joke, if it is a joke?"

Having talked it around in circles several times, and not making any real progress in resolving the note, they decided to let it go, at least for now. As the hour of midnight approached, they decided that they were getting a little too sober, and got the barkeep to fix them one more drink, in honor of St. Patty's Day. Dan got another double. They settled up the tab, with the cashier, and, as the countdown went on, "seven, six, five, four, three, two, one, Happy Saint Patty's Day!", Bill and Dan gulped down their last shots at Shennanigan's, and headed out the door. As they wandered toward the next bar, Bill decided that he had had enough, and suddenly stepped into the bushes to puke. When Bill returned, he looked like about five miles of bad road. They were fortunately just about a block from Bill's apartment. Dan and Bill escorted each other to Bill's apartment, and then got Bill into his place. Dan left Bill, and went off to get a couple of more drinks, this time at O'Reilly's Pub, a few blocks farther down Broadway. He had to walk across a small bridge, and then started to slowly realize that some of the lights on the nearby streets , and some traffic signals, had all gone down. Except for the street that he was on, a lot of the rest of the neighborhood was in the dark. Dan walked into O' Reilly's, and got another whiskey. After downing that shot, O' Reilly's lost their lights, too. The staff started to escort people out the door, by emergency lighting, and closed up for the night. Dan had gone in through the front door, and was escorted out the back.

Disoriented, and in the dark, Dan staggered about, looking for a landmark that he could identify. He finally found a comfortable place to sit down, and then passed out. The last couple of drinks were just a couple too many. The seat that he slept on felt quite good, and seemed, in his stupor, to be slowly rocking him, back and forth, gently swaying him into slumber.

When he began to wake up, he became conscious of the swaying sensation, that he had noted the previous night, and also that there seemed to be a breeze, and a good stiff one, at that! Dan opened his eyes, looked up, and saw that he was in a basket, with the riggings of a balloon attached. He realized that he must be up in the air! He looked over the side, and said, "Holy Shit! What the Hell happened?" Looking down, he was able to guesstimate that he was at least about a mile in the air! As the balloon continued on its merry, and wind-driven, course, Dan looked around in the basket. He found food, and water, some blankets and coats, and another note, again attached to a rock, just like the previous one. He tore into the strings securing the note, and read it :

"Good Morning, Sir Daniel! I see that you made the predicted, and correct, choices last night. You are to be congratulated in having chosen to begin your journey. You will be safe in your current modus of conveyance. Please do not attempt to interfere with the balloon. It knows what it is doing, and the winds know where to take it. Please just relax, and enjoy the ride! If you do attempt to disturb the balloon, the results are likely to be unpredictable. Balloons are such finicky and temperamental things! In your supplies, you will note that, in addition to the food and water that were placed so as to be obvious, I have taken the liberty to include your passport. Your first destination is Northern Ireland! I have chosen the altitude, and timing, so as to take advantage of special wind conditions. You should arrive, in about five to seven days."

"WHAT?! Northern Ireland?! What kind of a nut are you, anyway, and how did I get into this mess, and why Northern Ireland?"

Dan sat back, stunned. He realized that he apparently had really done it, this time! After thinking about it some, it became obvious that he seemed to be well provided for, and reasonably safe, for the moment, so it was time for a full inventory of what he had to work with. Plenty of food, and water, for one thing, and in the pack, with him, was : his passport, some maps, crude as they were, and some good maps, as well. He also found: 20,000 Euros, flashlights, and extra batteries, matches, first aid supplies, a small-caliber pistol, with 100 rounds of ammo, and a full first-aid kit. Pen, pencil, and paper. Three sets of changes of clothes. Two coats, and a raincoat. Extra shoes. New toothbrush, toothpaste, and dental floss. In one of the pockets, he found a couple of books, and a notebook. There were also a couple of knives, ropes, and a couple of decks of playing cards, chains, a plastic tarp, and similar stuff, whose immediate value was more obscure.

"Hmmmmm! Someone seems to be REALLY wanting for ME to go someplace, for reasons which would seem to be unknown, at the moment, but why Northern Ireland?"

Having banged it around in his head for quite a while, Dan realized that he was just spinning a hamster wheel, and going nowhere, mighty fast, by doing so. His ride, on the other hand, appeared to be doing quite nicely about where it was going, thank you! So, it was time for a nap.

While it would hardly qualify for a good nap, at home, in his comfy bed, Dan slept well enough, partly because of exhaustion, partly due to sleeping off the remnants of a hangover, and also out of a resigned boredom. Some of his dreams were not exactly pleasant. His subconscious was processing what was going on around him, trying to make some kind of sense out of the whole thing.

He must have slept for quite a while, as his watch told him a time that did not make sense, until he realized that he must have crossed at least one time zone, while he was out. While the ground below gave the illusion of appearing to move slowly, due to his altitude, it became fairly obvious that the balloon must be eating up the miles. Some of those things, whose exact identity could not be easily determined, must be several miles apart. Yet they came, and were gone again, in just a few minutes. From this, and similar observations, Dan was able to arrive at a guesstimate of his speed: About 60 – 80 miles per hour. Coming at his balloon, from the direction of the sun, was another raven. The raven landed on the edge of the basket, for just long enough to drop another message-rock, and was then immediately gone again, having flown back into the sun, so as to obscure its path, away from the balloon.

Dan grabbed up the message-rock, and hurried to get it open.

"Sir Daniel. You are on course, and on schedule. Please relax, and enjoy the ride. Eat some food, and dress warmly for tonight, as it will be a little bit chilly. Wrap yourself up well. In your provisions, you will find that I have taken the liberty of ensuring that there are sleeping pills. Night approaches, and your journey will be much more comfortable, if you are asleep. During the night, you will be passing over Manitoba. The winds were chosen for this route, to avoid the rather annoying paranoia going on in the United States, over Homeland Security. Your balloon will adjust its altitude, to about 12000 feet, to maintain the target course. Sleep well. Tomorrow, you will see Newfoundland!"

Dan wondered who the Hell it was, that is doing this, and why they would bother with him? What could he possibly know, or be able to do, that someone else could not be more conveniently chosen for, would be able to do better?

As the sun was going down, he decided that it was time to take a pee, and let it fly, over the side, down wind. It would probably evaporate, before it got all of the way to the ground, and it would probably not really matter, if it did not! So, he found the sleeping pills, and drank some water, and bundled up, very well, for the night, in dutiful compliance with the instructions delivered on the mysterious rocks. At least, so far, they had not steered him wrong.

As the dawn began to break, the light caused Dan to stir from his drug-induced slumber. When he awoke, he realized that he had forgotten where he was, for a couple of seconds. He sat up, and looked over the side. Once his eyes had adjusted, Dan was able to see the leading edge of a very large body of water. Soon, it occurred to him that he was almost to the edge of the Atlantic Ocean! Dan was startled, and the realization hit him, that he would soon be out over the open water, and if something went wrong, he was going to be swimming in one Hell of a pickle jar!

Dan got some water and food, having realized that the cold night must have drained a lot of his energy reserves. He was comfortable, but definitely not looking forward to any nights that might be colder! While munching away on his breakfast, he spied another one of the message rocks, that apparently must have been dropped, during the night.

"Hello, again, Sir Daniel! It was necessary for this message to be delivered during the night, as my usual couriers would otherwise be out of the area, at the moment. I anticipated that you would be checked out for a while, and would probably not see them make the drop, anyway, since it would be dark at the time of delivery. Now that you have passed over Newfoundland, your course will require a small adjustment in altitude, and the balloon has executed the instruction set. You will likely see that your altitude has decreased to 7000 feet. This was done to avoid the unstable aspects of the North Atlantic Atmospheric Vortex, and to ride the warm winds, generated by the North Atlantic Thermohaline effect. It will take most of today, but you should pass over land, near the southern tip of Greenland."

Dan wondered, "How the HELL do YOU know so much?! Who ARE you, anyway?"

He got out a piece of paper from his supplies, and wrote out a note : "Should it happen that I die during this journey, and this note somehow survives me, be it known that I was kidnapped, in a sense, in that I did not know, ahead of time, where I was going, or even that I was going there. I was already well on my way, before I knew that I was going someplace. Included, with this letter, are the notes that were delivered to me, the first one before my journey began, and the others, which were delivered while en route, all via bird couriers."

At about this time, the winds sped up, and the altitude decreased. From the position of the sun, and the estimated time of day, he seemed to now be traveling more-or-less northeast. The fury of the winds caught his unfinished note, and ripped it from the writing surface, and out of his hands. The note was gone!

After a few minutes, the fury of the squall had passed. Dan was startled enough to just sit back, and give the whole situation a good going over, before he did anything else stupid! It was time for some more food, while he chewed over the whole situation, in light of the recent events. Dan ate, and he must have dozed some, while eating, for several hours had passed, according to his solar estimates. He looked down, and saw that he was indeed near some land, that could have been the Greenland, as explained in the latest note. At about this time, Dan realized that he was now full of shit, and he dropped his britches, and hung himself over the side, and let it fly. It did not matter where it landed, since he was still well out, over the open water. If it beaned a shark, or whatever, it was likely to be a plus! So, what the Hell?!

Twilight came and went, and Dan bundled up, for another cold night.

Apparently, the entire night passed him by, as he awoke to find a new day. He stood up, and took a pee, over the side, again aimed down wind. He had long ago realized the value of the old saying, "We hold these truths to be self-evident: Never cough, sneeze, spit, or pee, into the wind."

While rummaging in his food supplies, he discovered that another "Present" had been dropped for him, during his latest slumber:

"Sir Daniel. The winds have agreed to make a small adjustment to your arrival time. You are now ahead of schedule. Iceland will be visible to you, before too long, somewhat to your north. We believe that you should be safely on the soil of Ireland, before the volcano erupts, in Iceland."

Dan remembered that there was a pair of binoculars in his travel repertoire, and he could just see the rumbling and smoke, of what was probably the volcanic plume mentioned in the note.

"Jesus! What the Hell else is going to happen on this trip?!"

The balloon continued on its course, slowly adjusting the altitude, as needed, to maintain its heading. Not long before dusk, a raven flew up to the basket, and made a drop. Dan grabbed the message rock, as the raven sped away.

"Sir Daniel. Your balloon will come upon the shores of Ireland, just at twilight. Round up all of your supplies, and be ready to go. Leave absolutely nothing behind! You will be coming in low, only a few hundred feet above the water. The volcano will provide enough cover, along with the darkness. In the confusion, no one is likely to be looking for a balloon. When the balloon touches down, get out immediately, with everything! The balloon will not wait long! Your arrival point should be just south of the border with Northern Ireland. Load your weapon, and keep it handy. We were going to send you south, tonight, but it will be better, with the volcanic ash, which is likely to be dumped about where you will be, that you improvise a hiding place, for tonight. If you are careful, and clever, you should be able to create a small tent for tonight. The ash will obscure your location, and you can rig up a passable dust mask with the supplies in your provisions. Stay put where you set up. The ravens will report your location. Our agents will contact you, in the morning. The password for the agents, two females, is 'Persistence wins all, in the end!' Your counter-sign is, 'Yes, the Gray Ghost has helped me, many times.' They will then reply, 'The castle is on the Queen's side.' Your answer is, 'Bishop, to Bishop 7. Shah Mat!' Our agents will already know what you look like. They have seen recent photos of you. The elaborations are to further protect you, since you will not know them, because you will technically be a spy, if you are captured by government agents."

"Oh, Great!" Dan muttered to himself, "That is just what I need! No one is going to believe the truth, and I do not have any other story for them!"

He did not have too long to stew about it, for the balloon was over land, and descending quickly, just as had been foretold. Dan had his backpack on, and looked around, one last time. When the balloon touched down, he jumped over the side. After just a few seconds, the balloon floated upward, and gained speed and altitude, as it was being escorted away, by the wind. Soon, the balloon was lost to the darkness, and the increasingly dense volcanic ash, drifting down.

There was just enough light for Dan to find himself a satisfactory excuse for a half-assed shelter, when it was combined with a tarp, weighted down with some fairly heavy rocks. A low, rocky cut in the side of a hill. The rain started to come down, hard. The volcanic ash caused the rain to fall, and the rain then weighted down the ash, in turn. The rain, Dan realized, was a good thing : otherwise, he could suffocate from the volcanic glass, which would form a concrete in his lungs, even with his improvised breathing shield. So, even though he would have an added misery, he would, at least, still be alive, to enjoy his misery!

"Boy!", Dan thought to himself, "It's going to be a long night." He huddled up, and tried to keep at least a semblance of warm and dry. After quite a spell, he finally drifted off, to visit the land of Nightmares.

2

When Dan awakened, just before dawn broke, he flinched, and grabbed his handgun, as a reflex action. He shifted his position just enough, to allow a hand to move the tarp an almost imperceptible amount, and thus give him a peek out, from under the tarp. The sky was just starting to lighten a little. Since the date was near the Vernal Equinox, and all of the Earth has about 12 hours of daylight, and 12 hours of darkness, around this time, Dan was able to deduce that it must be around 6 AM, local time. He pulled his stuff together, and got the backpack ready.

Just a few minutes later, there was a female voice:

"Sir Daniel, are you there?"

Dan peeked out from under the tarp, his gun ready, "Who are you?"

"I am called Orla. We are glad that you are safe. It was a tough, but necessary, journey, and Persistence wins all, in the end."

Recognizing the prearranged call sign, Dan replied, "Yes, The Gray Ghost has helped me, many times!"

The other female agent said, "The Castle is on the Queen's side of the mountain."

Dan then replied, "Oh, very good, then the game is won, with Bishop, to Bishop 7. Shah Mat!"

Orla said, "Well, Sir Daniel, this is Maeve. We are your tour guides. Grab your gear, and let us begin. We move south, immediately! Double-Time!"

The two women rounded up, and folded, the tarp, and attached it to Dan's backpack, and made sure that there was no obvious evidence left behind. Orla said, "Good. Time to go!", and immediately started the march south, at double time. Dan had to hustle, just a bit, to fall into place, behind Orla. Maeve brought up the rear, continuously scanning for obvious clues that might have been left behind, and checking the horizon behind them.

After a forced march, of over two hours, Orla called a break, near a ravine. "This is a good spot, for a quick stop. Down here, we can be out of sight."

Dan said, as he was catching a drink of water, and a snack, "Man! You girls can move! What are you, British Intelligence?"

Maeve said, "It is best for all of us, if we know as close to nothing about each other, as is possible!"

Dan let that sink in for just a few seconds, and then said, "Yes, I understand. Of course. So, are you allowed to tell me where we are going?"

Orla, after a quick pause, said, "We are taking you to a 'Safe House', for now. There, we will rest, and you will receive the next communication, from our couriers. That message will explain what comes next. Grab your stuff. We must be on our way. There is a storm coming!"

Dan did as he was told, as Orla and Maeve looked around on the ground, for obvious problems, and then they scanned the skyline, and the air.

Orla then set off on the march, at a blistering speed! Dan could hardly believe that she was still just walking. Maeve said, "Okay, time to move!"

Dan was running, at first, trying to catch up. Maeve took a last look behind them, and moved out, as well. On and on they went, through drizzle and fog, mile after mile. At one of their rest breaks, they were delayed, for a few minutes, from starting up again, because of a squall, which passed over them. Orla grabbed the tarp and set up a makeshift, and close-fitting, shelter for the three of them, with help from Maeve. The squall turned out to be only a little less than a "Micro-Burst." Rain, and locally high, down draft, wind speeds, with hailstones that would have actually hurt, if they had been any bigger. After a pounding of almost 20 minutes, the hail stopped, and the skies cleared, which brought out the sun, and the solar radiation caused a fog to form all around them. Orla said, "Time to go. Move it on out! We know which direction to go, by the position of the Sun, and the time of day. Watch your step!"

Orla and Maeve scooped up the tarp, and folded it up enough to attach to Dan's backpack. Orla then took off, with Dan and Maeve right up behind her. They made good time, even with the fog. Maeve explained that they were able to do so, because, while they could still see where they were going, it was more difficult for someone who might otherwise see them, to be able to do so, from any great distance. Hence, aside from the low probability of someone being out here, in this mess, they are likely to be okay, for now. But they must be ready for anything, nonetheless.

Eventually, Orla made up for the lost 20 minutes, and just a little bit more. They arrived at their intended "Safe House", which, on the surface, looked like an old, and long ago abandoned, stone shelter, from at least the Bronze Age, and probably much older, just before twilight.

Maeve said, "Good. I was not looking forward to traveling in the darkness."

Orla said, "Nor was I! That squall almost messed us up."

Dan said, "Wow! You girls are good! You made up for the lost time, in getting us here, without our having to do any running."

Maeve replied, "Running is to be avoided, when possible. You can generally only run for a comparatively short distance, and energy is consumed more rapidly than it can be drawn, and the waste products accumulate faster than they can be processed out, whereas you can walk many tens of miles in a day."

Orla found the stash of supplies, well hidden in the rocks.

Dan exclaimed, "You mean that THIS is the 'Safe House' that you mentioned? I certainly did not picture it being anything even remotely like this!"

"Of course," Maeve said, "That is precisely why it works! No one in their right minds would expect such a place to be anything more than what it is : A long dead remnant, from a dead family, and a dead time. A pile of rocks, carefully fitted together.   Many thousands of years old."

"Would it be all right if we had a small fire, to keep ourselves warm?", Dan asked, "No one could see any smoke, and the fire would be inside, below the eye view of anyone who might see it, and there are many twigs, and other pieces of wood around."

Orla said, "No. No fires. Your points are good ones, but someone would be likely to find the ashes of the fire, since we would not be able to hide all of the evidence of our having been here. This place works, because it is preserved as close as possible to the way that it was. We will have to put on some dry clothes, from the supplies as provided, and eat a cold meal, and cover ourselves up, as best as we can, for the night. In the morning, we will have to be up before dawn, to prepare to leave, and must be gone before sunrise, to avoid anyone associating us with this place."

They all did the appropriate changing of clothes, ate their meals, drank some water, and then took private potty breaks outside, and covered up the evidence. Just before they were ready to settle down for the night, a raven arrived, bearing a rock, with a note attached. It made a little squawk, and Maeve saw the raven first, and said, "Oh, well, hello there! I see that you have the next message, for Dan!"

The raven squawked again, and tossed the rock toward Maeve, and then turned, to fly away into the night. Orla said, "Thank You!", just as the raven headed off. Maeve handed the note to Dan, who opened it, to read:

"Congratulations, Sir Daniel! You have arrived at the first stop. You, and our agents, have done well, especially in compensating for the weather conditions. All are to be congratulated. After this note is read, the agents are naturally expected to destroy it. I can tell you that your itinerary includes a night in Tipperary, and then you will board a small boat, to be piloted by Charon, the Ferryman, who will take you across the Irish Sea. Charon knows where you are to be taken to. You will receive the next instruction set, at your room in Tipperary."

"Man!", Dan whined, "This sure is weird! Can you girls explain any of this to me? Why am I on this journey, for example?"

Orla said, "We are not allowed to discuss this with you, and we do not know all of the details, in any case. That is necessary, for the protection of all of us! All we can say is that, if something should go wrong, you will then have to continue on, to Tipperary, alone. Sir Percival will reconnect with you, through the Ravens, and he may then provide other agents, to assist you."

"So, who is this 'Sir Percival' anyway?", asked Dan.

Maeve replied, "Again, we are not allowed to discuss that with you. Let us get some sleep. I will take the first watch. Dan, you must always be ready to move, at a moment's notice, should something go wrong."

So, Dan and Orla settled down, and went to sleep, each in their own bedrolls.

In the morning, or rather at the appointed time, since it was still not yet dawn, Orla awakened them, and they all ate some food. Orla then went outside, to hide the evidence that any one had ever been there, and Maeve cleaned up inside.

They left the Bronze Age dwelling, just as the sky began to show the first hints of dawn. At first, they walked relatively slowly, to compensate for the poor lighting, and to give their muscles time to limber up a little bit. It also allowed them to put some distance between themselves, and where they had spent the night, before anyone could really see them, from any distance at all. After several miles, the dawn caught up with them, and a fairly large dog spotted them, and came over to challenge their pathway. Orla separated herself from the other two, and Maeve moved in front of Dan. Thinking that Orla was the easier mark, since she was alone, and isolated from the other two, the dog growled, and then leaped at Orla, who then dispatched the dog, with a single knuckle-punch to the side of the neck. Orla had broken the neck of a German Shepherd, in one punch! The dog died, right there, on the spot, and they continued on their way.

"Good," said Maeve, "You left a minimum of mess."

"Yes, I like it better that way." Stated Orla, "Right now, there is no obvious, immediate evidence, of what had just happened, here."

Dan asked, "Will Sir Percival teach me this stuff?"

Maeve replied, "We do not know what you will be taught, but we have been told that you will do good work, when you get to where you are going."

Dan said, "Gee, I sure wish I had a clue of what it is, that is expected of me, when I get there, wherever 'There' is."

Orla answered, "Well, whatever it is, we must get going again," and putting action to her words, headed off to the south, with Dan and Maeve right behind her.

After a couple of hours, they stopped for water and a snack, as well as potty breaks. The group positioned themselves on the shady side of a rock outcropping, to avoid the Sun, as much as to make it harder for someone to see them, from any likely distance.

Dan asked, "Would it be alright for me to ask approximately where it was that I landed, the other night?"

Maeve and Orla looked at each other, and both nodded in agreement. Maeve said, "We picked you up near Killarga, and I suppose that we can tell you where the first real stop is, now?" as she looked at Orla , who nodded, and said, "We will be picking up some bicycles, in Carrick-On-Shannon. We need to be that far away from where you landed, and also if we get them there, nobody will think that much of three people out for a bike ride. Since you already know, from Sir Percival, that you will have a night in Tipperary, we can confirm that much, too. Beyond that, we can say nothing more, at this time."

Dan nodded in understanding, and since they were done with their meal break, Orla got up, saying "Well, we must be on our way, again." They cleaned up their rest spot, and moved on.

Late in the afternoon, they arrived at the outskirts of Carrick-On-Shannon. Since they were all pretty well shot from the ordeal, they went to the Safe-House, operated by the agents of Sir Percival, and got rooms, and then got cleaned up, and took a short nap.

Since it was still early enough, they were able to eat dinner at a nearby café. It was close to dark, as they walked back to their rooms. Two very drunken sailors, apparently on leave, approached Maeve, together, and one of them said, "Hi, beautiful! Could we take you to our flat, for the night?" Maeve said, "No, thank you! I would rather not bother with it!" When one of them tried to grab her, Maeve had both of them down on the ground, and unconscious, with broken noses, in about three seconds flat, just as Orla was stepping up to help, if needed! They dragged the sailors into the nearby dark alley, and unloaded them into a dumpster, to sleep it off.

As they walked back out of the alleyway, they dusted off their hands, and Maeve said, "Come, Daniel, let us be on our merry way!" Dan was walking between them, and said, "Wow! I am impressed! How long ago did you learn that stuff?"

Orla said, "I started my training at age three." And Maeve added, "My brother used to pick on me a lot, when I was about two. I found someone who was sympathetic to my situation, and had arranged a private teacher, for me, when I was about three. By the time I was four, my older brother was himself being punished by a little girl, who was less than one half of his weight, and one third of his age. One time, he took quite a pounding. When our father got home, and asked what had happened to my brother, he was too embarrassed to tell his father the truth : that he had just gotten flattened by his little sister, whom he was picking on. My dad, suspicious, asked me about it. I merely shrugged, and replied, 'See No Evil!' My dad laughed, and my brother never bothered me, again! "

Dan could hardly believe his ears, but he did believe his eyes! Two big guys, each of them much bigger than Maeve, were now laying in a dumpster, with broken noses, and sleeping off their drunk. They all calmly went back to their rooms, and went to bed for the night.

In the morning, they rounded up all of their stuff, and picked up their bicycles, and got away from the "Safe-House." After about 20 minutes, they found a little café. Orla signaled for a stop, saying, "We should now be about far enough away, from the little nuisance situation of last night." She looked at Maeve, and asked, "Time for some food?" To which Maeve nodded.

They had tea and sandwiches, and then filled their water jugs, and visited the rest rooms. Soon, they were off at a steady, mile-eating pace, for Tipperary. There were a few unexpected delays. One of which, was caused by an overturned truck, which had been overloaded, with an unbalanced load. It was apparently going too fast, as it made a turn. Regular vehicles were stuck, in both directions, as they waited for the mess to be cleaned up, enough for traffic to resume. However, the bicycles, which they were riding, were able to get through, without too great of a difficulty, or too long of a delay.

After they had cleared the mess, Dan said, "Well, that certainly underscores the value of bicycles, in that type of situation."

Orla said, "Yes. I much prefer bicycles, on narrow country roads. They may not go as fast in normal situations, but we also do not have to pay for the ridiculously overpriced petrol, and it helps to keep our legs, and the rest of our bodies, in good shape!"

Dan nodded in understanding, noticing that both of these girls were not only slender and muscular, but actually beautiful. They could also take down pretty near anybody, lickety-split! He started to wonder if it might happen that he will be trained in some of this stuff? It would sure be nice to know how to do it!

Hours, and many miles, later, they found another little café, and stopped for food and water. Not long after resuming their trek, they encountered a large herd of sheep, being escorted by ranchers on horses, and by dogs. Their progress slowed down to a crawl, but they were able to keep moving. It took about an hour for them, and the herd, to pass through each other, sort of by osmosis. The sheep acted as a sort of permeable membrane. The bike riders diffused their way through the herd, waving at the ranchers, as they passed them, but they did keep moving.

Several miles after the, "Close encounter of the sheep kind", Orla was a little ways ahead of the others, and a dog jumped out from some brush, along the side of the road, and was seriously challenging Dan. As the dog jumped, Maeve, who had been riding behind Dan, reached behind her back, and whipped out a knife, and threw it, all in one motion. Her very practiced eye instantly made a kill, severing the dog's Aorta. Orla got back there, just as Maeve was cleaning up her blade, and putting it back in the sheath.

Dan said, "Sheeze! Thank You, Maeve!" She merely said, "Just doing my job!"

Orla grabbed up the dog, by the hind legs, and dragged it off into the high grass, off of the side of the road. She then came back, and said, "Excellent! The chances are that the buzzards will take care of the little pest, that you had to send on his way, before very long."

Maeve said, "Yes, if the ants do not strip the carcass, first. See right over there? That looks like an ant hill!"

To which Orla replied, "Oh, well, so it is, at that! Well, let us be on with our merry little outing! We can stop for water, and potty breaks, in a few miles, once we have left the area of our rather distasteful little incident."

As they resumed their journey, Dan was thinking about the last couple of days, and was struck by the observation that these girls are highly trained, and skilled, assassins, who are so accustomed to killing, or whatever needed to be done, that it affected them no more than it would bother him to swat a fly. He then realized that it was all a matter of degree. Western societies formally reject the notion of killing, but then do it all of the time, anyway, and in so doing, generate confusion in our children. If he were to become a trained agent, he would also have to overcome the confusion, and hesitation, which was programmed into him. The advantage that these girls had, among many others, is that they were trained for this, even before Kindergarten could begin to exercise the brainwashing that would follow in grammar school, and later in life. Many religions say, "Thou shalt not kill!", but then the "Followers" of those religions go out and kill each other in, "Holy Wars", under the delusionary belief that God is on their side, and theirs is the "Just Cause." It was all just an excuse to commit murder, anyway.

After about 20 minutes of riding, they reached a place where Orla stopped, and said, "There! This should do rather nicely. We can take turns in that clump of trees, right over there. Who wants to go first? The others stay here with our bicycles."

Maeve said, "Well, I think I will. Be right back!", and she walked off, to check out the clump from various angles, before going into it.

While Maeve was gone, Orla asked Dan, "Well, are you finding that you are starting to get a little bit into shape? You have done fairly well at keeping up!"

Dan said, "Thank You. It is only by extreme will power, and by ignoring the pain, that I have managed to keep up with you. By the end of the day, I am shot for the night! I collapse, and I immediately 'Check Out', for the night."

Orla laughed, and said, "Well, I suspect that you will get used to it. It only takes about three months, to get the worst of the pain behind you, for the first part of your training. Then comes the REALLY hard stuff! Less physical, but still just as demanding. It is easier if you start getting the appropriate training, from about age two, on. This is because the brain is still in its most pliable state, where it can make the wiring associations needed, as a part of its original wiring. We CAN adapt after we get older, but it is much easier if it is done while we are still very young. So, it helps if you do it right, in the first place."

Maeve came back, and said, "Okay, that spot looks good."

Orla then said, "Well, Dan? Your turn.", and Dan nodded as he walked toward the woods.

"Well," said Orla, "He is still a little bit green, but he seems to be willing to learn, and to work at it. So, it may be that Sir Percival chose well."

"Yes", said Maeve, "It seems that he is also fairly well educated, too, but I have not really attempted to deduce what his education is in.

There is too much other stuff going on, and it was not part of the assignment. That is one which I will probably leave to Sir Percival. Just getting him to Charon is enough of a pickle, at the moment. Dogs can be such pests!"

"Aye! They can, at that!" , said Orla, "Rumor has it that Sir Percival once slapped a very large dog on the nose, and the dog backed up, and sat down, and wagged his tail, as if to say, 'Yes, Sir!' "

They adjusted their bikes, and drank some water.

As Dan was coming back, Maeve said to Orla, "Well, as long as we do not have to leave anybody else in a dumpster, on this trip, I will be happy enough."

Dan said, "Well, that was interesting. I was watching the squirrels collecting some of the other nuts, that were in that clump of trees!"

Maeve laughed, and said to Orla , "Okay, your turn."

Orla went over to the potty area, while Dan was adjusting his shoes.

Maeve said, "I think Orla will want to go, as soon as she gets back. So, you should be ready to go. We are just barely holding schedule, with these various little delays. She will be wanting to push hard, if we are to make it to Tipperary, today."

Dan nodded, and got his water out, and took a good hit off of that. And reached for a small snack, and popped it into his mouth, while tying his shoes, and then got mounted on his bike, ready to go, just as instructed.

Orla came back fairly quickly, and got a last drink of water, and mounted up. She said, "Okay, let's do this!" And they all headed off to Tipperary!

Dan thought to himself, "Yes, it IS, indeed, 'A long, long way to Tipperary!'"

As Maeve had predicted, Orla did set a blistering pace, for many a mile.

Dan thought, "WOW!, What is she? A machine? Hmmm, yes, I suppose that she could almost be one. But if that is the case, then Maeve must be one, too. Perhaps this is what my 'Assignment' might be: To become an agent, for this Sir Percival?"

After this, Dan just focused on trying to keep up with Orla. He reached deep into his mental reserves, and blocked out the pain. After about an hour, Dan realized that the pain had gone away! He then pushed even harder, and was able to almost catch up to Orla. Maeve just stayed right behind Dan, regardless of his speed. Her job was to guard the rear, and also make sure that Dan did not get lost. Orla's job, on the other hand, was to not only get them there as fast as possible, but also to start to push Dan, in preparation for his next tests.

They arrived at the outskirts of Tipperary, just as the sun was setting. Orla led them to one of Sir Percival's "Safe Houses." They all carried their bikes up to their rooms, for the night. Then, they all got cleaned up, and rested for a few minutes. Maeve then knocked on Dan's door. When he answered, she asked, "Are you ready to find some food?" Dan nodded, just as Orla was coming out of her room. They left, to find a place to eat.

After dinner, Dan asked, "Would it be alright if I got a drink, while we are here? I always had this vision, of someday having a drink in Tipperary!"

Orla laughed, and said, "By all means! We could hardly deny such a vision! Just keep it down to one, but make it a good one!"

Dan motioned to the serving wench, who came over, and, Dan asked the girls if they wanted anything. They each said that the water is fine, so Dan said, "Irish Whiskey, on the rocks, make it a double, with a twist of lemon."

The waitress did as she was told, and returned to the table a few minutes later, with his drink. They all settled the bill, and Dan said, "A toast to Tipperary! Yes, it is, indeed, a 'Long, long way to Tipperary!' " Dan chugged down the double, and then said, quietly, to the girls, "My

Grandfather passed through here, in 1917, on his way to World War One." They all got up and left, and returned to their rooms, this time without any further incidents. Between being quite tired, and slightly drunk, Dan did not remember getting into bed, but he woke up at 0430. He realized that the girls would probably be getting ready to go, so he got dressed, and was fully packed, just as Orla knocked on his door. Dan opened it and said, "Hi." Orla asked if he was ready to go. Dan nodded, and grabbed his bike. The three of them hit the road at 0530, just as the skies were starting to lighten, in the east.

On and on, they rode: Clonmel, Carrick-on-Suir, New Ross. They stopped for food, and potty breaks, along the way, and then continued eating the miles. Finally, late in the afternoon, they arrived at Wexford.

Orla stopped at a pub, and said to the others, "You can get started, here. I will go see if Charon is actually there, and ready." Maeve simply nodded at Orla, who then set off to find Charon. Dan and Maeve locked their bikes, and went inside. They found a place to sit down, and the waitress came over, to ask what would be their pleasure. Maeve said, "Two iced teas, with lemon, for now." The waitress left. Maeve then looked around, and said, very quietly, to Dan, "We need for you to keep your wits about you, tonight. There is no way to foresee how this will work out. We are pretty sure that it is all in place, but there is a storm expected, and it may be a rough trip. Dan nodded, in understanding. He was still letting that sink in, when a Raven picked up a message rock, from the high shelf behind the bar, and flew on over, to land on their table. The raven dropped the message in front of Dan. Maeve said to the raven, "Why, thank you very much!" The raven winked at her, and flew back over to its perch, behind the bar.

Dan unwrapped the message. In addition to the note, there was also a small gold coin. Maeve said, "That is your payment fee, to Charon, for your passage. It is just a formality, really, as he already works for us, but it makes him feel special, and it works out nicely, when there is a storm coming. Put it in your pocket, for now."

Dan did so, just as the waitress came back with their iced teas. Maeve said to the waitress, "Thank You, for now. There will be more, once we have relaxed for a few minutes." The waitress nodded, and left again. Maeve said, "Okay, let's see the note."

Dan got it out, and unfolded it. They read it together.

"Well done!", the note started, "You are almost to the pick-up point. I have received word that Charon is ready, and the journey will begin, after dark. Our meteorologists say that the seas will be rougher than average, with North winds, steady, at gale force, gusting to 'Category 1' hurricane force."

Dan said, "Jesus! Can we do this?" Maeve replied, serenely, "Yes , Charon has been doing this, for a VERY long time!"

Just then, Orla came back, and joined them at the table. She said, "Charon is there, and ready. He is expecting us to arrive, just after dark. He likes it better that way! Is it time, for some food?"

The others nodded, and the waitress came back. They ordered from the menu, and got some more tea. Dan said that he wanted some fish and chips. Orla laughed, and said that was an appropriate choice, and the girls each got a grilled fish, with vegetables.

They all chatted about the usual nothings, and small-talk stuff, and complimented Dan about doing much better than expected. Dan said that he used to ride a bike a lot, in his misspent youth, and the girls smiled about that. The dinner came, and they all ate heartily, since they were hungry, and had told Dan that there would likely not be any more opportunities to eat, until they reached Charon's destination. Dan realized that they would not be able to tell him Charon's destination, just yet, so he did not even bother to ask.

After dinner, it was nearly dark, and close to time to go, so they paid up on the tab, and grabbed their packs and bikes, and headed off to Ferrybank, on the edge of the Irish Sea. Orla led them to Charon's mooring point. They all got on the boat, just as the winds really began to pick up. It was bad enough, with trying to control their bikes on the way there, but now the wind would have just knocked them over, or sent them crashing into objects. They stored their bikes, and packs, below deck, and Orla said to Charon, "We are ready when you are!" Charon looked at Dan, and Maeve said, "Hand him your passage fee!"

Dan approached Charon, with the coin in hand. The boat was nearly dark, except for a couple of very dim glows, coming from what appeared to be an instrument panel. Otherwise, the cabin was even darker. Dan's impression of Charon was that there was something quite spooky about this person. Charon was immensely tall, and very muscular, with hair down to at least his shoulders. His skin seemed to be quite dark, and wrinkled. His dirty, flat-black, clothes absorbed all of the light from the instrument panel. Somehow, this man seemed also to be very tired and bored, and about half again as old as time.

Even spookier was the fact that Charon said nothing, and almost did not even acknowledge Dan's presence.

Dan placed the coin in Charon's hand, without touching him, and then got as far back away, as he felt was polite. He sat down with the girls, and tried to repress a shudder. He rubbed his hand across his mouth, and sat there, spooked, as he wondered if he had just had a close encounter with Death himself, or perhaps Death's handmaiden?!

Charon started the engines, and warmed up the cabin. He went outside, on deck, to untie the mooring lines, and then he returned to the cabin. The throttle was brought up, and the boat began to move away from the dock, and out toward the open sea.

Maeve said to Dan, "Okay, we have cleared the rocks, and are now out in the open sea. It will be best if you will lie down, and try to sleep. The journey will take many hours, even under the best of circumstances, and obviously a North Wind Hurricane, on the Irish Sea, does not qualify as the 'Best of Circumstances'!"

Orla nodded, and they all laid down, and tried to be as comfortable as possible. Maeve and Orla quickly went to sleep, but Dan, tired as he was, kept getting tingling sensations running up and down his spine, while his hair stood on end. He kept one eye on Charon for some several hours, before finally drifting off, to face the demons in his nightmares. One of his dreams was of the Four Horsemen. He remembered, in his dreams, having read some of the works of Poe, including "The Masque of the Red Death." Dan had about as many entries stored in his imagination, as the average person, and they all seemed to want to make an appearance, tonight!

When Dan woke up, around Noon, the next day, after a very fitful night of unrest, he found that the girls were already awake. He found them in the galley, for lack of a better description, just sitting down and relaxing, as best as the circumstances allowed. He asked if they had been awake for long.

"No," Orla replied, "Just long enough to eat a sandwich, made from the galley stores."

Maeve asked if he was hungry, and pointed to the stores, in the cabinets.

Dan went over to look in the food cabinets, as he asked, "Have we been moving all night?"

Orla said, "Of course! Once Charon starts a journey, it will be completed! He has been at it all night. This is the way that he works. We will be able to make some better progress, now that the wind has let up, just a little bit. We should be getting there, shortly after dark, which is, again, the way that Charon likes it best, in any case."

Dan managed to build himself a passable excuse for a sandwich, and he then got himself some water, and sat down with the girls.

"Man! Those nightmares, last night, were real pissers! One right after the other! Some of them seemed to go on for hours, but I would wake up, and my watch said that only a few minutes had gone by, since the last time that I had looked, after the previous round of nightmares. Stuff from Poe, and from having watched too many of the old horror movies, and even worse, the TV reruns of some of the more recent horror movies, and from books that have not yet even been made into horror movies."

Orla laughed, and Maeve said, "That is Charon! He does that to pretty much everybody who travels on his boat. I had that experience for about my first four or five trips, and then I did not have any further troubles after that. He has always gotten me to wherever I needed to go, when I needed to travel this way."

Dan asked, "So, Who is Charon, anyway?"

Orla answered, "For us, he is the Ferryman. We were told that Sir Percival rescued him from a bad situation, and hired him to be available for special assignments. Obviously, he has done his job well. There have never been any problems with that account. Charon is very reliable. He will deliver you to where you are supposed to go!"

Dan thought about that some, while chewing on his sandwich. It actually did feel like he had been transformed, by the last several days, and now he was on the great crossing of the River Styx, complete with heavy seas, and a violent storm. The only thing that was missing was the sulfur fumes! Somehow, he had been changed, and he could no longer revert to what had he been, before. What could this Sir Percival possibly want, that would be worth this much trouble?

Maeve interrupted his thoughts, saying, "Oh, by the way. Do you remember the volcano, in Iceland, that required a bit of an adjustment to your schedule?"

Dan nodded, and Maeve continued, "Well, it seems that the sulfur dioxide fumes, from the volcano, have been picked up by the hurricane, and the north winds will soon be adding an extra bonus of very acid rain, to this trip!"

Orla said, "Yes, so we will need to get going for the 'Safe House', as soon as we get ashore. Fortunately, it is only a short distance to the first destination. We should be able to be there, in just a few minutes. We will then need to get into the showers, and changes of clothes, at that location. The staff there will take care of our bikes, and other equipment, to minimize the damage to those items."

Dan nodded wearily, "It was just a moment ago, that I was thinking that the only thing that was missing, so far, from this trip, was the absence of the 'Fire and Brimstone.' Well, I saw the fire, and the brimstone just caught up with me!"

Maeve laughed, and said, "There you go! Be careful what you wish for. Someone just might be amused enough, to make your wish come true!"

Dan thought about that for a while, and then asked, "Is there anything that we need to do, between now and the delivery point?"

Orla said, "No. It has already been done. We have also made sure that your stuff is ready, too. When Charon ties up at the dock, and puts out the gangplank, we go immediately. As usual, I will lead, and Maeve will make sure that you do not get lost."

Dan then said, "So, I guess that we are ready, then? I noticed that there are some decks of cards, in the food cabinets. Do you girls like to play cards?"

Orla looked at Maeve, and nodded. Maeve said, "Yes. That is a good way to kill a little time. Which games do you like?"

Dan said, "I am up for most card games. Rummy, Hearts, Crazy Eights, Pinochle, etc. If there are any games that you prefer, and I do not know them, I can usually catch on, quickly enough."

Orla said, "Well, Pinochle is a good choice. It is usually better with a fourth, but three-handed is fine, too. Is that okay with you, Maeve?"

Maeve smiled, and nodded, and Dan started shuffling the deck.

Many games went by, with Orla and Maeve winning most of them. Dan had gotten a double pinochle dealt to him, one hand, and was sweating bullets, while trying to save his meld. Fortunately, he had the good sense to not bid, after the opening, and the other two spent their divided trump early, and Dan was left with a jack of trump, after the dust settled. This was the high point of the game, for him.

As dusk settled in around their boat, Orla asked Charon if they were on schedule, and Charon nodded. She came back, and said that they would be there pretty quick, and then they all got ready for the jump-off point.

The winds had calmed down enough, so that the boat could tie up at the dock, just after it was plenty dark enough. Maeve had gone out on deck, to secure the boat to the dock. They all grabbed their bikes and gear, and split for the safe-house, with a stinging acid-rain coming down, and, also, some small pumice stones, about half of the size of a BB pellet. Orla led the way, and they all got there, lickety-split! They headed straight for the showers, and the staff decontaminated the equipment, and washed their clothes.

After they got cleaned up, and put on new clothes, Orla went off to the debriefing room, for a meeting with their local supervisors. When she came back, Maeve asked how it went, and Orla said that they seemed to be pleased enough. "They had a couple of little points, but I was able to justify the decisions well enough, since this is the kind of stuff that happens in the 'Real-World' field operations, and they let it go."

Maeve said, "Good. Okay, then, it is time for us to go catch some real sleep, for a change."

The staff gave them their room keys for the night, and they all flopped, and went right to sleep.

During the night, the winds returned to the full fury, that they had shown earlier, during their journey across the Irish Sea. Dan felt much safer, by comparison, and was too tired for any real dreams of note, so he slept straight through, until dawn.

When dawn came around, the girls were already up, and dressed. Maeve banged on Dan's door. Dan startled, and said, "Huh? Oh, okay, be right there. I just got woke up!"

Dan got dressed, quickly, and answered the door. "Okay, I seem to be awake enough, now. Now, what do we do?"

Maeve said, "Time for breakfast. We get to eat in a restaurant, downstairs!"

Dan said, "Good! Let's go!"

They all went downstairs, and found a booth. A waitress came around, and they ordered. Dan asked about what would happen, next.

Orla said, "Well, all of our gear has been washed, and treated. Portions of it have been replaced, due to various forms of damage. The representatives of Sir Percival have instructed that certain additional equipment be added to our repertoire, and the staff has followed those instructions. We have been assigned a vehicle, for the first part of the journey, to save time, and to minimize suspicions. We will have a trailer in tow, with our bikes on it, and the rest of the gear is in the truck."

A few minutes later, the food came. Maeve told Dan, "Eat well! It will be many hours, before you get another good opportunity."

Dan nodded, and then dug in. When they were all done, Orla said, "Good! Time to move on!"

3

After a thorough inventory, and vehicle check, Orla signed the equipment checklist, and they all got into the truck. Just as Orla pulled out of the garage, the rainy, gray skies darkened even more, and down came the hail, heavy enough to keep visibility down to about 50 feet, if you stretched your imagination that far! The hail came down for miles, as they slowly made their way in a direction that, as far as Dan could guesstimate, was more-or-less south. Perhaps the road was straighter than he thought, but the slow speed, and the weather, made each and every small turn seem to be more significant than it might have actually been. Finally, the hail let up some, but then the fog settled in, and Dan got around to asking if this was fairly typical weather.

Maeve answered, "Well, not really, but in the whole history of our working for Sir Percival, it seems to happen this way quite a lot!"

Orla added, "When I was first interviewed by his representatives about working for Sir Percival, I encountered a place where it was raining frogs, on my way to the interview!", Orla laughed, "It seems that there had been a small, local, twister, which passed over a pond, and sucked up a load of water, frogs and all, and then dumped them in front of, and onto, me!"

Dan's jaw dropped open, and he just sat there, in stunned silence, picking up the pieces of his jaw, which must have hit the floor and shattered, or so it felt to him. He was lost in thought for many a mile. Who, or what, could do this kind of stuff? Is this whole thing just an ongoing bad dream, that he might suddenly wake up from? It seemed to be real enough, and he doubted that his imagination could dream up this whole thing. Maybe he had gotten a hold of some psychedelic mushrooms, or perhaps someone slipped something into one of his drinks, and he might still wake up, in his apartment?

Although it was not even Noon yet, the sky grew darker, and seemed to be a mixture of various shades of gray. The fog turned into an even heavier rain, and Orla slowed down even more, which turned out to be a good thing, as out of the gray, a large tree gave way from its weakened, and already tenuous, grip on the side of a hill, and started sliding straight down, more or less vertically, until it hit a rock, which stopped the bottom of the tree, but the top just kept right on going down, and fell across the road. Orla had just enough time to come to a gentle stop.

Maeve said, "Well.....Shit!"

Orla picked up her cell phone, and put in a call to base.

After a couple of minutes of discussion, Orla hung up the phone, took a deep breath, and let it out.

Orla then said, "They want us to keep going. They have a fix on where we are, from the cell phone towers, and will have the tree cleared, and retrieve the vehicle. So, grab the gear, and the bikes, and lock everything else up. It looks like the 'Back-up Plan' just became the main plan, for now. Get your rain clothes on."

They all got dressed, and locked up the truck, and got the bikes off of the trailer. As they got the bikes worked over onto the other side of the tree, and were ready to set off for the next part of the journey, Orla took the lead again, but this time did not go racing ahead, setting a pace. They stayed pretty close together. Not only because it would be too easy to get separated, but also because no one could see all that far in front of themselves. The brakes on the bicycles would be too wet for them to be able to stop fast enough, if they were to attempt any real speed, as well.

Thus, they moved along for quite some time, and covered many a mile. They stopped, as needed, for potty breaks, and water. No one could see them, or anything else, so they would just move off into the fog, and take a pee, or whatever, and then resume the journey.

A few hours later, they found a dry spot, under a tree near the road, and Orla stopped there.

"Okay", Orla said, "Is anybody ready to eat something, yet?"

Dan and Maeve both nodded, and then they all got some of the provisions out of the backpacks, that they had been rather burdensomely carrying, for quite a while, and munched for several minutes, getting some reward from their burdens, for the trouble.

While chewing on his food, Dan was lost in thought: What if this seemingly strange stuff of the last several days was to be the "New Normal?" The girls seemed to not regard this as unusual, or if they did, they kept it to themselves. Perhaps his old life was the "exception", and this kind of stuff was what a lot of other people dealt with routinely? He had not considered his life to have been "sheltered", but perhaps it was?

After the short food break, they were all ready to move on again. The weather lifted, just enough, and Orla was able to go faster, so they made a little bit better time. Eventually, Orla stopped again, and the others caught up with her.

Maeve said, "Oh, good! We have reached the fork, in the road!" She then added, to Dan, "Well, here is where it gets more interesting!"

Dan looked up at the road, seemingly winding off into the clouds, going up the side of a mountain. He asked, "So, is it all uphill, now?"

Orla laughed, and said, "Oh, no, that would be too easy! We have to go up and down, many times, yet! The road will eventually degenerate, and the bikes will become almost useless. I hope that you have been on a horse, before?"

Dan rubbed his hand across his mouth, and paused for a couple of seconds, before he answered.

"Well, yes, I have, some, but that was under much better circumstances!"

Maeve said, "Well, these horses are well trained, and know where they are going. If you just give your horse free reins, and hang on, it will follow Orla, quite nicely!"

Dan thought, "So, where the Hell is this place, anyway?!"

Orla led off again, with Dan and Maeve following. True to her word, the road took many twists and turns, and went up and down several times, as it seemed to be gaining some altitude, over the long haul. The "Road", if you want to call it that, seemed to be petering out, and then got better again, for a little bit. Dusk approached, and Orla said, "Well, we have just enough time to set up the tent, before it gets too dark to see anything, in these trees, and this seems to be about as good of a time, and place, as any."

Maeve agreed, and said to Dan, "Okay, grab the tent stuff that they packed on your bike." She and Orla did the same, with the tent equipment on their bikes.

Dan did as he was told, and three of them had the tent up, and sleeping bags spread out in the tent, with just enough time left, before dark, for another quick snack. They all ate, and then settled down in their sleeping bags.

Dan slept soundly, with only minimal bad dreams, while processing what had been going on, for these last several days. By the time the first hints of morning rolled around, he was still thoroughly asleep.

Maeve bumped Dan, to see if he would stir easily, but not much happened.

Maeve then gave Dan a more persuasive nudge, and said, "Hey! Get up, and get your shoes on. It is time to eat, and pack up the tent, and move on!"

Dan opened one eye, as if he was signifying that he was sure that this had to still be a dream. He blinked, but it did not go away, so he decided to open the other eye, for confirmation. He stared for a couple of seconds. But, sure enough, it was real! So he got up, and pulled on his shoes. They all ate breakfast. Nobody said much, and mostly Dan just yawned a lot, between mouthfuls. He was too tired to think, or say, much of anything. Dan was also preoccupied, with imagining what he might find, when they got to the end of this journey.

The girls left the tent first, and Dan crawled out behind them. Once he started moving around, and the food started to work, he actually felt better, in the crisp morning air, and the sluggishness left him. Orla and Maeve did turn out to be every bit as seasoned, at this stuff, as he was thinking, a couple of days ago, that they just might be. They seemed to have acquired a special confidence, and competence, that he had to admire!

Everything got packed up, and they all drank some extra water.

Dan asked, "So, are we up into the clouds? I can see all of what, about 50 feet, if I use my imagination, to fill in what I cannot really see!"

Maeve laughed, and said, "No, we are not THAT high up! We are just in a valley, with a thick fog, all around us!"

Orla said, "Okay, time to go. We should reach the Horse Station about Noon."

Dan followed, thinking about this "Horse Station", and Maeve was right behind Dan. About once an hour, or so, they stopped for water, and potty breaks. The "road" finally permanently gave way to a narrow foot trail, on the side of the hills, mostly seeming to go uphill, a very little bit. Sometimes the pathway disappeared, altogether, for a distance, and then came back for a while. Finally, at about a quarter to Noon, Dan realized that he had not seen the trail, for a couple of miles. The bikes were just starting to become a chore, more than an asset, when Orla arrived at the Horse Station, that she had previously mentioned.

They all stopped and stretched, and traded in their bikes for horses. The crew manning the station looked over their gear, and attached it all to the horses, while the travelers took food and potty breaks, and got ready for the next part of the journey. Dan could not see much, thanks to the continuing fog, but he could make out a couple of buildings, and what seemed to be a large pasture, fenced off into smaller sections, and several horses, and some fairly large rocks, jutting up out of the ground, covered in a bright green moss, and a few trees.

Maeve said to Dan, "This part of the journey may be a little bit tricky, but the thing to remember, here, is that you are now riding something that has a little bit of a brain, as opposed to a bicycle. Sometimes the horse may get confused, but it is still smarter at knowing where it wants to go, than a bicycle is! Your horse has also been trained to follow Orla's horse."

Orla checked her watch, and then looked at the clock on the wall, behind the service desk, to verify the time, and the counter person smiled, and said, "Chwarter wedi un!"

Orla smiled back, and said, "Diolch!" She then waved, and left. Upon returning to the horses, she found that Dan and Maeve were already saddled up, and waiting. Orla mounted the lead horse, and they all rode off into the fog. As they rose higher, the fog lessened, but the trees and brush became thicker, apparently due to reaching a place with more average rainfall, or perhaps better soil. On they trudged, for many a mile, sometimes going up, sometimes down a little. The pathway, obscure and meandering as it was, still seemed to be the route of least resistance. Dan could see no obvious improvements, that could be easily made. The trail looked like it had been worn into the earth, since time out of mind. The nice thing about riding a horse, Dan soon realized, is that he could reach into his bags and grab a snack, or a drink, without having to stop. The going was slow, but they kept going.

Finally, as dusk approached, and just as Dan was starting to think that they might have to set up camp for another night, they arrived at a place where the earth flattened out. They rode on for another mile, through gloomy, wind-worn trees, some of which, while not really tall, could be several hundreds of years old, with gnarled and broken branches, and quite large trunks. With nightfall close at hand, they broke into a clearing, and then Dan saw a magnificent stone building.

While it might not qualify as a castle, as in the sense of the images conveyed, when one thinks of the magnificent old castles, from the "Middle Ages", it was certainly the closest thing to a castle, that Dan had personally ever seen. The horses, realizing that they were near the end of yet another journey, wanted to speed up a little bit, and Orla let them do so. The horses went directly to their stable, where the attendants were waiting.

The front attendant said, "Welcome, Orla and Maeve, and you must be Sir Daniel! Welcome! You are all right on time! We will take care of your stuff, and you may proceed directly to the main entrance." They dismounted, and stretched, and moved around a little bit, as the attendants took control of the horses, and unpacked their burdens.

Orla then led them to the main entrance of this splendid structure, seemingly all stone on the outside. Dan tried to grasp more of the edifice, but it was simply too dark to pick up much in the way of details. They stepped into the security entrance, and the guard greeted them, "Noswaith dda, Orla and Maeve, and are you Sir Daniel?"

Maeve said, "Iawn. This is Sir Daniel. We have all traveled many days, in many different ways, and through many miles, together!"

Dan thought to himself, "Boy, that is for damned sure!"

The guard said, "Well, then, welcome! Please all sign in, and proceed to the guest quarters. And Orla, the board wishes to have you proceed directly to the Administrative Office." Orla nodded, and looked at Maeve, who then said, "See you at the guest house. I will get Dan settled." Orla went to administration, ready for the usual ritual of debriefing, and accounting.

Maeve led Dan to the guest house, and got the keys to their rooms, for the night. The staff had already made sure that each assigned room had replacements for all of their clothes, as well as soap, shampoo, shaving equipment, towels, etc.

Maeve said to Dan, "Get cleaned up, and dressed. It may just turn out that we all end up crashing for tonight. But try to be ready for anything! We will probably get a chance to eat, later. I just don't know for sure what they will have us do, tonight!"

Dan, too tired to say much, just nodded in understanding, and Maeve left him to get cleaned up, and did so herself.

After Maeve got out of the shower, and had dried off, Orla knocked at Maeve's door. Maeve opened it just enough, to see a smiling Orla, just coming back from the brief meeting. Orla gave Maeve a "Thumbs Up", and a broad smile!

Maeve said, "Oh, good! See you shortly!"

Orla went to her room, and Maeve returned to dressing, and getting ready.

When Orla was cleaned up and ready, she returned to knock at Maeve's door, and they both proceeded to Dan's door, and knocked. Dan was dressed and ready, as Maeve had instructed, and opened the door.

Orla said, "Good, you are ready! We have been invited to the dining hall. You will be meeting some of the people who invited you here, and there is plenty of good food and drink, waiting for us!"

So, they all proceeded to the dining hall. When they walked in, there was a general round of applause awaiting them. Orla made the formal introduction, announcing that Dan had arrived. Orla and Maeve each took turns introducing Dan directly, to many people.

Maeve said to Dan, "Just do the best you can. There is probably nobody here that actually expects you to remember their name, out of the dozens that you will meet tonight."

Everyone eventually sat down, and the person who had been chosen to lead the ceremonies said,

"Well, I wish to formally welcome Sir Daniel, to join our organization, on behalf of Sir Percival, whom you will likely meet tomorrow. He has been detained by another matter requiring his attention, this evening. Meanwhile, we are all to enjoy this occasion, and have lots of good food and drinks. Dan, we will discuss your assignments, tomorrow."

Dan wondered, once again, what that ominous word, "Assignments", might mean, as the serving staff distributed the menus. He then focused on what to order for dinner. When the waiter came around, Dan said, "I will have the Atlantic deep-sea cod fish and chips, and could I get some scotch, on the rocks, with a twist of lemon?" The waiter nodded, and asked if there was anything else that he wished at the moment? Dan said, "No, that will do, for now. Thank you." The waiter then moved on, to the next person.

Some time later, all of the food and drinks began to arrive, all at once. Dan realized that there must be much more to this organization than he had assumed up to this point, just from the size of the serving staff, and the probable size of the cooking staff, and the administration, and who knows what all else, that he had not even seen yet?

After the meals and drinks were polished off, and a few more short speeches were made by various people, the gathering began to die down, and people slowly exited the scene. Orla eventually said, "Well, it appears that we are about done here, for tonight." Then Maeve said, "Yes, it does look that way." Shortly later, the Master of Ceremonies asked if everything had been satisfactory for this evening, and Dan replied, "Yes, it was splendidly well done! Thank you for putting this all together for me. I am very honored!"

The MC then replied, "On behalf of the staff, I am honored that you were pleased. We hope that you will be very happy here!"

Dan said, "Well, if today was any sign of what follows, I think I just might be!" Dan and the MC shook hands, and Orla and Maeve escorted Dan back to their rooms, for the night.

Dan locked the door to his room, got undressed, and flopped into bed for the night. His sleep was a strange mixture of wonder and excitement, and dread, as he waited for the morning, when he would be expecting to find out what they wanted him for. The dreams were too numerous to track. Some of them were apparently very short, and others dragged on, taking little commercial breaks, while other dreams played out, in short flashes, and glimpses of what was, and what might be.

4

Dawn came early, to Dan. He could have used another couple of hours of sleep, but his adrenalin, and curiosity, got the better of him. Thus, he was already up, and dressed, and just lying down on top of the bed, resting and thinking, when Maeve knocked on the door. "Dan," she said, "Time to get up!"

Dan opened the door, and Maeve said, "Oh, you are dressed already! Are you ready for breakfast?"

Dan replied, "Yes. Let's go!"

Maeve knocked on Orla's door, and said, "Hi. We are ready."

Orla answered the door, and then they were all off to the dining hall. She said, to Dan, "We get to eat, and then we will deliver you to the Assistant Operations Manager, for a private meeting, at 0900."

As they walked outside, Dan could begin to see, for the first time, a hint of the size of this operation. There were many buildings in all directions, as well as a fenced, and walled, compound that stretched as far as he could see, from his limited position. Dan said to the girls, "So, just what is this place, and what do we do, here, and how big is it?"

Maeve said, "The administration will give you some clues, at 0900. If you accept the assignment, they will gradually reveal more to you, on a 'Need to know' basis. For right now, it is time to get yourself some good food, for you may be a while, before you get an opportunity to take a lunch break."

Orla said, "Yes, on my first day, it was about seven hours, before I got lunch! So, it is time to eat!"

They all headed for the dining hall and ordered breakfast. Dan, keeping in mind what the girls had said, got some extra food, so as to be ready for what followed. They chatted about the usual nothings, while they ate. At 0845, they delivered Dan to the secretary for the assistant operations manager, who said that Mr. Jones would be with him, shortly. Maeve and Orla then left Dan in her hands, and went off to do whatever they were going to do.

After about ten minutes, Mr. Jones came out of his office, and said, "Hello, Dan. You probably do not remember me, but we met last night. In the confusion of all of what has happened to you, over the last several days, and with the rather large number of people that were at the welcoming dinner, I would be surprised if you remembered much of anything about the dinner!"

Dan replied, "Yes, sir, that is very much true! I think I may remember your face, and possibly a few other faces, if I saw them again, but no names stuck with me, that I could immediately recall. Everything is still a fast-moving blur."

They shook hands, and then Dan followed Jones back to his office, where he invited Dan to sit down, and closed the door. Jones then said, "So, you are probably wondering what this whole thing has been all about, for the last couple of weeks?"

Dan laughed, and said, "Yes, sir, I HAVE been wondering what it was all about, ever since I woke up in the balloon, that first time, just as I was passing over what was probably about Saskatchewan!"

Jones laughed, and said, "Well, we do apologize for the rather dramatic invitation to join our little organization, but Sir Percival wanted you, and told the group to make sure that we got you, before anyone else did! What Percy wants, Percy gets! He has not been wrong yet! One of the reasons for that rather large amount of 'Front Money', was not only to ensure your safety and convenience, just in case something went wrong, on your way here, but also to entice you enough, to let you know that we were serious about getting you."

Dan let that sink in, for just a couple of seconds, and then said, "So, just what is it that your company wants with me?"

Jones answered, "We have reviewed your background, with a fine-toothed comb, over the last couple of months, and we believe that your qualifications, both those on paper, such as schooling and degrees, and also those that are more of a personal nature, such as your psychological profile, and work ethic, would be a very significant asset to us."

Jones then continued, "We have a need for a Materials Scientist, and Metallurgist, 'in training', in addition to many other things that you will be learning about, and doing for us, over the next several years. The work hours will be long, and most of the rest of your time will be spent studying, so you will be quite busy, and not have much free time, but that is another reason for why you were selected : you tended to work extra hours, without pay, just to try to get the job done."

Dan said, "I am honored to even be considered for such a job, but surely you could get someone else for this type of position, who was already much better qualified, who could 'hit the ground running', so to speak!"

Jones then explained, "Yes, that may have been a possibility, but not with the overall package already in place. Besides, as I said, Percy wanted you, and he gets what he wants! We are prepared to start you at 65,000 Euros, per annum, with a full benefits package, which you can read about, as you are filling out the paperwork, and you can continue collecting your retirement, from the job that you just left! You can even just let it accumulate in a bank, in the States, if you wish!"

Dan asked, "So, are we actually in Wales? I have been kind of confused about just exactly where we are, and what about my having to go through immigrations and customs, and other stuff, both here, and in Ireland?"

Jones said, "Yes, we are in Wales, and while the Irish government has been informed of your passage through there, unannounced, we have also explained to their customs officers, through our agents, that you were escorted through, by our agents, and nothing untoward was done along the way. We carry enough clout, so that they just accepted our assurances on the matter, and since they are over-worked anyway, they let it go. Our staff is also handling the matter with London, right now. Since Sir Percival has connections to the peerage, it should be a simple enough matter, especially if you do not leave our premises until it is all fully resolved, to everyone's satisfaction. In a few days, or at worst, weeks, you will probably have an offer of dual citizenship tendered to you, for Wales, and the United States."

Dan said, "Wow! So, can you have someone show me around, and how soon can I start?"

Jones answered, "Well, we can take you to another room, to fill out the starting paperwork, which mostly consists of the usual nonsense that you have already done many times before, on other jobs, plus there are non-disclosure agreements, to protect the confidentiality of what you will learn, and do, here, and non-competition agreements, and official security checks, which will be handled by the government, to make sure that you are not some secret agent of a terrorist organization, and some more specialized stuff, which might be loosely considered to be part of the usual nonsense. But we already know almost everything about you, that probably anyone would ever care about! For instance, we even know about every girl that you ever dated, and very nearly every book that you have ever read, and every teacher that you have ever taken a class from!

"We can have you start after lunch, today. That will give you some time to fill out the paperwork. As for, 'Showing you around', that will be done in stages, on an 'As Needed' basis, related to the performance of your duties. What you will start out doing, will be some things that might be considered to be crude, and old-fashioned, and perhaps even backwards, by modern standards, but Percy wants you to learn the organization, from the bottom-up! From the VERY bottom! In so doing, you will have the full comprehension of the job. In so doing, you will become fully qualified, in ways that we could not really get an actual metallurgist to be willing to learn, except on paper. It is an interesting study, to realize the number of 'High-Powered' people out there, who have advanced degrees, who truly cannot change a light bulb! It seems that modern academics has somehow failed us!"

Dan laughed, and said, "Well, I can definitely change a light bulb!"

Jones laughed, and replied, "Yes, we know. Believe it or not, that WAS one of the personal qualifications, which we considered! Well, are you ready to move off to the auxiliary office, to start on the paperwork?"

Dan nodded, and then Jones extended his hand, and Dan shook it, and then Jones said, "On behalf of our organization, let me formally welcome you! Let's get you started on the forms."

They went to the room, where the forms were already neatly organized, and Jones said, "Please make yourself comfortable. You should have everything you will need, already here. Many of the forms are already filled out for you, and just need to be carefully reviewed, and signed. If there is anything that you need, just ask the secretary, Miss Griffin, for help."

So, Dan started wading through the stacks of paperwork and reading material. After a little while, Miss Griffin asked Dan if he would like a cup of tea, and what would he like with it? Dan said that lemon and sugar would be nice, to go with the iced tea. She returned promptly with the beverage, and asked if everything was clear enough in the paperwork? Dan laughed, and then replied, "Yes, it is just fine, but there is quite a pile of it!"

Miss Griffin smiled, and replied, "Well, you are privileged, and for that, you get to have EXTRA paperwork, and reading material! Sometimes being 'special' can be a curse!"

Dan laughed again, and said, "Yes, I have always believed that it is better to attempt to remain obscure, and unnoticed, when possible. Unfortunately, I sometimes get detected anyway. It seems to have been the nature of most of my jobs."

Miss Griffin said, "Well, let me know if I can be of any more help."

Dan said, "Thank You!", and he then returned to the business at hand. He completed the required forms at just about lunchtime, and handed them over to Miss Griffin, and said, "So, where do we eat, around here?"

Maeve appeared in the waiting room, and said, "I can answer that! You are going to lunch with me, and Orla, and we will show you the Cafeteria. We will return you to Jones after lunch, and then you will begin your training."

So, off to the cafeteria they went. Along the way, the girls introduced him to various people that they ran into, some of which, it seemed to Dan, that he might have seen the night before, but they all handled it well, pretending that they were just now meeting, for the first time. Dan got himself a Club Sandwich, with French Fries, and an iced tea, with lemon. Orla and Maeve each got a bowl of clam chowder, and a sandwich. They all chatted about general stuff, somewhat related to the job, that they could explain, without revealing any actual organizational secrets, such as the annual rainfall, and typical monthly temperature averages, and the populations of various cities.

After lunch, they surrendered Dan back to Jones, and wished Dan "Good Luck!" Jones said that he was sure that Dan will do just fine.

Jones added, "Well, Dan, my secretary, Janet, will take you to the locker room, and you will put on some coveralls. Miss Griffin will then lead you to the elevator, and escort you down to Purgatory, where Frank will be waiting for you. The work will be hard, but Sir Percival wants you to learn the organization from the bottom up. The VERY bottom! Once you achieve the required skill set, and understanding, Percy will send you on, to the next part of your training."

So, Dan got his coveralls assigned, and got into them, and then he and Janet took the long ride down to Purgatory. The elevator door opened, and as it happened, Frank was just walking by at the time. Janet said to Frank, "Frank, this is Sir Daniel. Sir Percival wants him to start here, and learn all of the finer points of the job, and to develop his physical strength, and motor skills, before he is moved up to the next level of his training."

Frank said, "Oh, okay. Come on, Dan. Thank you, Janet."

The elevator door closed, and Janet took the return ride up. Frank pointed at the wall, and said, "Grab a shovel, and follow me!"

Dan did as he was told. Frank pointed to a large hopper of coal, and said, "Just start shoveling the coal into the open door of the furnace. Make sure that you drink enough water. The restrooms are right over there. It is hot down here, so take it easy at first, and just do whatever you can. This is to develop your physical strength. You are apparently not in bad shape, for your age, but this will improve you quite a lot! Just pay attention to how you are feeling. We have salt tablets, too, if you need them."

So, Dan spent the next several hours, learning for himself the mechanics of how to efficiently, and safely, shovel many tons of coal. At first, he just did small loads per shovel, but gradually learned to do it a little bit better. Some of the pieces of coal were a little too big, or too heavy, for him to lift at this stage, but Dan had noticed a sledge hammer nearby, and broke up the larger pieces, into more manageable sizes.

At the end of the day, Frank said, "Okay, come back tomorrow. You will spend the whole day here, and then you will start to REALLY shovel coal!" So, Dan hung up his overalls, and took the long elevator ride back to the surface. Exhausted, Dan stopped at the cafeteria for some food and drink, and went back to his room. He got into the shower, and soaked his sore and tired muscles. He went to bed early, after taking some aspirin, and extra water.

The next day, Dan went back to shovel more coal. He improved his technique, and also learned how to judge better when a piece of coal needed to be hit with a hammer. To optimize the time spent working the hammer, he learned to set aside some of the larger pieces that he would need to break up, before he would be able to shovel them, and then grabbed the hammer, and smashed several large pieces into smaller pieces, all at once. At the end of the day, Dan rode back to the surface, exhausted. Each day, the process was repeated, and he got much better at shoveling coal, and he became much stronger. He started making notes, in a spiral notebook, about what worked the best, and how well he had done, and how much stronger he seemed to be getting. After several weeks, he began to feel so much better that he would go for a walk, at the end of the day, and then gradually began to run short distances. Eventually, he was able to run farther, and faster. After three months, Jones called Dan in one morning, and said,

"Dan, I understand that you are doing much better at shoveling coal, and improving your strength. You are now ready to be shifted to your next opportunity. We will still be having you shoveling coal, for a while longer, part time, to help maintain the strength that you have just acquired, but we will also transition you to sieving molding sand. This sand has just been through a casting process. By now, you have had an opportunity to study, and memorize, the maps we provided you with, a couple of months ago. Tomorrow, go to the sand room, at the usual time that you were doing for the coal room. They will be expecting you. For the first couple of weeks, you will do the sand room, in the morning, and the coal room after lunch. After about two weeks, we will shift you to the sand room."

The next morning, Dan showed up at the sand room. They put him to work, shoveling sand up off the workroom floor, and loading it onto a vibrating shaker screen. Most of the sand was slightly damp, having been moistened, for ramming up around the molding pattern. This made the sand heavier, and because the sand was also being held together by the surface tension of the water, the shovel was able to hold much more sand than it did of coal. As a result of this, Dan soon deduced why the sand room was the next step in the physical development process : A shovel full of this stuff required much more effort to lift up onto the shaker. After spending the morning shoveling sand, he was looking forward to a comparatively lighter load of shoveling coal.

For the next couple of weeks, he shoveled sand in the morning, and coal in the afternoon. At the end of the day in the coal room, after the two weeks were up, Frank said to Dan, "Well, it looks like they want you to be in the sand room, full time, now, so you won't be needing to come back down here, at least for a while."

Dan said, "Thanks for having me down here. I have learned a lot about coal, and how to shovel it, and got some good muscles along the way!"

Frank said, "Yes, you did! You were starting to get pretty good at it, too! Well, see you around. We will most likely run into each other, now and then. Good luck!"

They shook hands, and Dan boarded the elevator, for the long ride up.

The next day, Dan reported to the sand room. They had him continue shoveling sand onto the sieve all day long. Again, Dan gradually developed his shoveling technique, and his strength, so that he could haul more sand per shovel load. The sieve was sized so that the individual grains of sand could drop right through, onto the conveyor belt, and be sent back to the casting room, but the larger pieces were dumped into a trough, and diverted along another conveyor belt, where they were rolled out, to be flattened. Foreign materials, such as metal flakes from the casting process, were separated out, and the rest of the sand rejoined the casting process. After a couple of weeks, Dan noticed that someone had replaced his shovel with another one, which was a little bit larger. He did not say anything, and instead just figured that it was all a part of the process. A few more weeks went by, and the shovel was again replaced, by an even larger one. By this time, the shovel, and the amount of sand, had about reached their optimum size. Dan had also managed to have enough energy left in the evenings, for a few minutes of reading, before he passed out for the night, from exhaustion. He learned that the sand is mixed with Bentonite clay, when the sand is new, and freshly oven dried. The clay arrives as a dry powder, and the sand/clay mix is tumbled together, dry, in a mixer, to help optimize the uniformity of the batch. This was a part of why the sand was so heavy, and why it held together so well on the shovel. The powdered clay helped to fill in the voids in the pure sand. The clay helped to hold the water in the sand, and the water also helped to fill in the remains of the sand voids. This, when combined with the fact that this mixture could be lifted as a very full shovel, with almost vertical edges, and often a couple of feet deep, was why a shovel load, full of the sand/ clay/ water mix, could become very heavy. The sand/clay mix was prepared with dry ingredients, for ease of mixing, and to help ensure greater uniformity. The mixing would be very difficult to do, once the clay got wet. It would want to stick to everything, and it would form clay clumps in the molding sand. Thus, the reason for why it was done dry.

Dan soon spent a day in the sand/clay mixing room. He opened, and dumped, and shoveled in, bags of dry Bentonite clay into a hopper, which was feeding a giant tank, about the size of a railroad tank car. When the mixing process was complete, the sand/clay mix would go into a holding tank, where it was kept dry until needed.

After a few more days of shoveling sand, Dan was told to report to the carpentry room, where they showed him how to cut wood to the right size, and construct molding boxes that would fit together correctly. The boxes would then be fitted with little extension arms, and with little steel pins, that would fit into the overlapping board extensions, so that by pulling the quick-release pins, the casting could be removed quickly.

When Dan had finished building his first box, one of the carpenters had him fill the box with loose, wet, molding sand, and try to lift it. Dan was only just barely able to do the lift. The carpenter then handed Dan a hammer, and a block of wood. Dan was then told to ram the sand down solidly across the entire surface of the sand in the box, to a uniform depth. The carpenter then said, "You saw how you had a full box of loose, and wet, sand, to start with. You have also just seen how far down that seemingly solid sand could be easily compressed. That extra space becomes more weight needed to fill the box. People get hernias trying to lift a full box of rammed-up sand. Don't do it! Get a hand truck, or fill your casting box, while it is on a rolling platform."

After lunch, Dan was sent on to the pattern rammers. Here, he learned about how to correctly locate a pattern into the sand, so as to avoid having the molten metal burn right through the box, and thus possibly leak out onto the feet of the metal pourers.

John White, the rammer supervisor, said to Dan, "We have started you with a very simple pattern, with all sides tapered, so that it can be easily extracted from the sand, and poured. Do not worry about any screw-ups on this pattern. You are almost guaranteed to screw up your first several test pours. There are simply too many things that can, and usually will, go wrong, when you first start doing this kind of stuff. Many of these things that will go wrong, are things that you could read about in a book, and it would not mean a thing to you, until you start doing the work. We could tell you stuff, until we are just blue in the face, and it would only go in one ear, and out the other. A lot of it is variable, depending on how well conditioned the sand is, what the exact grain size is, how much clay is in that part of the batch, the temperature of the spray water, and on and on. Depending on what the shape is of the pattern, and the composition of the pattern, and so on, it all is handled very slightly differently, and sometimes a LOT differently! A pattern man can, and often will, spend years learning about how to make a pattern work, correctly, and a sand rammer can spend years learning how to work with the various sands and patterns that he will encounter. Sometimes, a pattern will have to be split into more than one piece, and fitted with pins, and other little tricks, so that the pattern can be removed from the sand, and create a castable void into which the molten metal charge will be poured. Even the most beautiful patterns are absolutely worthless, if they cannot be removed cleanly from the sand, so that the pour can be made, and an accurate casting representation of the pattern retrieved, after the metal has cooled. We do not always use wood for the sand boxes, but they are cheap, and easily made. They are also quite versatile, and they can often be easily modified, when needed."

John then handed Dan a sketch of the pattern box, that he wanted Dan to build, complete with measurements.

John said, "Go over to the saws, and the wood supplies, over there, and select the materials specified, and build this box, pretty close to the specs. When you have finished with your pattern box, bring it back here, and I will look it over, for any obvious problems, and then when it is ready, we will give you the first of the test patterns, that will be part of the learning program."

So, Dan did as he was told, and found the supplies, and the saws, nails, hammer, screws, and the variable-speed, reversing, drills. And Dan built the box as close to the specifications as he could. When he thought the box was ready, he brought it back to John, who looked it over, and decided that Dan's box passed inspection.

John then said, "You were probably wondering about the box with four sides, and the interlocking pins, and no fixed top or bottom. This would be a pretty suspicious box, for most purposes, but for us, this is just what we need, to illustrate some of the techniques that are often needed for what we do, here."

Dan nodded, and then John added, "Well the easiest, and most effective, way to get the point across, is just to get started. Take your box, and attach the bottom to it. Turn it upside down, to do this. Then flip the box back over."

Dan did so, and then John said, "Here is your first pouring pattern," as he handed the pattern to Dan, "Study the pattern for a short time, and see if you can deduce how to best place the pattern so as to most efficiently achieve the desired pour. It is how well the pour turns out, that decides, more than any of us, in most cases, how good of a job you did. Often, the arbiter of your skill as a foundry man is simply the laws of physics. They will determine the success, or failure, of your efforts, much more effectively, and impersonally, than any of us."

The pattern was approximately a rectangular solid. Dan noticed that it seemed to be slightly smaller at one end, than it was at the other. He took out a tape measure, to check this, and John said, "Very Good! You have a keen eye! One end is, indeed, a little bit smaller than the other one. What does this tell you?"

Dan admitted that he was not really sure what that was about, and that it could mean any of a number of things.

John agreed, and said, "Well, here is where the education, in the school of, 'trial-and-error' starts. It is our most effective teacher. So, what I want for you to do, first, is to simply put some sand into the bottom of your box. Let's start with making the sand about three inches deep."

So, Dan did just that, and John then told Dan to ram the sand down in the box so that it was a uniform depth, and flat, smooth, and hard.

Dan tried to do this, but he quickly discovered that it was not doing what he wanted it to do. John said, "What do you think happened, here? Think about sand when you walk on the beach. On the wet sand, it packs easily, and you can walk on it pretty well. When you try to walk on dry sand, it just slides around, and can be much harder to walk on. You have clean, pure, and dry, sand in your box."

Dan said, "Oh!", and dumped the dry sand out of his box, and back onto the pile.

John told Dan to put a shovel full of sand into a bucket, and then grab a small garden trowel, and dump in a load of powdered Bentonite clay into the bucket. "Now, put the lid on the bucket, and roll it around on the floor, to help mix the clay uniformly into the sand."

After Dan did this, John had him open the bucket. John then reached into the bucket, and pulled up a handful of the sand-clay mix. He shuffled it through his hand, feeling the texture of the mix. John had Dan pick up a sample, and do the same.

"Note how this feels! Run it around in your hands, and handle it in various ways. Run it between your fingers, and squeeze it together. Look closely at this mix."

Dan did so, and then John added, "I would say that you are about a half a trowel short, on the Bentonite."

So, Dan added the instructed amount of Bentonite, and put the lid back on, and rolled the mixture around on the floor, just as he had previously done. After several minutes, he sat the bucket upright, and pulled off the lid. John grabbed another sample, and said, "Much better. Run your hands through it, and repeat the little tests that we did just a few minutes ago."

Dan did this, and John watched Dan's hands, and the behavior of the sample.

John said, "Okay. Good enough, for now. Grab that spray bottle, over there, and we will start getting the sand watered down. Start with a few squirts of water into the mix, and then start turning over the sand, as you squirt in more water. Once the sand starts to allow it, use the trowel to excavate a cavity into the sand, and then squirt the water into the cavity, too, all the while squirting in water, and mixing it all together."

Dan kept mixing, and squirting water. Once John thought that there was almost enough water in the bucket, he said, "Okay, put the lid on the bucket, and roll it around, just as we had done when the stuff was dry."

So, after several minutes of mixing, John figured that it was time to sample the contents of the bucket. Dan pulled off the lid, and he and John both took out samples of the sand.

"Okay," said John, "Good enough for now. Now, how would you put the pattern into the sand box? Do you remember what we did, just a little while ago?"

Dan said that he thought so, and proceeded to try. He put about three inches of sand into the casting box, and then rammed it down, using the hammer and the various little blocks of wood, and got it all flat, and fairly smooth.

John said, "Now, measure the depth of the sand, by shoving a small wire into the sand, until it reaches bottom."

Dan did so, and used his thumb to keep track of the depth. He showed John how much sand was in the box.

John said, "It is now time for a test of what you have just done. Pick the box straight up, and carefully turn it over, without bumping it on anything."

So, Dan did this, and the sand promptly fell out of the box!

"Okay," said John, "That is what I had thought! You did not ram the sand hard enough! Do it again, and strike it down harder, this time! This is another example of the kinds of things that can really only be effectively learned in the schools of 'Trial and Error', and then you graduate, to the school of 'Hard Knocks.'"

So, Dan did it all over again, and rammed it harder, this time. Only part of it fell out, and then he got the sand to stay put on the third try. "As you do this stuff," John said, "You also have to keep in mind that the water is evaporating, and that will change how the sand behaves. So you want to eventually learn to keep the bucket covered, and add water to the mix, as it is needed, if you take very long on doing this stuff. Also, there are times when you will be covering the casting box, to help keep the water in."

"So, now," added John, "have you given any further thought to the pattern that we are going to be casting, in light of what you have just been learning?"

Dan admitted that he had not really done a whole lot of thinking about that, just yet, and John said,

"Okay, in the interests of a little bit of efficiency, I will provide you with some clues. Since you need to put the pattern into the sand, which way would you put the pattern into the sand? The answer might be easier than you think, if you will remember that the pattern has a slightly irregular shape."

Dan said, "Well, there are six faces to this pattern, and four of them are supposed to be identical, so that really only leaves three possible, effectively different, alternatives. While it might be possible to use one of the four identical sides, I suspect that it is the ends that we are interested in here. So, it would be the top end, with the larger base, that I would guess would be up, and I would want to have some sand on the underside of the casting, to prevent the heat from burning right through the bottom of the box."

John said, "Well, you are half way right, sort of. Go ahead with your idea, and put the pattern into the box the way that you want, and then start on the ramming up of the sand!"

So, Dan tried out his idea, and soon discovered that he was having trouble ramming the sand around the pattern. He stopped, and looked a little bit puzzled.

John said, "Okay, there are a couple of things wrong, here. First off, the pattern is upside down, for these particular sizes of pattern and box. You might be able to have it be upside down, if you have an oversized box, but then you will have extra weight in the box. This extra weight could be okay, for us, since we have the equipment to handle it, but some places will not have this capability. So, this is another parameter to be considered. So, take out your pattern, and then turn the box over, and dump out the sand. Then ram up another bottom layer, of about the same three inches deep. Then put the pattern in, with the larger base, face down."

Dan did as he was told, and then John said, "Now, place a couple of inches of sand all of the way around the pattern. When you start ramming the sand down, try to do it uniformly around the pattern, so as to minimize the amount of pattern movement which occurs. As each layer of sand becomes solid, then add another couple of inches, using the hammer and blocks, and other stuff that you have at your disposal, for the job."

After doing several layers in this fashion, Dan realized that he was going to run into a logical contradiction, and he said, "If I keep going like this, I am not going to be able to get the pattern back out of the sand!"

John said, "Very Good! You figured it out! So, what are you going to do to solve this problem?"

Dan thought on this for about a half a minute, and then said, "Well, first off, it seems to me that the 'bottom' of this box, should be the top!"

John said, "Okay, and then what?"

Dan said, "Well, you went to all of the trouble to make sure that I built a box that I could easily disassemble, so there must be a reason for that! If the pattern tapers down to allow it to come out of the sand, then the larger face must be down, and that would mean that the three inches of insulating sand that would be on the bottom would need to start out on top of the pattern. So I am going to try something out."

John said that would be okay, and then watched as Dan dumped out all of the work that he had just done, again, and this time put the pattern in first, with no sand under it. Dan then rammed up the sand solidly all of the way around the pattern, covering it completely in the sand, and then hammered in some more sand over the top of the pattern, to the three inch depth. After this, Dan reflected on the fact that he still had a void in the top of the box, and then rammed in enough sand, to bring the sand all of the way up to even with the top surface of the box.

Dan paused for a minute, and then John said, "Okay, you are on the right track. Now, what?"

Dan said, "Well, my thinking is that I want to attach the cover face to the top of this box, and then turn the box over."

John said, "Okay, you are doing fine. Take a shot at that."

Dan attached the cover face to the box. And John said, "Now, you will want to turn this over, very carefully, without lifting, or bumping, it. It will be very heavy!"

So, Dan and John managed to successfully reorient the box, and Dan then removed the top, which was formerly the bottom, of the box.

John said, "Okay, it all looks good! To make sure, take a hammer, and a block, and then tap around the edges of the pattern, to test the solidity of the sand. Lay the block down, long ways, right up against the edge of the pattern, and then tap lightly, and uniformly, along the length of the block."

Dan did this, as John watched. John nodded in approval, and said, "Okay, let's get the casting box onto a hand truck, and go to the kiln room, just down the hall a ways. By the way, that little operation that you just did, with flipping a pattern box over, is called a 'Single Roll'. You will eventually run into patterns that will require double, and triple, rolls, and many other fancy maneuvers, to get the desired results from the casting."

John opened the door to the kiln room, and held it open, so that Dan could wheel in his charge. John then said that, in the interests of safety, he would do the pour, this first time, so that Dan could watch, and get a feel for what happens here. "There is too much that can go wrong, and there is no time to explain what to do, once the crucible leaves the kiln. It is best for you to just watch, this time. Put on the safety equipment, hanging on the wall, over there." John pointed to a wall, and likewise proceeded to get dressed, himself. John removed the pattern from the sand, so that the void was ready for the metal.

John told Dan to stand clear, but be ready for anything, as almost anything can happen, when there is molten metal running around loose. John opened the kiln door, and there it was : Dan's first glimpse of what he would probably soon be working with, himself. The lighting of the room was just very slightly subdued, to enhance the effect of the kiln. The kiln was aglow, with a heat that was bright red-orange, and Dan could feel some of the heat, even from where he was standing. John secured the tongs around the crucible, and lifted the magical, molten charge from the kiln. John moved the crucible into pouring position, and emptied the contents into the void, where the pattern had been. John returned the empty pot to the kiln, and closed the kiln door, and turned off the heat to the kiln.

John said, "This is our small-scale room. We use it for demonstrations, and for teaching purposes. A disaster with a small amount of metal is bad enough! Multiply this little bit of metal by about 5000, and you could begin to get an idea of what goes on, here! Okay, come on over here, and watch the show. It should be about safe enough, by now, as long as you do not do anything stupid."

So Dan moved in closer, and watched, fascinated, as the bright orange glow began to subside a little bit. He noted that, even though the metal was still glowing hot, and still molten, that he could see the bright reflective silver of the surface.

John closed the door to the kiln, and said, "The temperature of the metal, and the kiln, was around 1600F, when I opened the door, to make the pour. By the time I was able to get the crucible emptied, it was probably about 1450F, which is a pretty good pouring temperature, for this casting. As the metal cools, it will shrink, and depending on what you are making a casting of, that shrinkage could be a very important consideration, in the design process. It all depends on what you are making, and what kind of metal you are using. Most of the time, you will want a pattern that can be retrieved from the sand, and that can mean, depending on the shape, and other considerations, that a pattern has to be made in pieces, often out of wood, in such a way that it will perhaps have interlocking pins, to hold all of the pieces in alignment. The pattern may have multiple segments, spread out over more than one casting box, and may involve multiple rolls, and sometimes portions of the sand mold may have to be shaken out, and remade again. At other times, a consumable pattern is a better choice. For this pattern, and for the purposes of the demonstration, none of this was done, to keep it simple. The 'Shock and Awe' effect, is what was desired here. About all that most people manage to retain from this, is the wonder of watching the metal coming out of the kiln, and being poured, like water, into a sand mold. For many of the visitors, this is the first time that they have been this close to anything this hot, and a very primitive feeling, a sort of a 'memory', perhaps, buried deep in the collective subconscious of the species, can arise.

"Often, a casting can be used just as it is, once it leaves the sand. We also may have to do some hand work on it, such as filing or cutting. The original creators of the first primitive machine tools had to do it all by hand, but we now have the ability to use the improved versions of those early proto-machines to help us do the work, in most instances. That brings up the next consideration in the design of a pattern. Sometimes we have to leave additional material on a casting, that will have to be cut away, at the appropriate stage of manufacture. This material may be needed, to make the machining steps easier, or sometimes, to make it possible to machine the piece at all. After the piece has been shaped, the excess material may be removed, or it can sometimes be left, even though it no longer serves an actual function. It depends on the final function of the casting. If it is for our own use, such as an experimental design test, we might just ignore it, if it does not interfere with our purposes. If the machine is a finished design, for sale, we will likely remove the unnecessary stuff, for the improved appearance of the finished product. Well, that is about enough to think about, for now. Since it is fairly late in the day, and the casting will be several hours cooling off enough to be safely handled, we can call it a day for you, at least in this room. We can dump out the casting in the morning, and take a look at how you did, on your first experimental pouring! Follow me to my office, and I can suggest some books that you could check out of our library, and start your studying, tonight."

So Dan followed John back to his office, and John wrote down the names of some of the books that would be in the library, and would likely be the most effective at this stage of learning. John added that there would be more experimental learning castings to follow, as needed, to help Dan with the development of his overall abilities. They parted for the evening, and Dan dropped by the library, to obtain the assigned reading material. He checked out the books, and as he was walking back to his room, Dan noticed a fairly tall, and slender, girl going into one of the kiln rooms. He stopped, and thought about that, for a few seconds, realizing that he did not remember seeing her before. He decided that he had enough else to do, and since he had no idea who she was, figured it was likely to be one of the fairly frequent visitors that come here.

Dan dropped off the books at his room, and decided that this would be a good night for fish and chips, at the cafeteria. He ate dinner, both thoughtfully and mindfully, thinking about his new lessons, and also with some distraction, wondering about the mysterious girl, who walked into one of the kiln rooms! After dinner, he went for a brief walk, and then returned to his room, to start learning some of the details of metal casting. He was fascinated by the material, and found himself quickly absorbing the contents of the books. A few notes were all that was needed. The rest of it stayed in his mind, as it all made perfect sense, and seemed to crystallize within the framework of his own mental organization, and life experiences, even though he had not done any of this before. He hit the shower, and then fell asleep, with his face in a book. After a short time, Dan woke up enough, to put the book aside, and turn off the light. His dreams were a rehearsal of what had been done today, and what he had learned, and read, and thinking about tomorrow, and the unknown girl.

By morning, Dan had pretty much forgotten about the girl, as he was reviewing, and collecting, his thoughts about the casting he had made yesterday. He got dressed, and ate breakfast, and returned to where the casting was waiting, from the previous night. John was already there, and he had Dan pull the box sidewall pins out. John handed Dan a trowel, and said for him to start digging into the sand, until he found the casting, and scrape away the excess sand. Dan then knocked the casting gently out of the pile. At which point, John handed him a wire brush, and waited to see whether Dan would know what to do with it. Dan used the wire brush, to remove the residual sand that did not easily come off with the trowel.

John said, "Okay, let's put the casting up on the bench here, and look it over."

Dan then lifted it up, and put it on the bench. John carefully looked over the casting, and then said, "Well, what do you see wrong here?"

Dan said, "Following from what you told me yesterday, and from what I have read, last night, it seems that I had a couple of soft spots in the sand, from when I rammed it up."

John said, "Okay, that part is good. Did you notice anything else?"

Dan thought for a couple of seconds, and then said, "Well, there are these little marks, over here, but I do not immediately place them."

John said, "Those are little steam trails, where the sand was too damp, near the edge of the casting. Sometimes, you will see those as little blemishes, if you are lucky. Other times, the steam will bubble up into the casting, and perhaps render it useless. In a really bad case, if there is enough water, there can be an eruption of metal, and that hot molten metal can be thrown everywhere, including on you! There is a fine line between not enough water, and too much water. Various factors can come into play here, such as how much water there is, and where it is concentrated, and how much of a head of metal pushing down, from above, there is. Also, the size range, and the distribution of the sizes, of the sand grains, and the amount of clay that is in the sand, will be factors. I deliberately did not tell you about venting the sand, since there was enough other stuff for you to think about, the first time, and it was just a learning experience, anyway. Today, however, we will be building on where we left off yesterday. We will be doing another pattern, today, and it will be more involved, and present more learning opportunities for you. But first, we want to make a note, in passing, of another important point about casting. Turn the casting over, and set it down on the table again."

Dan did so, and then John said, "Notice how the top of the metal left a little bit of a divot, where the metal shrunk as it was cooling? This is another property of castings that has to be considered, and often compensated for. Shrinkage may seriously affect the castings. Thin areas will cool quickly, and solidify, and often rob the heavier, and thicker areas, which cool more slowly, of metal. Sometimes a casting may pull itself apart, if the sand is rammed too solidly in the wrong areas. Also, the casting may solidify completely on the outside, and yet leave a void inside, due to the shrinkage of the still molten metal on the inside. The trick is to get the sand to do what you want it to do. To be solid where you want it to be solid, and to be solid enough to hold together when the metal is molten, and then collapse at the right time. They spent centuries learning how to get the results that they wanted, and it is really an art form, with a rudiment of science that had evolved around it. Each batch of sand is different, as is each batch of metal, and each pattern. But they had figured out how to do it well enough, by the middle ages, so we should be able to figure out what they did, even if it sometimes will take us years of training. Fortunately, we have some pretty good books now, to help us avoid making absolutely all of the exact same stupid mistakes, all over again, every time. So, today, we are going to have you step it up a notch, and that begins now."

John told Dan to load the casting onto the "reject" pile, in the corner, for now, and the said, "You will note that the kiln is on, and heating up. In many instances, you would have to build another box, just to size for the next pattern, but we already have one handy, so we are going to have you re-sieve your sand, from yesterday's pattern. The screen is over there, and so is the shovel."

Dan took the hint, and re-sieved the sand, and cleaned up the floor, including scooping up the small little metal fragments that are often found in the sand, after casting. He proceeded to get the sand to a preliminary conditioning, with a spray bottle, while John grabbed Dan's next pattern, and brought it over to where Dan was.

John said, "This pattern will present new opportunities for demonstrating a simpler, but still more realistic, casting situation. Study it for a couple of minutes, and tell me what you see, and perhaps how you would handle it for casting."

Dan did so, and noted that he had been presented with a wood pattern, again. It was shaped somewhat like a concrete pier block, except that it had "feet" sticking out of it, on two sides. Sometimes, an abutment for a bridge might be of this shape. It was a small pattern, about four inches by six, and about four inches high. Two of the sides were almost vertical, and the two sides which are adjacent to the feet, had, perhaps, about a ten degree angle, down to where the feet projections began.

Dan said, "Well, I note that it comes apart, with the bottom part having the feet, and the top part has the sloping pier shape, and that there is a third piece, over on the other table, and a little pin-hole in the center of the top part of the pier."

John said, "Okay, good so far. How would you approach this for making a casting?"

Dan thought about that for a couple of seconds, and then said, "Well, it looks like I would have to make a split box casting, and the sides are all sloped, so as to help to provide some clues of how to approach this, so if it is okay with you, I would like to try to follow some deductions about the casting box, from the shape of the pattern?"

John nodded, and then Dan grabbed a shallow wooden tray, and rammed it full of sand, to about the maximum amount that the tray would hold, and then struck off the excess sand, so as to leave a flat surface. Dan then grabbed a four – sided, framed, unit, with no top or bottom, and placed this piece on the table top, having noted that this piece had little cross-sticks, or ribs, in it, to help with keeping the sand from just immediately falling out, when the frame was lifted, after ramming. Dan located the pattern in the frame, and started to ram the sand around the pattern. Afterward, he decided that it was time to try to lift his work, and then most of the sand just dropped out, onto the table top!

John said, "Well, what do you think happened here?"

Dan said, "It would seem that the sand was a little bit too dry, and that I did not ram it hard enough."

John said that those were likely good guesses, as he ran his hand through the pile of sand that had previously been in the frame. So Dan wetted the sand down more, with a spray bottle, and then used the trowel to stir it all together, so that the mixture would be a little more uniform. Dan then rammed the pattern back up into the sand, extra hard this time. John had Dan try lifting the tray frame again, and the sand held, and stayed where it was placed. Dan looked relieved, and John said, "It will likely be okay for this exercise, but it might also need a little bit more Bentonite, in the future. So, now what would you do?"

Dan nodded, and then grabbed the third tray frame part, and placed it on top of the second part, which had just been rammed up. He then located the round, riser portion of the pattern in place on top of the pier shaped piece.

John interrupted here, "Note that the pattern portion, which is already in the sand, had a little hole in the bottom of the foot part. This was to test your observational skills."

Dan said, "I had noticed that! I just did not know what to do with it! I guess I should have asked?"

John said, "That would have been good! The two pieces of this pattern also serve a role in other casting patterns, and that is why they were not permanently assembled together. See if you can install the locking screw, from the table over there, without having to redo the ramming on your current work frame."

Dan managed to do so, with difficulty, but it got done. Dan then resumed with the ramming of the sand around the slightly tapered cylinder, after using the alignment pin. John noted that the melt metal was almost ready for pouring. He had Dan carefully suspend the frame at just enough of an angle so as to be able to remove the pattern from the sand. Dan managed to do so, with only the very slightest loss of sand, which he was able to blow out of the way, and then put the frame down, on top of the bottom layer. Dan then carefully removed the tapered cylinder from above, just as John was opening up the kiln. Dan put on his safety gear again, and watched as John made a pour, into Dan's mold.

Again, it was fascinating to watch this molten metal come from the kiln, and then be poured, almost like water, into a cavity that he had made in the sand, albeit that this cavity was much more involved than the previous one. John said, "Okay, that is enough, for now. Come back after lunch, since it is almost that time, anyway."

Dan nodded, and got out of his gear, and wandered off to the lunchroom. He picked up his food, and was looking for a good place to settle down, when he saw Maeve waving at him, so he went over to join her.

Dan sat down, saying, "Hello, Maeve! Long time, no see!"

Maeve said, "Yes! I have been on special assignments. The usual 'Hush-Hush' stuff."

"I understand", Dan said, adding, "I am still learning some basic skills, for what may be a special project, that I still have not got a clue on!"

"Yes", said Maeve, laughing, "That is usually the way that it works, here! If you pass each phase of your training, then you might get to learn a little bit more!"

Dan then asked, "Is Orla around?"

"Yes", said Maeve, "She might be here shortly, but then again, maybe not! Rehearsals and review, and so on, for the next thing, whatever it may be!"

So, they ate their lunch. Dan commented, "I could not help but to realize, from observing your skills and organization, during my recruitment trip, that you must have spent a lot of time in preparation for it."

Maeve said that this was frequently the case, since they got the harder jobs, but that she could not say any more, and asked how much time Dan had served in Purgatory, when he first started.

Dan replied, "Well, I lost track of it, exactly, since a good portion of it was spent in bed, collapsed, after dinner, for the night, for at least the first several weeks, just to get up, and do it all over again, the next day. However, I think it might have been about three months, even though it seemed like it was a terminal ennui. It appears to have done me some good, though. I might just have a few more muscles, now, than what I had before!"

Maeve said, "Yes! It does look like you might at that! Well, unfortunately, my lunch is up, and Orla seemingly was not able to make it. I will tell her that I saw you."

Dan said, "Oh, okay. Thank you for having me join you for lunch, and please tell Orla 'Hi!', too!"

Maeve left, and Dan finished up his food, and wandered back to learn about how the latest casting turned out.

Dan got back to the casting, just ahead of John. John then placed his hand just above the casting, to feel the radiant heat, and said that it was likely to be okay to open the casting, and then checked the surface temperature of the casting, with an infrared-sensing instrument.

He said, "Well, it is safe enough for us to take out of the sand, but just make sure to not actually touch it. Put on your leather gloves, and face protection, and leather coat."

Dan did so, and proceeded to release the casting from the sand. He found a couple of little spots where the sand had fallen away from its intended place, and landed in the bottom of the void, creating a slight bulge where it had fallen from, and a little divot, where the sand had landed. There were also a couple of fins, where the metal had seeped into the spaces, at the boundaries between the sand boxes.

John said, "Well, all in all, that is not bad, especially for the second try! You will get better. All you have to do is just critique your own work, being honest with yourself about what likely went wrong, and being very careful to address those areas, while continuing to maintain and improve your skill in those places that you did good in. Since you have already had the safety instructions, and now know where all of the stuff is, and have studied how to operate the kiln, you should be okay in here. I have now been given other things to do, for a while. I can watch you from my office, on the camera, and if anything goes wrong, or I see that you are about to do something unbelievably stupid, I can be here really quick. There is also a voice link, so that you can yell for help, too. So, since you already have been shown where the wood shop is, make yourself some patterns, and then experiment with where to best split them, and how to do multiple rolls, and some of those things that you have been reading about, and watching the instructional videos for. For some of this kind of stuff, being left to figure it out for yourself, is really the best way. The important thing to remember here, is that this is an inherently dangerous activity. We can minimize the dangers, by being thoughtful about what we do, but there is always a risk in dealing with molten metals. Aluminum, while bad enough, is comparatively less risky than magnesium, and cast iron, and so on. By the time you are handling molten cobalt, and then tungsten, you should be ready to handle most anything else, at least as far as temperature goes. Magnesium, for example, is best handled in one of our special rooms, made just for the purpose. You enter a sealed room, and then place the sand box in the room, in a designated place, and leave the room, and then close the gas tight doors. The air is then replaced by dry, moisture-free, pure argon. You melt the magnesium in the kiln, and then pour the casting. After the metal has thoroughly cooled, and we can aid in speeding up the cooling, by a refrigeration system, the argon is collected back from the room, and re-purified. The magnesium casting is then safe enough to handle. One thing to remember about magnesium, is that it is the last element, as you move up the electromotive series table, that has any chance of surviving in the pure state, for any length of time. Everything else above it, is just simply too reactive to be found in the free-state in nature. Even magnesium needs to have carefully controlled conditions. The basic, 'Green-Sand', casting technique is modified by the addition of boric acid, or another inhibitor, to the sand, and the sharp corners need an extra thick fillet, compared to aluminum. We can also add small amounts of other elements to the magnesium, to provide better properties than what the magnesium would have, alone. However, you will be playing with aluminum for quite some time, before we show you what to do for bronze and cast iron. You should have a little bit more free time, now, in the evenings and your days off, to study chemistry and metallurgy. A little bit of thoughtful research on your part should show you areas that are of special interest, for you. Have at it, and show us what you can do!"

Dan said, "Thank you! That is just the type of free-floating assignments, that I like the best!"

John then left Dan to do his own experimenting, with sand and aluminum.

After several days of this pattern, Dan happened to be leaving his workroom, at just the right time, to see the ghostly image of the same girl, moving so smoothly and gracefully, that she was seemingly floating as she walked. He attempted to follow her, to see where she went, but he quickly lost her, probably into one of the doors that was then locked behind her.

Dan was again shaken by this girl. He had almost forgotten her, after the first time, because it had been long enough, and he had enough other stuff to think about. Dan figured that he should let it go, and get back to his room, and get to work. He would need to show them what he could do, probably sometime soon.

Dan soon developed more complex casting patterns, and built special boxes for his patterns, and learned the techniques, such as double, and triple rolls, and false bottoms and tops, which would then be shaken out, and re-made. He learned how to compensate for shrinkage, and how hard to ram the patterns, in selected areas, so as to avoid having a casting tear itself in half, from having the sand rammed too hard in the wrong places. Soon, he was approved for using a larger crucible, and more metal. Dan then developed an interest in learning how to make simple machines, from scratch, and began to study books on how to do this. After making a pattern toward achieving this purpose, Dan would then make the casting, and do the clean-up work, such as filing off any fins, and other rough spots on the casting. Soon, he learned how to make a finished surface optically flat, with selective application of files and sandpaper, and polishing compounds. He then used cold-rolled steel pieces, to provide hardness and wear resistance to certain areas of the machines that he made. By selective and thoughtful application of the available tools at each step, Dan soon arrived at his first, self-made, metal lathe. Then, using the metal lathe, and those other items that were previously available, he made himself a simple milling machine, and some of his own cutting tools. The little pieces of steel, that were discards from other areas, could then be sharpened to be his cutting tools, for working the aluminum castings. They had to be sharpened a little bit more often than some of the harder metals might, but he was able to find the scrap material, and there was little or no cost for the scrap.

Next, Dan created a metal shaper, from castings, and loose hardware parts, and other items that he was able to requisition, such as electric motors. Each machine that he made, then aided in the development of the next one. Soon, he discovered that he could use the exhaust hood in his work room, usually used to carry the fumes outside, from other operations, and then he started to experiment with some materials that might be much easier to work with. Styrofoam patterns, made from the extruded Styrofoam, could be easily cut and shaped with hand saws, and other simple tools. Once the pieces had been shaped and glued together, he could attach pieces of steel to those areas of the pattern, that would otherwise be badly deformed during the sand ramming process, by using adhesives, such as caulking. The caulking would burn up, and the steel pieces, if they had ends that extended beyond the pattern, would remain where they were placed, by virtue of the sand, which prevented them from falling into the void, and spoiling the casting. This really sped up the manufacturing process, and the only trade-off was that, if he screwed up the casting, he would have to remake the pattern entirely. There were still instances in which he would want a wooden pattern, such as if he wanted multiple copies of a pattern. Mostly, however, the consumable patterns worked out very well. It was just another material that he had to learn to work with. By using the tools that he already had, and those that he had made, he was able to move progressively up to larger, and more sophisticated machines. Eventually, he had made some really good stuff. Then one day, he thought it was time to ask John if he was on a good track, with the items that he had made, so far.

John came over to Dan's little work room, and started studying the creations in great detail. John told Dan that he had been watching Dan's progress, with amusement and admiration. Almost single handedly, Dan had derived for himself some of the basic machine tools that were used for a full century, until the computer came along, and then really shook things up.

Unknown to Dan, John had been sending progress reports to Mr. Jones, who was then forwarding them to Sir Percival. All were pleased about what Dan had done, with minimal interference, essentially unsupervised. It supported the basic philosophy of Sir Percival, that if you hire good people, who have the right material in their personality, and turn them loose, within reason, to follow their interests, the results can be surprising. It was one of the places that the basic education systems in many countries went wrong. By insisting, from kindergarten, on a "One size fits all" approach, under the dubious pretenses of "efficiency", we stifle, right from the start, almost any of the free spirit of creativity, that may have been ready to bud from these young minds. By burying them in boring activities at school, and planting them in front of TV sets at home, these children often quickly give up any of their own thoughts, and submit to the demands of the "Educational System." A "typical" grade school, in particular, but it is also true of high schools, is just a "Zombie Factory." The first year or two, should be a thoughtful evaluation of who may have the spark of useful curiosity, and in what areas, and evaluate how to best serve those children. Instead, we train them to not think. There are children out there, who learn to read, well, long before the age of three. Those children are already years ahead of children who are just starting to learn to read in first grade, and yet the early readers still have to put up with the same very basic, and now boring stuff, that they had learned, sometimes on their own, three years earlier. Some children, who otherwise appear to be average, are really quite brilliant, and this may be hidden behind a handicap. Improved testing methods would be extremely beneficial. Suppose, for example, that we had another Newton, with an absolutely brilliant mind, who could make great advances for civilization, that was just kept in a room all by himself, just because he had a handicap, and was a little "difficult" to handle? Is this a price that society is willing to pay? Is it "fair" to the child? Eventually, a "Judgment Call" has to be made, but we should err on the side of caution. If Newton had died, as it is reported that he almost did, on the first day of his life, would we have gone to the moon in 1969?

Fortunately, some of these children get through the stifling swamp of our current K-12 system, anyway, but at what cost? Perhaps they were lucky to have a teacher, or a mentor, or a friend, or relative, that inspired them, and then managed to keep the flame of desire alive. By the time they get to college, it is a little bit better, but even here we stuff dubious "Graduation Requirements" down their throats. It is claimed that these "Distribution Requirements" are there, to make the student a more "Well-Rounded" person. In reality, the distribution requirements tack years, and many thousands of dollars, onto the student's bill. What, besides money, is being "distributed?" Most of those courses that are stuffed down the student's throat are vomited back out, and forgotten, just as quickly as possible, after the course requirements have been completed, anyway. Many departments would have to shut down entirely, at many schools, because they have no value to the students of those schools. Get rid of certain departments, and cut down the number of credits that are required to get a Bachelor's degree, and college will go a long way toward becoming "affordable" again. Thus, more students would graduate from college, but then we just create another problem: If everyone has a Bachelor's degree, we have just upped the basic standard. Assume that everyone now starts to get a bachelor's degree, then they all have the same "advantage." An advantage to everyone, becomes an advantage to no one. The same thing happened, years ago, when the basic standard was an eighth grade education. Those few who managed to go to high school were at an advantage, simply because they had been lucky enough to have the opportunity to get through high school. In the 1960s, the graduating Early Boomers all thought they could get an advantage, by going to college. The very first ones to get through did find an advantage, in that they were at the leading edge of a wave that would want to follow them, hoping to get the same advantage. The first ones out, got the teaching, and managerial, and science jobs that there were many vacancies available in, and waiting for them to fill. The rest of them had an increasingly difficult time with just getting a job at all. It was much like the basic "Pyramid Scheme": the first ones in, and the first ones out, will come out to be well ahead. Many of the rest of them will be lucky to do a little better than break even, and quite a few of them will just lose their shirts, being lucky to get a job pumping gas, with the station owner complaining about them being "Overqualified."

What do these students do then? Stay at home with parents who cannot afford them? Go back to college, to get the next higher degree, if they can manage to survive these additional requirements, and either way, tack so much money onto what they owe for college, that virtually none of them have any hope of ever paying it off? Even if the lucky ones manage to get a Ph.D., there are so many of them out in the market place, that they cannot get teaching jobs, while competing for an ever shrinking pool of positions, as the available money for supporting such positions dwindles, partly because of tax cuts that got pushed through, by those who managed to get through the educational system, first, so as to cut down on the competition, for those jobs that require whatever level of college it is that they managed to finish.   A few of those may go on to get other degrees, as well. But eventually one runs out of life, and cannot long continue such pursuits.

Dan found himself to be quite inspired by the words of praise that he received, and then focused his thoughts on how to develop even bigger, and better, machines. Soon, he reached the physical limits of what one person could easily do alone, with the work space and equipment that he had.

It was at about this time that Jones called for Dan to come to his office. Dan learned that Sir Percival was quite pleased with Dan's progress. It had been decided that he was now ready for some of the "Hot Stuff!"   Dan's new work area would be in the "Cast Iron" room, and this would involve better crucibles, and gas-fired kilns, and even more protective gear than before.

The next day, Dan was in the Cast Iron work area. He was not surprised to find that there was only the basic instructor there, and only for just a few minutes, to make sure that Dan knew about the most important stuff. Dan was considered to be a "Big Boy", now, and could probably manage to figure out what was where, and how to use it.

Someone had to figure out all of this stuff, in the first place, so he could probably figure out most of what he needed fairly quickly, too. In the interests of safety, the main thing that the visiting instructor did, was to make sure that Dan knew how to turn on, and off, the gas for the kiln.

So, Dan started with making a "Consolidation Melt", from the pieces of scrap Cast Iron, which would easily fit into the crucible. As room in the crucible became available, more pieces were pre-heated, and then added to the crucible. While the melting and super-heating went on, Dan made himself up a simple pattern, so that he could test the properties of the cast iron. Soon, the metal, and the test pattern, were ready. The pour was made, and the consumable Styrofoam pattern went "poof!", and ignited, with the metal filling the void. The exhaust system carried the fumes out to the scrubber. It was time for lunch about then, and the casting would be quite some time cooling enough to be extracted from the sand, so Dan turned off the gas, and got cleaned up, and went to lunch.

After lunch, which he tried to not hurry through, in his excitement of wanting to see what happened with the cast iron, Dan was just going back to his new work room, when he happened to see the same mysterious girl, again seemingly floating down the hall, going toward the administration area. Dan was starting to become more curious about who she was, and tried to follow her. She disappeared into the restricted area, where the REAL "Big Boys", including Sir Percival himself, were. So he turned away, and went back to the task at hand, which was learning more about Cast Iron. Still, he was damned if he could keep his mind off of her, and completely on his work. He found that the casting was of a quality that was okay, for a first effort, but some improvements in technique were necessary.

Dan fired up the kiln, and loaded the crucible with scraps, including a re-melt of the casting that he had just made. Since it was a colder start for the new melt, with more metal, it gave him more time to get ready for the pour. He prepared two consumable patterns, so as to help with optimizing both his time, and the gas usage. About an hour and a half later, Dan was ready to pour, so he suited up, and did the appropriate safety procedures. The door to the kiln was then opened, and for the first time, he began to really appreciate what he was about to do here. The previous pour was quite small, but this one was almost a full crucible, of white-hot metal! Even the radiant heat from this pot, and also from the open kiln door, would have been enough to set clothing, and ordinary materials, on fire, at some distance. However, Dan was well schooled in how to do this stuff, and he managed to pull it off, even with some small sparks and spurts coming from the sand box. Still, after THAT one, he decided that he needed a break, and returned the empty crucible to the kiln, closed the kiln door, and turned off the gas. He waited around for a little while, until the risk of danger had mostly passed, and then got out of his heat suit.

Dan decided that he needed more than a break, so he signed out, for a couple of hours, and got himself a double scotch, on the rocks, with his traditional twist of lemon.

While thinking about what had just happened, and the girl, he realized that he was now just slightly saner, at the moment, since he had a drink in his hand. He sipped at the drink, with a little straw, and pondered what he could munch on. He waved at the serving wench, and said, that he would like a plate of sglodion. Just as the French fries arrived, he saw Maeve, and waved at her. Maeve came over, but could not stay long, since she and Orla were just returning from their latest assignment. They chatted for a minute, and then Dan asked Maeve if she knew that fairly tall girl that seems to float into the main administration area, every now and then.

Maeve said, "It MIGHT be Sir Percival's God-child, from the description that you have given me! But I could be wrong, too. In any case, I need to get going, and don't quote me on that!"

Dan said, "Right. Hear no evil! Speak nothing! Thank you, and it is always nice to see you. Perhaps Orla could join us, sometime?"

Maeve said that it might be nice, but that they were almost always out on an assignment, or getting ready for the next assignment. But she would relay the thought to Orla, anyway.

So, Dan finished up his plate of French fries, and paid the serving wench. He sat there for a little bit longer, thinking about the mysterious girl, and sipped on the remnants of his drink. The " 'God-child' of Sir Percival?" He needed to think about that one, for quite a bit longer, but he also needed to return to the casting, that he had just made.

5

Months went by, and Dan developed his skills, and was then approved for more exotic metals, and trained in, and learned about on his own, various techniques. He continued to work, mostly on his own, for long hours. He read all of the books on casting that were available to him, in their library, and then sought out new books, and devoured the knowledge contained in them. Except for brief walks, about one or two per day, he spent the rest of the time absorbing chemistry, physics, metallurgy, materials science, and mathematics. Eventually, he requested permission to attend the University, and pursue a Master of Materials Sciences degree.

The next day, after the application had been received by Sir Percival, Dan was called to a meeting with Mr. Jones. Jones had also reviewed the application.

Mr. Jones said, "Come on in, Dan! Sit Down! Sir Percival is most pleased, with your great progress, and was quite tickled to receive your application, to pursue an advanced degree, and he immediately approved it, and instructed us to grant you a pay raise of 500 Euros per month, and to cover whatever expenses are associated with your pursuit of your degree, including time off from your normal activities, as needed. We have forwarded your application to the University that you have chosen, directly to the appropriate contacts, that we have in place, to ensure the optimum opportunities for success. We have agents in place there, who will assist you as much as possible, in ways that we have determined to be effective, and efficient. Some of them are very knowledgeable secretaries, and teaching assistants, as well as certain professors, who while nominally employed by the University, actually work for us. We get what we want, and they receive extra compensation, to help them with having the ability to do research. By submitting a grant to a private foundation, namely us, we provide funds, and equipment, and sometimes specialized expertise, to help them with successfully fulfilling the ridiculous requirement, that they often face, of 'Publish, or Perish!', as if though teaching classes was not enough. You can start at the beginning of the next term! By the way, we also just received your certification of dual-citizenship for the United States, and Wales! Sorry for the delay on that one! It seems that Sir Percival had to twist a few arms in Parliament, and on Downey Street! "

Dan said, "Wow! Thank You!"

Jones asked if there was anything else, for right now, and Dan said, "No, I think you more than covered anything that I would have thought of, to ask about." Dan and Jones shook hands, and Dan returned to his work, in developing his skills in metallurgy.

Dan left, to return to his work area, but before he got there, he decided to eat lunch instead, so he went to the cafeteria, and decided that today would be a good day for fish and chips. He requested a large plate of fish and chips, and an iced tea, with lemon.

As he sat there, eating his food, he was also lost in thought, again. Who, he wondered, is this Sir Percival, and what about the mysterious girl, that he would see floating down the hall, every now and then? How does Sir Percival have the power to "Twist a few arms", as Jones said it, in Parliament, and on Downey Street? He was promised a meeting with Sir Percival, many months ago, but that never happened.

However, he was being well treated, and left to work for himself, without any of the usual bullshit, that would likely come with a job like his, at his level of pay. He had heard of similar situations, where people were well treated, and left to pursue their own interests, wherever they may lead, without the definite expectation of obtaining certain results, such as the ones that are IBM Fellows. Was he being groomed for a form of Fellowship? Most of the time, if the right people are left to pursue such interests, they can develop good things, once they are freed from the distractions, and time wasters, of the usual daily crap that we often consider to be normal living. Working here, Dan had a support staff to take care of the cooking, and the cleaning, and shopping, etc. If he needed, or wanted something, he only needed to tell the appropriate person about it, and then it got done. An organization that could do that must be much larger than he had really had the time to think about. When it was time for the Dentist, he received a notification about when his appointment was scheduled for, and the Dentist was also an employee of Sir Percival. This also applied to many other specialists.

Dan was so lost in thought, that he only happened to look up in time to see the mysterious girl, floating out of the cafeteria. Since he had just finished his food, he grabbed what was left of his tea, and carried his plate to the drop spot, and attempted to follow her. Once again, she disappeared into the restricted area. This time, he happened to see that she turned to go into a different direction than usual, when she reached the restricted zone. Dan turned away, again. "Who is she? What does she do?", he thought to himself.

Dan returned to his work in the casting area. By this time, he was once again in search of new skills, and new materials to work with. He began to research how to work with various forms of high-temperature ceramics, and had already developed, for himself, a small, low-pressure, liquid propellant rocket motor. By keeping the combustion chamber pressure fairly low, the chances of a catastrophic failure were greatly reduced. He had once experimented with a simple homemade liquid propellant motor. He was able to cut the bottom portion off of an Erlenmeyer flask, and fire-polish the cut edges. He then modified an Erlenmeyer vacuum flask, by adding another spout to the one that was standard issue, about one inch up from the bottom, on the opposite side. The flask that had the bottom cut off was then inverted, and fused, neck to neck, to the flask with two spouts. He then had attached two rubber hoses, one to each of the glass spouts. One of them fed in ordinary air, from a small compressor. The other supplied the 80% Ethanol that he had made, and distilled, for himself. Once ignition was achieved, he could adjust the air, and the fuel, flow rates, so that he could watch how the combustion process occurred. By controlling the pressure of the air input, he controlled the combustion chamber pressure. If the combustion pressure exceeded the air input pressure, the air could not enter the chamber, and the motor would shut down. As long as he paid close attention to the whole operation, he could be reasonably sure that things were under control. He was only able to do fairly short runs, otherwise the throat area would have the possibility of melting, or eroding, from the concentrated heat, and speed, of the combustion gases, which were at the local speed of sound. By doing this work behind a shield, and watching with an array of mirrors, he was reasonably safe from whatever could be likely to go wrong. That, however, was not his first foray into the liquid propellant arena. His first try was to use a small retort, and coat the inside of the retort with 70% isopropanol, and drain out the excess. He would then take a match, and hold it near enough to obtain an ignition from the condensation spout. The flame would slowly travel up the neck, until it reached the bulb, and then flash all at once, with the combustion gases zipping out the condensation spout, with an audible sound, similar to "ZZZZippp!" After obtaining several successes in these trials, he built himself a small, and crude, low pressure liquid propellant motor, made from water pipe fittings. Here, he could use compressed air, at a higher pressure, and acetone. He continued on this way, until he reached the limit of what he could reasonably, and safely do on his own.

Dan now had access to much better equipment, and a good support staff. He began to understand, and envy, how it was that the famous people of the earlier times could do so much : They were rich enough, to be able to hire people to take care of the usual day-to-day stuff, and thus leave themselves free, to explore their own interests. Their money allowed them to obtain the fame, and secure their places in the history books. Thus, many of them were able to buy their way into fame, rather than die in obscurity and oblivion. Other people, just as smart, or often even smarter, were buried and forgotten, or only made a minimal, and unrecognized, impact. Perhaps they managed to write a small book, but the book was never removed from the library shelves and studied, and eventually was discarded by the library staff, because it had crumbled into dust. It was too bad that the same things had to be discovered, and rediscovered, time and time again. Each person, and each generation, had to re-learn the same boring stuff, time and time again, from the ground up. Wouldn't it be nice if there were some way to speed up the process, such as by implanting a "Knowledge Chip" into the brain? Then, humans could start to make some real progress. The only problem there, is that there would have to be some way to discard the "Knowledge" that was shown to be in error. Religion, for example, is superstition, and does not form a knowledge base. There would be groups that would attempt to have their religion implanted on the knowledge chip, and inserted into the brain. Thus, the knowledge chip could become a form of implanted brainwashing. Dan then concluded that the knowledge chip is probably not the best idea, after all. It appeared that the way forward would be to load a computer program that was well constructed, with the appropriate coding, so that the computer could access, and rigorously test, when needed, a data base loaded with what was then considered to be "known." Those items which cannot be established as known would then be placed into a "suspect" status, to await further evaluation. In this way, humans could be freed from having the burden of learning learn everything, over and over again.

Of course, humans would then need to be dependent on computers, but we are heading that way, anyway. There is now too much knowledge for any one human to absorb, and use. Thus, the need for specialization. Advanced life forms, based on carbon, would be too susceptible to extinction. But they would have to be advanced enough, to have the ability to use their brains for purposes beyond just pure survival. We are at a transitional state. The successor to man will be his machines, for he would not allow himself to be openly subject to the will of another life form, except one that he would create. If his machines then replace him, then the successor to carbon would be silicon. Silicon, as a direct life-form, could not achieve the number, and variety, of complex molecules that would appear to be needed. Once the computer arrives at the ability to store sufficient knowledge, and the capability to reproduce itself, and transfer a copy of all of its acquired "Knowledge" to its "Children", then man could be in trouble. One way that man could be supplanted, would be to be extirpated, such as by a disease, which would be of sudden origin, and enormously contagious, and then suddenly deadly. Another way would be an asteroid strike, in which the entire planet is rendered uninhabitable. Even here, a few humans could survive, just as a few mammals did, 65.5 million years ago. It would then be an open question of whether humans could re-populate the planet, in time to avoid being surpassed by another species, but humans would have the advantage of already being smart enough, to start with. Another species would have to acquire the brains to do us in, even though almost all of the acquired knowledge, up to that point in time, would very likely be lost, and we would then have to start all over again, almost from where we were, thousands of centuries in the past. A computer, on the other hand, loaded with sufficient knowledge, and the appropriate algorithms, which are just another form of knowledge, and the ability to make tools, and copies of itself, etc , could then take over the Earth. Computers could also make copies of themselves, and send them off to inhabit other planets, using just the knowledge that man already has, and machines could be built to go to places that man could never hope to reach. Man is a creature of the Earth, and would appear to have a great deal of difficulty with long-term space travel. One apparent problem, with long-term space travel, would be the limited gene pool, on board the spacecraft. So, unless Man finds a way to significantly speed up space travel, to relativistic speeds, or to safely, and reliably, place himself in a state of suspended animation, the population of the spacecraft would be severely inbred, before reaching its destination. However, Man is also a crafty creature, and thus could not be totally counted out of the game.

By this time, Dan had just realized that he was working on auto-pilot, while his brain had been off wandering about, in the land of daydreams. He returned his focus to the task at hand. His casting had turned out to be near-perfect, for the engineering purposes that he had sought it for. Other castings soon followed, and then Dan designed for himself, a series of machines that he could use to make other machines, each better and bigger than the ones before, with advanced features that were forwarded to the administration staff. Some of these ideas were patentable, and the appropriate patents were filed for.

When the time came, Dan shipped off to the English-language courses, at the University of Wales. Dan also added a few courses, to help to improve some of his very basic knowledge of Welsh, or Cymry. He found that the staff that he needed was already in place, and that he was able to devote his full attention to the courses. It turned out that he had acquired almost all of the needed knowledge on his own, long before he got to the school. Thus, he had little difficulty, and completed the requirements early. His thesis was on how to turn silicon-boron-carbon-nitrides into ball bearings, starting with Bucky Balls. These, then became ball-bearings, with a toughness and hardness to replace steel, and then he figured out how to grow them, like crystals. Jones, Meave, and Orla, all showed up when he was handed his diploma, along with the title of Master Of Materials Science. This work turned out to have such an enormous, and immediate, impact on the world of machines, that Sir Percival's organization had already had it patented, by the day that the degree had been granted. In recognition of this extraordinary achievement, Sir Percival had forwarded a letter to the peerage, and to the Palace. A week later, Dan was before the Queen, to be knighted! Dan was now the "Sir Daniel", that Percy believed that Dan would soon be, when he was hired.

6

Upon returning to work, following a short vacation to recover from his ordeal, Dan was called to a meeting in Jones' office. Dan would now become the head of his own little department, with a pay raise to 8000 Euros per month, but first he was to get his long-awaited meeting with Sir Percival. Jones then led Dan down the hall, and through a maze of hallways, with enough twists, and turns, to get him lost, several times over. Jones explained that this was done for the purpose of protecting Sir Percival. Only a few people had ever met him, and all were sworn to absolute secrecy, under the penalty of death, at the hands of Percy's trained assassins, including Der Sniper! His assassins were everywhere, and had been trained as "Sleeper Agents", authorized to make a kill, when necessary, without getting prior approval, which helps to show the level of training, and loyalty, that Percy had instilled into his agents. Percy took care of their families, in the event that an agent was captured or killed, with life insurance, and a pension, and other forms of protection and assistance, for the rest of their lives, including a rescue service for those who were captured, which at least rivaled the very best in the world, including hiring former agents that had retired from the various governments. Through the power and special skills of his staff, Percy's Agents were also programmed so as to "erase" from their minds, any knowledge related to their employer, in the event of problems, thus rendering themselves useless, to any captor seeking to learn any information about Sir Percival. They were subjected to the special techniques of the "Feline Mind Meld", thus protecting Sir Percival from those on the outside.

Dan noticed this strange reference to a cat, but kept it to himself. Jones brought Dan to the office, and home, as it turned out, of Sir Percival. Upon entering Percy's office, Jones and Dan sat down. After about one minute, a beautiful, silver-gray, long-haired cat entered the room, and hopped up into the chair behind the desk, and started typing on the keyboard. The screen had been turned, so as to face the visitors. The words began to appear on the screen, followed by the output of the voice synthesizer!

"Welcome, Sir Daniel! We finally get to meet, in person! Sorry for the delay in this meeting. A number of circumstances interfered with our doing so, before now. But I am most pleased that it has finally come to pass. I am a special breed of cat, called a Nebelung. That is a variation of the Russian Blue. One of my relatives appeared on the cover of the OCT, 2003, issue of 'Cat Fancy' Magazine. You are probably wondering how it was that I learned how to type, and form words, on the computer. That started one day, when I walked across the keyboard, and combinations of letters appeared, and then, the voice synthesizer, that my guardian had left turned on, began to attempt to spit out the words that I typed. I became intrigued, and I then taught myself to use the system, to communicate words and then thoughts, and whole sentences. Eventually, I was able to form complex thoughts, and communicate ideas. My guardian then had a special system created, just for me, with larger than normal keys on the keyboard, to make it easier for me to type. It turned out that I have the special gift of a brain that is superior to that of many humans, and I just needed for someone to provide me with a means to get my ideas out of my mind, and into a form where humans could understand them. I take in your spoken words, and communicate back to you, via this keyboard and screen, with the additional help of the voice synthesizer."

To say that Dan was stunned would be quite an understatement! Here was a cat, communicating words, and thoughts, and ideas, in roughly the same way that Stephen Hawking was forced to do so, now, because of his ALS. The thoughts inside of a brilliant mind would have been lost, without the ability to communicate with the outside world. Koko, the gorilla, had learned a sign language, and developed the ability to reorganize those words, and thoughts, in new ways, and finally to communicate with another gorilla, as well as with humans. It also occurred to Dan that it might be possible to teach a dog to communicate this way, with humans and other dogs, if the keyboard were sized appropriately, and the humans willing to commit themselves to trying to do so. It might initially require a massive effort, but with care, and selection of those traits that were most desirable, through a couple of generations, it could be do-able.

Percy then continued : "I am aware that you have been intrigued, and fascinated, by my beautiful god-child, Cinderella. She is actually the child of my guardian. Cinderella, would you please come here, and meet Sir Daniel?"

Cinderella then appeared from around the corner, where she had been seated, listening to the conversation. To say that she was beautiful, would be a minor understatement. She was tall, and thin, and had long, deep black, hair.

Dan and Jones stood up, and Cinderella blushed, and curtsied, saying, "Welcome, Sir Daniel! I am most pleased, and greatly honored, to meet you! I hope that I am found to be worthy of the wait, that has taken so long!"

Dan said, "Dear Lady, the honor is mine, as well! I have seen little glimpses of you, once in a great while, from a fair distance, and you are every bit as beautiful as I had imagined!"

Cinderella then replied, "I thought, and hoped, that we might get to meet, formally, when Sir Percival was ready for this meeting to take place. Until that time, it was not my place to hurry the meeting, so I just merely disappeared as quickly, and gracefully, as I could, whenever I had been spotted by you."

Dan said, "Well, you sure could disappear, with speed and grace! You seemed to float away, just as though you were a ghost. Sometimes it was so ethereal, that I wondered if I had been having a recurring dream."

Cinderella then continued, "I was taught how to walk with speed, and quiet grace, by Percy, and his agent, Der Sniper."

At this time, another human entered the room. Before anybody else could say anything, Percy's voice synthesizer was speaking, "Sir Daniel, I wish to present my Guardian, Jack! Cinderella is Jack's daughter."

Dan recognized him immediately, and said, "Jack! I thought that you were dead!"

Jack replied, "No, Dan. It was necessary for everyone to think so, because I performed some very critical, and highly sensitive work, as an agent of the United States. Things got awkward, to say the least, and the President made arrangements for me to be relocated, here. They had a protected situation waiting for me, and since I could already speak Welsh, it was something of a plus. Percy's organization grew quickly, and my having bought him a voice synthesizer was one of the smartest things that I have ever done! Dan, Cinderella is your first cousin. I am aware that you may think that you could not marry her, but I happen to know of a number of countries, including right here, in the UK, and Wales, as well as some states, within the United States, where you could marry, should the two of you eventually choose to do so. I mention this up front, because I am aware of the interest that Cinderella has expressed in you, and that you have apparently shown similar interest in her. I am not attempting to plant any ideas in the heads of either of you, merely to state that the antiquated, stereotyped, prejudice against first cousin marriages, is only rarely born out in fact. A few instances of bad results, from years ago, do not warrant any continuation of the legal and social prejudice, in the face of modern technology. The increased risk roughly corresponds to a woman in her early 40s, and they now have genetic testing available to help ensure that obvious problems are terminated. They are also certainly NOT telling women in their 40s, that they cannot have children! There are even many advantages to such a marriage, since you have often grown up together, and have a long and common history of knowing everything about each other. If they still want to be together, after all of that time, then they must really like each other! It will often allow you to keep a collected wealth within the family, as well.

"We should also remember that marriage is now only a legal, and social, convention : They could live together, and have children, even without the 'Blessing' of the State. Marriage was originally set up, so as to assign the financial responsibility for providing for children of a woman, to a specific man. This became necessary, so as to relieve society of the burdens of providing for children that were abandoned by the father, since the mothers often could not provide for the children, alone. Religions, which can be used as tools of the rich, then added covenants and regulations about such things, and then had the Bible declare that it was a 'Sin' against 'God', to have children, without marriage. It is not a sin against God. There is no God, for it to be a sin against! The Bible was written by man, and not God. It is only a financial problem, that some of the wealthier members of society, who did not want to provide for the children of the poor, would otherwise have had to deal with!"

Dan then said, "I am most honored to have any possibility that Cinderella might be interested in me, and I wish to explore that possibility with her, if she will have it, but how did you arrange the balloon ride, and the trained Ravens?"

Percy answered that one, through his voice synthesizer:

"Well, I have the special advantage of being able to employ the world's best weather forecasters, and there are birds who wish to work for me, for they realize that most cats will not try to bother them, out of respect for, and fear of, me. Der Sniper is one of the most feared, and efficient, killers on the planet. He is also a sweetheart, as long as you do not cross me! We make sure that the word gets well circulated, from those kills that he has had to make. You do not see Der Sniper, before he strikes, and we have the ability to easily, and completely, obliterate pretty much any trace of any target, that we can get within 35 miles of! Unmanned Drones, and Surface-To-Surface missiles, make that job so easy, that it is just merely kitten's play! All that I, or Der Sniper, have to do, now, is just to push a button, and you are gone! The rest of the story is easy enough, at that point. Well, I see that it is about time for me to participate in a scheduled conference call, so I need to have everyone excuse me for leaving so suddenly. Dan, we shall talk again, but it may be a while. Thank You."

So, Percy hopped down, and left the room. The others took the cue that the meeting was over. Jack returned to whatever he was working on, and Jones returned to his office. Dan and Cinderella left together. Dan immediately got lost trying to figure his way out of the Feline Mind Maze that Percy had designed. Cinderella led Dan out of the maze, and they went to a private cafeteria, which would explain why Dan only rarely got a glimpse of Cinderella, and never saw any of the others, anywhere else.

7

Cinderella and Dan then chose a secluded corner in the cafeteria, where they could keep an eye for anyone who approached. After a few minutes, a waitress arrived, and presented them each with a menu, and a glass of water. Both of them requested an iced tea, with lemon, while they studied the listing, and when they were ready, they closed the menus, and placed them on the table, which was the signal for the waitress to return.

After they had placed the orders for their food, and the waitress had left, Dan started up the conversation.

"I must say that my having woken up, in a balloon, and finding myself on the way here, was quite a shock! About the closest thing to any comparison, that I have encountered, for a situation like this, was Dorothy, taking a ride, in the tornado, on her way to a stroll down the Yellow Brick Road!"

Cinderella laughed, and replied, "I can appreciate that you would have wondered about what you were getting into! I actually thought that it was a master stroke, for Sir Percival to be able to maintain communications with you, through his private courier service. These are no ordinary ravens! They are specially trained, for the rigors of long distance, high speed travel. The raven agents that are based in the US, receive their instructions through a special network, and the message is passed along to the agents, for special delivery. The ravens that handle the sea communications, over the North Atlantic, are of an even higher class, and might be thought of as, 'Ninja Ravens.' Percy thought that it was necessary to maintain contact with you, to make sure that you stayed calm, and did not do something that could get you killed!"

Just then, the meal had arrived, and the waitress brought refills on the drinks. After the server left, Dan then said, "Well, I actually was initially so startled by the whole thing, that I might have attempted to do something to scuttle it, but fortunately there was a fresh communication from Sir Percival, which considerably calmed me, and after some time, I became more intrigued about who could pull off something like this, and why they would want me."

Cinderella answered that one, "Well, my father had told me much about you, going back a very long ways, and I had realized, from his descriptions of who you were, and the various things that you had done, that you could be someone that I really wanted to get to know. I would sometimes have a few minutes, at the end of a day of working with the kiln, and drop by to have a chat with Percy, about you. Percy is very wise, and he would ask me questions, through his computer and keyboard, about what it was that I would like to have, and what I thought about various things. He would often take considerable time, and showed me great kindness, and insight, about helping me to identify what I wanted. Not just merely what I thought that I wanted, at that particular moment, but instead to truly understand what it was that I really wanted. These were really deep, and probing, questions. So, it seems that you were someone that was about as close to a perfect fit as would be ever likely to be found, and Percy decided, as he had wrote to me, 'First Cousin laws be damned! You are going to have the opportunity to explore whether you can find happiness with Dan!' So, as it happened, it was learned that you were just about to retire from your previous employer, and Percy began his preparations to bring you here. Little by little, I became aware of the whole elaborate setup, that he had concocted, to pull this off. I was about as honored as anyone could be, that he would do this, for me! I am not yet permitted to tell you very much of this, at this time, but I am sure that you have already pondered what it would take for an operation of this magnitude to be pulled off. The whole logistics portion was a nightmare, all by itself. He consulted, for example, with his long-range weather forecasters, almost daily during the planning process, and getting the Raven Network ready for the new, priority assignment, required the special services of Der Sniper, who personally traveled to the United States, to supervise the job. We could not just simply 'Invite' you to come here, in the usual social conventions, because Dad was pretty sure that you would be a 'No-Show', in the common parlance, for a whole laundry list of reasons. Dad was not able to call you, or write to you, because he is officially dead, as far as the rest of the world is concerned. Percy thus needed to bring you here, and the planning was marvelously rewarded, when he learned that you and Bill were going to celebrate your last day of working. The rest of the process took about a day for Percy to finalize the preparations, and then to guide you to the waiting balloon, by virtue of manipulating traffic lights, and 'Power Outages'! After that, you, of course, know the rest of the story!"

Dan let that sink in for a moment, while they chewed on their lunch, and then said, "As I learn more about this, I am coming to realize that this whole operation is much larger, and even more sophisticated than I have previously thought, and I already had a suspicion of its size."

Cinderella said, "Well, all I am allowed to say, right now, is that the initial guess, that you speculated on, to Orla and Maeve, was much closer to the mark."

Dan said, "You mean about 'British Intelligence?'"

"Yes", answered Cinderella, "But it goes far beyond even that! You are now a member of a very secret society! There are very few who have ever even heard of our organization. Whereas, there are many who have heard of British Intelligence!"

They finished their lunch, and Dan wondered about where the waitress was, with the tab, for the meal, and Cinderella explained that Sir Percival was covering this one. So they continued to chat for a while, and Dan then asked, "I understand that you are making your own machine creations. Would it be alright if you could show me what you have been working on?"

Cinderella then blushed, and said that she would be honored to show what she had accomplished. She extended a hand for Dan, and then led him down another long series of hallways, and down several flights of stairs. Dan was long past lost by this point, so he asked, "How do you know where you are going? There are no markings of any kind anywhere along the way, or anywhere in this entire facility!"

"Yes, that is true!", Answered Cinderella, "All of this is done for the protection of Sir Percival, and my father. It was designed as a 'Feline Mind Maze.' Most of the people who work here, in the administration area, have a very high level of spatial intelligence, and quickly learn how to get around, without maps of any form, aside from the ones that are stored in their minds. The very few copies of the plans that exist, are kept locked in various safes, behind bolted doors, with security cameras. Only those people, who have reached the full Enlightenment of the 'Feline Level Nine', are even close to beginning to understand how it all works, here!"

Eventually, they reached the room that Cinderella called her "Studio", and she unlocked the door, and turned on the lights.

The modest word, "Studio", that Cinderella had chosen as the name, and description, of her workplace, had hardly prepared Dan for what he saw, when she had unlocked one of the inner doors, and turned on the lights, leading Dan in by the hand, before letting him wander around, and marvel, in jaw-dropping amazement, at what he saw.

This room was truly her own workspace, and it was at least the size of a football field, and that was just the initial room that he could see from where he stood.

"Down here", explained Cinderella, "I have my very own space. I spend quite a lot of each day here, and I have often not left this room for several days at a time. I have my own private underground bunker house, complete with bath, kitchen, shower, laundry, bed, etc., just like you would have in a normal house. There is a continuous air change, and cooling, provided by air ducts. As you will no doubt have experienced for yourself, when there are several kilns running at the same time, it can get quite hot. In this space, it can get even hotter still, as I have been privileged to be allowed to have special equipment that is not readily available in most other similar places. Everything has been designed to be as close to fire-proof as is possible, but even so, if something should still go horribly wrong, there is a manually activated system, to flood the room with Argon, to suppress the fire, with additional backup systems, which I can activate, as I make my exit, that will further suppress any possible fires, and cool things down, with Liquid Nitrogen."

They walked around, with Dan looking at various things, and Cinderella continued, "This is my electric-arc kiln, and that one, right over there, is my magnetic induction kiln, and the next one is my gas-oxygen kiln, that uses liquid oxygen, and cyanogen. My favorite one of all, which I have only used just a couple of times, because of the initial cost of the fuel, and the eventual destruction of the kiln, by the heat, is over there. I only fire it up, for use in studies of new materials for nose cones, for re-entry into Earth's atmosphere. That one uses liquid oxygen, and lithium metal, and can achieve over 13000F, hotter than the surface of the sun. I can retrieve, and reprocess, most of the lithium, by electrolysis, so that is not a real issue, and we have our own cryogenic manufacturing facilities, so it can be thought of as almost a self-sustaining, recycling and re-use operation. The cost comes from the fact that it is quite difficult for me to recover absolutely all of the lithium, for reprocessing, since it is boiled away by the intense heat generated. Sir Percival operates his own solar and wind power network, and has nuclear reactors, so that we can run all of our equipment, without having to worry about losing power. We have achieved many great inventions, and some of these are licensed out to others, with a payment of royalties to us."

As the tour continued, Cinderella led Dan into many of the side rooms.

"This is one of my pottery studios," she explained, "My work is sold all over the world, but most people are never allowed to even suspect who really made it."

Dan studied many of the pieces in great detail, and was marveling at the intricacy, and level of beautiful detail, shown in all of the works. Even the painting, and the final firing, were flawless. The work was of a "World Class" quality. It was about as fine as would be found anywhere.

Cinderella then led Dan to the next room, "In here, is my chemistry lab. I have, or can get, virtually every substance in existence, if I want it. Even those that I cannot get, I can make myself. If I really want some substance, I will just take another substance apart, down to its atoms, and then manipulate them to be what I want from them. The only things that I cannot really manage, are those where the geometry, or thermodynamics, or other physical limitations, prohibit the desired compound from existing. In the next room over, is my 'High Energy Physics' lab. While I do not have the scale of the CERN project, I have built my own Betatron. It has over five miles of carefully hand-wound wire in it."

Cinderella walked back into the main area, with Dan following.

Dan said, "I noticed that you have many machines of various sizes and persuasions, and they are all quite beautiful."

Cinderella answered, "Thank You! Like your own very nice work, I reasoned out, and created from scratch, all of my machines. Eventually, some of my machines grew to the point where I needed larger facilities, and higher temperatures, as well as special equipment. Most of this equipment, I made myself, just as you have done. Once the size of the projects, and my skill level, warranted it, Sir Percival hired some lab assistants for me. My helpers would take care of stuff that required more than one person, to be able to achieve. The machines that I can achieve my best work on, are variations of the miller, although sometimes an operation is easiest to complete on the metal lathe. Well, that is the 'Three Dollar Tour' of the main area! I would now like to invite you into my own humble little abode, so that you can see where I live."

Cinderella took Dan by the hand, and they went down a couple of hallways, still attached to the main studio. She then unlocked the door, and Dan followed her into her little home. As she led Dan around, and turned on the lights in various rooms, one by one, Dan noticed that one of the rooms was a well-stocked library, and on one of the walls, he noticed some of her certificates. She then wandered off, for a minute, and on the way out, offered to bring Dan back an iced-tea, with lemon. Dan accepted this, and was lost in thought, reading her various certificates and degrees, and some newspaper articles about her.

Bachelor of Arts, Chemistry, University of Wales, age 10.

Bachelor of Arts, two foreign languages, French and Welsh, University of Wales, age 12.

Bachelor of Fine Arts, Metalsmithing, University of Illinois, age 18.

Master of Materials Science, California State University, age 20.

Bachelor of Arts, Mathematics, University of Washington, age 14.

Master of Arts, Mathematics, University of Oregon, age 16.

Master of Arts in Teaching, Welsh Literature, University of Wales, age 21.

Dan soon realized that he must have read some of them out of order, and it was just about then, that Cinderella returned, with the refreshments.

Dan then said, "Thank You for the drink, and WOW! I am impressed! How does one get a Bachelor's in chemistry, at the age of ten? Most places would not even let you hold a test tube, at that age!"

Cinderella explained, "Well, I was reading very well, long before I was three, and I was reading science at four, and my father started me out, very carefully, in Chemistry at the age of five. Because of his position, and prestige, and resources, he was able to get me the very best private tutors, and I was 'Tested Out' of grade school, and High School, with an IQ of, 'Greater than 170'. I was allowed, after demonstrating skills and knowledge in chemistry, equivalent to a college Senior in Chemistry, and an appropriate level of maturity, to take the college courses, and whizzed right on through them, often completing an entire term's work, in a weekend, and then taking the final exams. Similarly, for the other departments. Once the skeptics became believers, it became even easier, and all of my professors, including the whole Department Of Chemistry, attended the commencement ceremonies, where I was admitted to the title of Bachelor Of Arts, in Chemistry. I was able to get the foreign language to be Welsh, because it was already documented that my first language was English, even though I often used Welsh more than English, at that time. If you have noticed that the degrees are from a wide, and scattered, variety of places, that is primarily because it was places that were conveniently near where my father was working at the time, usually for, or associated with, the CIA.

"I have often thought about doing a Ph.D., but so far I have not found the particular inspiration for doing this. I must confess that I thought that your thesis subject was a masterpiece of inspiration and imagination, though! But, I just might be 'Schooled Out', by now, as I seem to be primarily interested in working with my kilns, making my pottery, and creating ever more useful milling machines, and with your new knowledge of Materials Science, we can make even better, and stronger, milling cutters, and then use these new cutters, and some of the other knowledge that we have achieved, individually or collectively, to create new, and more sophisticated machines. I would like to make a whole new class of milling machines, that would allow us to really make something good, but right now, I am searching for the right vision of what this might become."

Cinderella then paused for a minute, and was lost in thought.

Dan studied her, and they both sipped on their iced tea.

He then said, "There seems to be another subject that is troubling you, is that right?"

Cinderella replied, "Yes, that is true! There are many of those, but the main distractions have been you, and also, I received a letter from one of my former instructors, and in this letter, he has asked me a seemingly simple, and innocent question, and as I studied the implications of his question, I realized that this apparently simple thought, would lead to the creation of a whole new branch of mathematics, if I were to choose to pursue it. But I just do not know if it is one that I want to pursue. Thus, I have to decide if I will follow up on it, or just simply develop and outline the idea enough, for another person to bring this new gift into the world. Since I have a Bachelor's and Master's in math, I am sort of 'Honor-Bound', to at least pass this along, in the event that I choose to not go any further with it, on my own. I once discovered a new, and very fast, method of doing multiplication. It was just a simple transformation. I played with it a lot, and verified that it worked correctly. Unfortunately, I lost the piece of paper that I created this on, and I have never been able to reconstruct it. It is as though it is a hole of lost knowledge. I remember that it existed, and that I discovered it, and even wrote it down, and used it several times, but I cannot even begin to reconstruct this method, even as simple as it was. How much more could we have done with that? It seems that we will never know, now. Thus, because of this tragedy, I am now even more acutely aware of this new gift, and I have to try to deal with it wisely. I even once asked Percy if he thought that my multiplication discovery could be retrieved with a Feline Mind Meld, but he said that there are some things that even he cannot retrieve, if they are truly gone, and since I have tried to retrieve it on my own, in various ways, for so long, it would be unlikely to work. He did say that he would try, if I was really being bothered by it, but since this is only an occasional thought, now, we should probably wait for a while.

"Often, I find myself collecting little thoughts, and notes, on pieces of paper, throughout the day, sometimes when I am in the middle of something else. These thoughts are scattered over many subjects. Some of them, I am able to hang on to, for long enough to write them down, and others flit into, and then out of existence, about like subatomic particles. These are truly complex visions that will frequently defy attempts to organize them into a meaningful form. Sometimes, they are like the flashes of vision that one might remember from a nightmare, only they are in the middle of the day, when one assumes that they are as wide awake, as they are usually ever likely to be.

"So, it sort of comes down to a matter of whether I want to do a Ph.D. in mathematics, which I am not sure that I have the drive for, anymore, or whether another area is more personally relevant, to me. If I had received this inquiry, shortly after I had finished the MA in math, I just might have done my Doctorate in the creation of an entirely new branch of math. Or, am I truly, and totally, burned out on theory? The amount of time, and creative energy, that I devote to working in my own space, creating works of immense beauty, and practical value, seems to sort of answer the question for me, but if it is okay with you, I would like for us to start a little collaboration on various projects, and then we can see where that will lead us. We might inspire each other to greatness."

Dan then thought on her suggestion for a short time, while sipping on his tea, and remembering that genius, and madness, are often two sides of the same coin, and he then asked, "Do you have any particular ideas, or projects, that you would like for us to develop?"

Cinderella thought on this, for several minutes, before answering.

"Well, I have a few projects that I have hoped to pursue, which come up, when I lay in bed at night. Again, it is a poorly defined idea, but I have wondered if it might be possible to use my experience with the liquid oxygen and lithium kiln to provide sufficient starting energy, when combined with liquid Xenon, and a nuclear energy source, to propel a small ion rocket, to speeds that we can only dream of achieving, with our current technology. However this would take years, and perhaps trillions of dollars to achieve, if it could work at all. I am also aware that such a project would require at least the cooperation of the entire economy of Europe, or at least the United States, and because of the launch of a large amount of nuclear material, would have to be a very open project, so that the rest of the world would not go into a panic mode, fearing it as a ruse for a nuclear first strike. I also know that there are attempts currently being made for developing the Xenon rocket. So that is a sort of generalized little grand vision of mine. It is not practical, but if one is going to have daydreams, they should at least occasionally be a little bit extravagant! Sometimes, an idea can be scaled down, to something that just might be 'Do-able.' In this case, however, it would almost certainly just be another one of those delusions of grandeur.

"However, as far as a practical idea for a project, we have both accumulated some experience in the creation of milling machines, and since Sir Percival has offered to create a whole department, and put you in charge of it, we have the best chance of getting all of the approval needed to get things going. But first, we need to work up a practical vision of what can be achieved, and how to do it with a minimum of cost, and risk."

Dan was fascinated by listening to Cinderella, and the descriptions which she gave to her visions, and by the level of complexity of her mind. He asked, "Do you have any sketches, or drawings, of what form, shape, or size, you would like to have such a project to take?"

"Yes," answered Cinderella, "come with me to another room!", as she took Dan's hand, and led him to yet another project area.

As they walked farther into her home, they soon arrived at a room with all manner of beautiful drawings on the walls.

Dan asked, "Did you do all of these, yourself?!"

"Oh, yes!", replied Cinderella, "I first started to teach myself to draw, when I was about four. I quickly discovered a love for architecture, in a practical sense. The truly ornate, and extravagant, building formats are not really for me, but I learned how to draw, and color, the work, to present it as the highest form of its vision. While I can admire the work that is sometimes realized, I also learned that the typical architecture teacher has a personality that does not work for me. I did find ONE, and she was already as good as any of the teachers that I had found anywhere, in any subject, and it was her very first class as a teacher. If I could have taken all of my Architecture courses from her, I might have decided to get a Master of Architecture, rather than some of my other pursuits. Unfortunately, even though she said that she loved teaching, she quit after her first term of teaching, and as I said, none of the other architecture instructors were, even the least bit, satisfactory for me. I suppose that one could say that they struck me as temperamental and, well, flaky!

"Since we are here on the subject of a project for a mutual collaboration, I have a drawer filled with drawings of possible projects, and we can flip through them, if you would like, but I also have another file of thoughts and ideas for experiments, to see if any of them will stimulate your curiosity, but my particular need, and one that we just might be able to develop into a form that would require the least actual investment from Sir Percival, is for a whole new class of milling cutters. Since we now both have a Master's in Material Science, we have nominally arrived, at least, at the minimum practical combined knowledge, that will allow our collaboration to have a reasonable chance of success. Milling machines have been very well developed, by others, as well as by ourselves, but the real need is for an optimal milling cutter, one that will require a minimum investment, at least during the initial development, and conceptualizing process. It will be quite some time, barring an unexpected breakthrough, but the vision that I have had for a long time now, is for a short-range laser.

Conceptually, it appears to violate the laws of physics, as we understand them now, but we have been surprised before, in the history of physics and chemistry. My idea is basically for a sort of a 'Light-Saber', like they showed in the movies, about thirty or forty years ago, and within this short, very precision length, high energy beam, would be an energy equivalent to that of the surface of the sun, on the basis of watts per square meter, or energy intensity. By some process, which we would need to devise, the length of this beam would be adjustable, and terminate with a square, flat end. One version of this might be to choose a series of high-frequency sine waves, and have them arranged so that they largely cancel each other out, except at a precise distance from their points of generation, where the waves would all combine to produce a single plane, where the energy density would be sufficient to vaporize any known material, and thus provide a clean, smooth surface, that would be at least as good as 'Optically Flat.' Any known material, coming within the range of this beam would be instantly vaporized, but material beyond the length of the beam would remain unaltered. The movement of the beam would have to be controlled by a high-precision, computer-guided operation, that would essentially scrape off atoms, one layer at a time. The resulting surface would thus always be optically-flat. In this way, we would eliminate the need for, at the very least, flat-faced, end-mill cutters, and possibly some of the other ones, as well. Working time requirements, for finishing parts, would be greatly reduced, sometimes to the point of being little more than just the setup time, required to load the part onto the machine.

"One possible form of this, would be to have a crystalline cylinder of some sort, containing a lasing material, whose energy terminates at the end boundary of the crystal, and the resulting 'shock wave', caused by the material discontinuity, is what generates the intense heat that vaporizes any material that is inconsistent with the material of the lasing medium. The beam would function as a sort of high precision 'tweezers', in that it could pluck individual atoms off of the surface. The ability to pick up, and move, an atom off of the surface requires that work be done on the atom, and to move a lot of atoms, although each individually takes only a relatively small amount of energy, there ARE a lot of atoms, to say the least, and collectively, the process of removing material can take a lot of energy.

"Mostly, however, this has just been another little mental vortex of mine, something that my mind strays into, now and then. Each time this happens, I eventually seem to wake up, sometimes hours, or even days later, and realized that I have not eaten at all during this time, and have just barely drank enough water, to keep from getting really sick. I had one time when this happened, and I wrote an entire master's thesis in math, along with all of the proofs, et cetera, as it would be for the final presentation of the finished work. I received approval of the topic on a Thursday, and then I presented the finished product, on the following Monday afternoon! I have only the vaguest, and most fleeting, dream-like, images of the very feverish possession that took over my mind during this process. My thesis advisor was shocked to have the completed project, just a weekend after the topic was approved, and even more shocked, by my physical appearance! He called the Campus Nurse, and arranged transport to the Student Health Office. After a quick evaluation, the Nurse had a car from campus security drive me to the hospital. It was not quite bad enough for an ambulance, but there was a sense of urgency. The security officer brought my admittance information to the hospital with him, and thus sped up the process, since they did not have to ask me very many questions at the emergency room, during the check-in phase, which is just as well, since it seems that I was only a few steps away from a real problem! My mind went into a fugue state, and focused only on the objective at hand, which was generating a finished thesis, and neglected the care of my body, and therefore of the mind itself, in the process, and almost killed me, doing it! I had to take some pills, and spend some time locked up in the Psych Ward, and do a rehabilitation therapy thing, and learn how to manage myself better.

"Well, I got my Master of Arts, at age 16, as you will probably recall, from having looked at my 'Rogue's Gallery', hanging on the wall, and I was then 'Strongly' advised against pursuing a Ph.D., at least for a while, since it was the concern of a great many people, who were in the position to know quite a bit about what had happened, that I literally might not survive the program, without having someone around, who would be in the position, and have the authority, to supervise me. Looking back at it now, I would have to agree that they might have been right! So, as you may have noticed, after I finished the MA in math, I went to some of what were, for me, progressively 'lighter' subjects, and lastly, the MAT in welsh Literature. About the only 'bump' in that road, was the Master of Materials Science, but I had a lot of help with that one, since I had just done the Bachelor of Fine Arts in Metalsmithing, and Percy had a staff to take care of the rest of the daily living stuff, for me, such as food and laundry, and making sure that I took care of myself. He thus had made it about as easy as it could be, for me.

"After that was done, I realized that I had still not gone to a level that was 'light' enough for me, and I sat at home, for months, reading Welsh literature, and Fairy Tales, and going ever deeper into the history of Wales. It was a wonderful therapy for me, and may have been an absolutely essential step, on the road back. An older woman had told me a story that contained a cautionary note. She had lost her brother, from his pursuit of a master's degree. He had no trouble with getting a Bachelor's, and then went on for a Master's, after a few years. The demands placed on him, caused him to die of a stroke! At autopsy, they found that fully half of his brain had shriveled away. Percy is most kind to me, and I was allowed to have whatever time and support I needed to find my way back to some place of stability. I found the inspiration for another program, and most likely for the last time. I finished my MAT in Welsh Literature, at age 21. In a sense, I went back to an adult form of the childhood that I had largely skipped over, without even knowing anything about what it was that I had missed, when I went from age three, to about age 18, in just a couple of years! I have been in a therapeutic recovery mode ever since, up until very recently, shortly before we actually met. It finally ended, when I learned that you were on the way here, in a balloon, of all the crazy stunts! Sir Percival is one of the very few amongst us, who could have pulled that one off, without getting you killed!

"So, during the 'waiting period', before we were formally introduced, I determined that the most productive thing that I could do, was to develop new and better milling machines, and also mostly to concentrate on the production of high-quality art pieces, that Percy could sell, to offset the cost of providing for me, when I was not doing too good. And that is why I have been quite torn on how to approach the question that I was asked, recently. The one from the professor, that I had realized would open up a whole new branch of mathematics."

Dan sat quietly listening during her long story, absorbed by her every word.

Cinderella continued :

"Sometimes, I wonder when we will reach the limits of the amount of knowledge that humans can effectively absorb in a lifetime, and what will we do, then? With the amount of knowledge exploding all around us, in a wide and varied collection of fields, how does one even begin to be a responsibly educated member of a society? As our knowledge grows, the ability of the population to grasp it, gets increasingly overwhelmed, and an increasingly large portion of the people turn to a belief in various forms of magic, to compensate for, and provide alternative explanations for, those things which they do not understand. As Arthur C. Clarke had observed, 'Any sufficiently advanced technology is indistinguishable from magic.' Well, of course, one form of magic is religion. Imagine that one: we end up going full circle, and in our systematic attempt to get away from religion, through the diligent development of actual knowledge, of how things really work, we end up driving people back to religion, to provide them with some comfort for the things that they now can no longer understand, and many of them now no longer even try to understand! We end up going back to the very ignorance that we have spent at least four million years trying to shake. We become smarter than ever, and also remain just as ignorant as ever, at the same time. Because we remain just as ignorant, there are a great many people who then end up with no understanding of how things work, even in relatively simple things, such as politics, where a significant portion of the poor allow themselves to be manipulated into voting for the very forces that would abuse and destroy them, while making the rich ever richer, using the very religions that the poor now turn back to. The Rich manipulate the poor, using a 'Divide and Conquer' strategy, using political 'Wedge Issues', such as abortion, and the right to keep and bear arms, to split the poor into two camps. The rich do not give a damn about abortions, and the freedom to have them. If they want an abortion, even an illegal one, and they have sufficient money, they can get one performed safely. It is also part of how they keep the poor, poor. They also do not care about whether the people have the right to have guns. The rich can buy guns, and they can buy security guards. While it is still an important personal liberty, the Second Amendment has been effectively out-classed by technology. The right to 'Keep and Bear Arms' has been largely rendered obsolete, in the face of advanced strike-fighters, loaded with laser-guided bombs, and chemical, and nuclear, weapons. Its value, for being able to oppose tyranny, is now greatly less than it was in the 18th century. There are some provisions, in the US Constitution, that will soon be in serious need of being updated, due to technological changes, such as how to have a resolution between the freedom of the press, and the right to have a fair, and unbiased, trial by jury. Another issue, now, in the United States, is the struggle for healthcare reform. There are those who have said that they voted for 'Hope and Change' and now claim that they got plenty of hope, but very little actual change. The reason that they did not get any actual change, that they could see, is because they failed to get enough change in Washington, to be able to push through the change that is actually needed. The system is designed that way, so as to have it so that only one third of the senators can be voted out in any one cycle, and thus allow time for people to 'Forget', and to give the rich time to devise compensating strategies, to retain control of the situation. Too many of the poor people voted for the rich. If the poor ever wised up, they could out-vote the rich every single time, and make the rich pay their fair share of taxes, which is just the very thing that the rich absolutely do not want to do. Even Thomas Jefferson was concerned about that one. I think he was the one who had wrote something about the 'Tyranny of the Majority.' But here, even the rich often overlook something: what they attempt to do, is to get rid of taxes, thinking that they will become richer in the process, and they do, when they compare themselves to the poor! But the rich also have others to consider, and that is their fellow rich competitors. If they eliminate a tax, and show more money on their balance books, and all of the others who are equally rich, from the same tax loophole, now also have more money as well, and they then compete for, and drive up the prices on, the same goods and services, and also end up no better off than they would have been, if they had just left the taxes alone, in the first place. What they need to do, instead, is to find clever ways to increase just their own personal wealth, perhaps through innovation of a new good or service that people need or want, at an affordable price. Instead, they whine about all of the regulations and taxes, and how those regulations get in the way of getting stuff done. How do they think that the poor feel about that? There are many among the poor who could build their own homes, at a much more affordable price, except for all of the real bullshit regulations, that practically force them to buy a house, from a builder who has made the house so big that the prospective buyer now has to involve a bank in the process of obtaining the house. The National Debt in the United States has exploded ever since Reagan got into office, even with money being taken away from schools and road maintenance, and other vital services. The rich got richer, and everybody else has to deal with what is left. If the roads fall apart, and a country cannot even move goods and services from one place to another one, then they will very quickly be in a very deep hole of doo-doo! Right now, for instance, there are literally thousands of bridges that are unsafe, and need either serious repair, or to be torn down, and replaced. Try to get a truck across a bridge that has fallen into the water! If things get bad enough in the US, the rich can move to Canada, or another country, and take their money, and security guards, with them, and the poor have to deal with the mess that the rich left behind, just like with the 'Black Death', of The Middle Ages. The Rich fled the towns, where the poor were being left to die by the thousands, and retreated to the relative safety, and security, of their country estates, and closed the gates, and posted their security guards, to guard them, and waited for the storm of disease, and the violence that followed, to run its course.

"Virtually all of human history can be explained through one of three motivations : Money, Religion, and Sex. When one examines those three motivations closely, we find a single underlying motivation : The perpetuation of the Self. Sometimes, the best way to achieve the perpetuation of the Self, is by looking beyond the narrow Self, and helping to provide for the common good, which magnificently, a few of the very richest are actually doing that! For instance, if a civil war resulted from a class struggle, and many of the very richest were killed, would those rich people have been better off, if they had instead contributed more to the common good? This is not to say the rich must always feed the poor, for example, for then the rich would also become the poor, and then more of the poor would make more babies,(which, by the way, is a good argument for making sure that birth control, and education on the same, is freely available for women), but rather if the rich were to try to remember that they, too, could have ended up being poor, except for the accident of having been born in, or maybe having married into, a wealthy family, or having made a lucky investment, or, what the Hell, having hit the lottery!

"What is really needed in the United States, is for a constitutional reform, such that we use the technology that we now have available, and have a random draw, live, on television, by social security number, for determining who is 'elected' to the House of Representatives. In this way, the various groups of the population would, on the average, be fairly represented, in proportion to their numbers. Money would be completely removed from the equation. The lobbyists would not know who to try to elect, since everyone is running, because no one is running, and the person who is elected could not be influenced ahead of time. This would also have the advantage of largely destroying an entire industry, which is dedicated to the influencing of the population to vote for 'So-and-So.' Women would receive fair representation, as would minorities, and the elderly, etc, over the long haul. In any given election, they might not be fairly represented, but that is still better than it is now. Of course, convicted felons serving time, at the time of the election, could not serve, and there would be other reasonable exclusions, but, by and large, it would be a much fairer system than the one that the US has now. A Member of Congress serves the entire state. There would be no districts, to squabble over, every ten years, as one group attempts to gain an advantage over the other group. If your number comes up, you are drafted, and must report for training for your new job, just like in the military. The Federal Government would guarantee that your previous job will be there for you, after your service time is up. Note further that this system does not necessarily prevent you from being re-elected. It just makes your being re-elected, as unlikely as your having been chosen was, in the first place. It also would largely eliminate the monopoly of lawyers in the House, since lawyers would only be present proportionally to their numbers. This would likely result in   the bills being moved through Congress becoming much smaller, and easier to follow, rather than the mind-boggling crap that they frequently put out, now. Bills that are many thousands of pages, and are so big, that no one has actually even read them, to see what kind of garbage is being sneaked into the Bill, on its way to becoming law. Some may say that those chosen this way would be easily bribed, but it may actually be just the opposite, as some of the selectees may realize that this is their ONE chance, to maybe TRY to make a difference. In any case, it will be unlikely to be any worse than the mess that they already have!

"Even if we turned to computers, to solve some of our problems, we might someday reach the point where even the time required to complete the data transfer, from one machine to another one, would exceed the probable lifetime of said machine. Just in terms of the amount of knowledge required, and the speed of processing the data, alone, it might eventually happen that H. G. Wells's vision of the Morlock and Eloi, in 'The Time Machine', will come true, but for a different reason than the one that he had suggested, which had to do with the workers living under the Earth, and the Ruling Class living on the surface. In this new way, the robots would have all of the knowledge, initially with the human's blessing. After a while, the humans would become excessively dependent upon the Computer and the Robot. Humans have a habit of becoming incredibly lazy creatures, when given a half of a chance. Eventually, the humans would start to lose their 'edge', and begin the slide toward senility, as a species. If we last long enough, the successor to man will be his machines, and the successor to carbon will be silicon. Carbon is the enabler that allows machines, and therefore matter, to acquire sufficient knowledge to substitute silicon. Carbon, alone, has sufficient range and variety of possible compounds, to allow life to easily develop, as far as we can see, now, anyway. This is not to claim that in an entirely different set of initial conditions, things could not occur differently, but as it stands now, carbon is it. Even if we, or another life form, manage to find a faster processing chip, or a way to pack more memory storage into a smaller space, we will eventually hit certain fundamental limits that we probably cannot do very much about, such as the speed of light, or the number of charged particles that we can cram into a very small space, or even the number of electrons in the universe. Suppose, for example, that there are 10 to the power 100 electrons available in our universe, and that we make a machine that uses absolutely every last electron, and our hypothetical computer has the ability to detect the presence, or absence, of every single electron, within its assigned space. If the electron is present, the machine reports that digit as a 1. If not, then the machine reports the digit as a 0. If the electron is locked in its little box when it is not being called upon to vote as 'Present', then the computer recognizes it as 'Absent', and the number zero is assigned to its location. This then gives us the 'Binary', or two-option, state, and the largest number that could exist in our universe is then,

$$2^{\left(10^{100}\right)} - 1$$

Which is to say that the number, 1, is written with a hundred zeroes following it, and that number would then indicate the number of powers of 2 that would have to be multiplied together, and then all of those powers of two would have to be added together, and 1 would be subtracted from the total. So even in the entire universe, there is a finite number, perhaps very large, that represents the largest possible number, which can be represented in our universe, and thus the largest possible number that the mind of man or machine, or another life form, could represent, at least with a binary machine. This number then becomes our practical statement of 'Infinity', or the maximum integer that we could ever achieve, using our present conception of a computer. We COULD get fancy, and allow electrons to be 'borrowed' from boxes that would be zero, anyway, and thus extend our working number range, and some tricks like that, at the price of introducing 'Holes' in the number system, beyond the normal value of the 'Maximum Integer', but the point is still the same: there is an upper limit to the computer numbering system. Attempts to move beyond the maximum integer of the 'Complete Set' could have consequences for the technique of Mathematical Induction.

"Similarly, there is a lower limit, on how close to zero a computer number could get, and still be different from zero, even with a hypothetical computer, made from all of the available electrons, in the entire universe.

"Of course, it is possible to teach a computer to manipulate symbolic quantities, according to the rules of algebra, of both, finite, and trans-finite quantities, and that could then allow man to bypass this limitation on his machines, when it is needed to do so. I once played around with the inversion of matrices, as a solution technique, for curve-fitting of data points, and it absolutely pissed me off, to have the computer routinely give me an error message, such as 'NEARLY SINGULAR MATRIX!' So, I finally bypassed the limitations built into the usual arithmetic set, in the compilers, and wrote a program to generate Five-Thousand-Digit-Arithmetic! The numbers were created, stored, and manipulated as, usually, single-digit integers. Thus, I could handle numbers that would be small enough so as to be considered to be almost infinitesimal, for most practical purposes, but were still extremely important to me. Sometimes, for example, I found that the desired number, which I hunted for, was different from zero, only after over three hundred decimal places!

"Unfortunately, when I attempt to focus on a lot of this stuff anymore, I quickly get a severe headache, so what I have found that I have to do, now, is when a thought comes to mind, I have only a very small amount of time, in which to write it down, in enough detail, so that I can then, perhaps, return to it, from time to time, when a thought comes up, which relates to the previously recorded thought. Over time, I can still collect these ideas, but I usually cannot, at least at present, safely allow them to take over my mind, as would have previously happened. One time, I became so locked into an infinite, runaway, thought loop, that I was seriously locked out of reality, for several days. When my staff realized that I was in really bad trouble, they called for help, and my father came down, with the doctor, and they were ready to cart me off to the hospital. Percy had told Dad that he wanted to see me, before they loaded me into the wagon. The doctor said that we had to go, now! Dad told the doctor to wait for a few minutes, and Percy hopped up on top of me, and began to massage my forehead, and my neck. He also began to stare into my eyes, while placing one paw on each side of my head, and manipulating my neck. After this, Percy placed his head up against my forehead, and stared directly into my eyes for about a half a minute. Shortly after he completed this, he said, to Dad, though his voice synthesizer, ' You can take her to the hospital, now! Thank you for stopping this, for a minute. If you had not done so, she would have died of a stroke, before she even reached the hospital! Cinderella had a blood clot, that was blocking portions of her brain! I have relieved the problem, temporarily, but she needs treatment, and an infusion of fluids, to compensate for that which has not recently been replaced!'

"The doctor started to say, 'What the Hell does HE know about it.............?!'

"Dad just said, 'Shut up, and keep an open mind, and get her transported, NOW!'

"So, they loaded me in the ambulance, and Dad went along. Well, to make a long story short, another doctor eventually learned that there might be a much broader meaning to the term, 'Alternative Medicine!'

"So, I have rattled on for quite a while! Sorry about that! Sometimes, I get started, and lose track of when to stop. Would you like some more tea?"

Dan answered, "Yes, please!" as they both stood up, to stretch.

They walked around for a little bit, to restore their circulation, and Dan followed Cinderella to her kitchen, and she poured more tea, and added some fresh lemon slices.

"So," continued Cinderella, "That is the short version of why it is that I have to be very careful, and kind to myself. I no longer have the luxury of allowing whatever portions of my brain it is, that do this stuff, to simply run away. If that does happen, I, at the very least, end up being the victim of a runaway train wreck. My genius appears to be at least partly the result of some form of brain damage, in which the normal control mechanisms, which would otherwise use chaos to break up the self-referential feedback loops, fail to operate, possibly due to an organic, or chemical, or genetic defect. Each time this happens, it increases the probability that I will not recover from the effects. The usual MRI scans have not been greatly helpful, since it appears that I would have to be in the machine, at the time that it starts, and because that is something that is difficult to predict, inconvenient, and rather expensive, there have not been any serious attempts to get this done, yet."

Dan said, "WOW! So it would appear that we should approach any such project, that might place great demands on your brain, slowly and, cautiously. Would it be safer, and sufficiently satisfying to you, if we worked on doing your artwork, for now? Would Sir Percival be happy enough with this, at least for now?"

"Yes", answered Cinderella, "I agree that we must proceed slowly, with minimal risk, for now. Both the personal risk, to me, and the financial risk, to Percy. I am quite certain that Percy will be very supportive of whatever we work on together, as the friendship, and the love, that Percy and I have for each other, is deeper than most humans would ever be able to fathom. I have been the recipient of his kindness many times, and he has devoted many evenings to me, including several sessions of the Feline Mind Meld. I long ago lost count of exactly how many times Percy has done this for me, although I am sure that it is somewhere well past 40 times. Since he started devoting some entire evenings to our doing this, I gradually learned to really understand, and Percy has said that I will soon achieve the rank of 'Grandmaster of the Full Enlightenment', of 'Feline, Level Nine!'"

This really caught Dan's attention, so he asked, "Just what is it that is meant, when you say, 'Feline Level Nine'?"

"This is a unique way of being", responded Cinderella, "Where the brain's thought processes are rewired through certain exercises, and in other ways. Some of these exercises are physical, such as learning how to do special stretches, and a range of motion that is beyond that of most humans. Most of them are more of a mental nature, such as learning how to patiently sit, and concentrate, or how to walk so gracefully that one appears to float."

"Yes!", Dan interrupted, "I HAVE observed you doing that many times, such as floating down the hall!"

"That is one example," Cinderella continued, "Another one is the ability to sit patiently, comfortably, in one position, for several hours, motionless, with full concentration, awareness, and consciousness, without being bored, while maintaining great intensity. Some forms of human pursuit, such as Yoga, can be helpful, for preparing to learn this. Some of the human schools, for example those that teach variations of Ninjutsu, and Dim Mak, are somewhat similar to the methods, as well as some Sniper schools. The candidate must learn, along with a great many other things, how to achieve total mind control. One man I know has mastered this so well, that he has received very serious surgery, without any anesthetics! The surgeon had his doubts, and therefore had an anesthesiologist standing by, just in case, but this was not needed, and the surgery was a full success.

"The brain can learn to have conscious control of the heart rate, blood pressure, respiration, etc. Another man, now dead, upon learning that he would have to spend the rest of his days in a nursing home, decided to just turn himself off, and quietly expired, during a nap, within just a few hours after being told of what he would have to do.

"While this is merely an anecdotal description of the answer to your question, it does provide at least a vague notion of some aspects of Feline Level Nine. The Feline Level Nine is a way of living and thinking, and being, through various forms of training, that allows for optimum enhancement of the whole person, body and brain. This makes it possible for someone to easily do things that would kill, or at least, severely injure, most people, who have not received the appropriate education, and rigorous training, that is needed. Many cats, and some humans, have special personal traits, which either aid in their arrival at the appropriate characteristics, or which at least minimize the number of bad habits, that would have to be unlearned."

Dan asked, "What kinds of things are you speaking of, specifically? Can you show me any of the simpler examples of how one starts to learn some of this stuff?"

"Yes!", answered Cinderella, "Come with me, to another room!"

She took Dan by the hand, again, and led him down another series of hallways, still within her home. After about two minutes or so, she opened a door, and turned on some more lights. They walked in, and she closed the door behind them.

"I have to keep this door closed," she explained, "To preserve the exquisite acoustic properties in this space! This is my sound training laboratory. There are hundreds of speakers in here, and the walls have been carefully developed, so as to optimize the sound qualities. Could you tell which speaker it was, specifically, that made a single sound, for less than a second?"

Dan answered, "I am afraid that out of all of these speakers in here, I could not even begin to hazard a guess!"

"Well," answered Cinderella, "That is one of the things that you would have to learn, if you were to attempt to pursue 'The Enlightenment!' And then, to make it even more interesting, after you have started to grasp the basics of doing this, we then have you blindfolded, and you sit in a chair, which slowly revolves around, and randomly translates you about, in the room, and you will notice that the speakers are fixed up, so as to allow them to move about in the room, as well."

Dan asked, "Why do you do this? It seems to be quite elaborate."

Cinderella explained, "Because humans have generally become much too dependent on just one of their senses : The eyes. Suppose that we ended up in a place where, for whatever reason, we could not see, even if we still had perfectly good eyes? Perhaps it is the middle of the night, in a power failure. Or maybe the car breaks down, after dark, in the forest, and the flashlight is dead. Most of us would only be able to slowly move about, at best, and be lucky to avoid being injured. By developing, and optimizing, our other senses, we have a better chance at success. If we are able to use sounds, somewhat analogous to what a bat could do, but specifically tuned to human abilities, we are enhancing our ability to survive, and thrive, in a variety of situations.

"Further, there are other special abilities, which we can enhance", Cinderella said, taking Dan's hand again, "Come with me!"

After a few minutes, they arrived at the next room.

"Where are we now?", asked Dan.

"In this room, I have developed, through the guidance of Percy, and Der Sniper, specially chosen and placed items, such as the rug which you stand on. The function of which, is to allow some training in how to detect motion in the room, even slow motion, in which you are blindfolded. Once you start to grasp some of the abilities required, you can detect someone walking slowly through the room, even though there is no noise made in the auditory range of the human ear. This ability is achieved, by learning to detect small disturbances to the air in the room. One can learn to do this, partly, by becoming exquisitely sensitive to such changes, through the very small temperature differences on the skin, from the rate of evaporation, or the movement of the hairs on the skin, caused by minute air movements from an object, or person, moving around, nearby. It is also the reason that I do not like fans. They overload my finely tuned sensory network, and generate false information. When possible, I will avoid being in rooms where there are fans.

"Would you be able to detect someone quietly dropping a dime, on a rug, 50 feet behind you? I can! I have also done it, even with shoes on. I feel the vibrations, even through the shoes, on the bottoms of my feet."

"As a further improvement, along with this, I have learned to hear, through walls, for example, by placing my fingertips on the walls, which I have further enhanced by learning to read braille, blindfolded, to provide a back-up plan for my sight, and also to greatly increase the adaptability, and flexibility, of my brain. The more cross-wiring, and redundancy, that I can achieve, the wider the range of situations that I can easily adapt to. I once detected that an earthquake was coming, and walked out of the building, several seconds before stuff started falling off of the walls! In this particular case, I felt the P-wave, several seconds before the S-wave hit. People have talked about how animals get all uptight, just before a quake hits. Humans can learn to do this, too.

"If we learn to pay attention to our eardrums, we can also use them to detect anomalies, such as a sudden change in air pressure, however small and momentary it might be. This might mean, perhaps, that someone has started a fire nearby, say for example, by dropping a match onto the starter fluid, to ignite charcoal briquettes.

"Another feature of this room is that the speakers, which are controlled in position, volume, rate of movement around the room, etc, also have the added feature of being fitted with small LEDs, to allow one to learn to position where they are, in a dark room, when you are not blindfolded, and the sound emitted is near your auditory limit. This helps to fine tune the brain, and your ears, to where the sound is coming from, and can enhance your ability to detect low sounds, especially if you are very young. All of this stuff is easier, if you start doing it at the earliest possible ages that you can. Orla, for example, had told me that one of the ways that she achieved hands that can literally crush bones was by being made, as a part of her very earliest training, as prescribed by the Grandmasters that she was learning from, to carry glass mayonnaise jars around, all day long, one in each hand, filled with progressively heavier loads. Each day, they would add a few more pennies to each jar, and she would have to hold the jar, by the rim, with just the fingertips, in opposition to the palm of the hand. When she was able to satisfactorily do one size of jar, say a 1 quart, then they switched to a 2 quart, and then a gallon jar. If you think pennies are not very heavy, then try carrying an entire jar full of them all day, every day. They get heavy in a hurry! And, if you are young enough at the time, you can get strong in a hurry. Combine this, with the other strength training, and the martial arts training and discipline that she received, and she was breaking 4 X 4s, at the age of four! It was not long after this, that she started to receive training in how to throw a knife, and soon arrived at the ability to consistently make a 'Kill Shot', even on a moving target. Maeve, as I understand that you have witnessed on your way here, has quite similar abilities."

Dan said, "Yes, I have indeed witnessed this, and I was quite relieved that she was able to do this, especially once my realization of what had happened, finally caught up with me! So, it would seem that one must devote a large portion, if not all, of your life to these pursuits, if one would become good at it?"

"Yes," Cinderella answered, "And that is one of the reasons that you only rarely see Maeve, and almost never see Orla. They spend quite a bit of time on all of their training, and planning, and rehearsals for each mission. The planning is down to the most minute of details, and with elaborate contingency and backup, and even then there is still the unknown factors of random chance that require the ability to 'Think On

Your Feet', as the saying goes, even when you are somersaulting through the air, to dodge a bullet that you sensed, just a small fraction of a second before it arrived at the place where your brain was just at!"

"Good God!", Dan interrupted, "She must lead a very interesting life!"

"Yes," replied Cinderella, "She reminds me of the ancient Chinese Curse: 'May you live in interesting times!' But, at least for herself, she has chosen this pathway, and she is a natural for it, as is Maeve. Sir Percival pays them very well, for what they do. I cannot go into details of what they have done, but you must have already realized, for yourself, that they have done really critical missions, not only for the United States Secret Service, but also British Special Forces. Even by association with us, you are now a target of those who would be eager to learn more about us, and it surely must have occurred to you, even before now, that if we could not rescue you, we would have to kill you!"

"Well, it has, indeed, gradually dawned on me, over several months, that such would likely be the case!", Dan answered, "Fortunately, I do not know much of anything."

"I have no doubt that this is true," replied Cinderella, "But the perception is that you COULD know something, and if captured, you would suffer horribly on that account, alone! That is why you must remain inside of our little complex. When you were working on your Master's, in Materials Sciences, at the University of Wales, you were, unknown to you, one of the most carefully, and secretly, guarded persons, in the British Isles!"

"So", said Dan, "I am starting to realize, even more, just how important I was, to Sir Percival, that he was willing to pull his top agents off of the many other jobs that they must have waiting, just to escort me here?! I was already plenty flattered, a long time ago, that this was done."

"Yes, Sir Daniel, you were brought here, not only for the work that you have done, and will continue to do, but more importantly, to Percy, you were brought here, for ME! I have, indeed, fallen very deeply in love with you, and you have shown me reason to believe that you are in love with me, too!"

"Besides", said Cinderella, laughing, "If you were to attempt to escape, as I was just explaining to you, we would have to kill you! Even with the little bit that you know, you now know too much! At the very least, Der Sniper would have to erase your mind!"

Cinderella locked her arms around Dan, and planted a long, hungry, and deep, kiss on his mouth.

After about a minute and a half, they "Came up for air", so to speak. They remained in each other's arms, and Dan then returned the kiss. Cinderella blushed, and took Dan by the hand, and led him to another room in her house, turned on the lights, and said to Dan,

"My staff has prepared this room, just for us! The Laundry people have noted your sizes of clothes, and preferences of sheets, blankets, pillow cases, and so on. The dresser, and the storage areas, have been appropriately stocked, accordingly. Thus, there is no reason for you to need to return to your apartment. Your toothpaste, tooth brushes, et cetera, have all been duplicated as well!"

Cinderella then started kissing Dan again, as she slipped her hand down inside of his pants. Not long after that, they were undressing each other, while still kissing. She laid down, on the bed, and Dan entered her. She went into orgasm immediately, and while he shot his first wad, hard and deep, he just kept right on going! It was more than 90 minutes later, with Cinderella in a state of extended sexual orgasm, the whole time, that Dan came again! After they stopped, she described what had happened for her as,

"It felt like I was being swept up in a tornado! It just went on and on! I was pulsing and throbbing the whole time! I have never felt so alive!"

With both of them now being freshly invigorated, they took a shower together. Later, they ate dinner, and then spent a slightly more subdued evening in bed with each other, enjoying their newly established physical closeness, with more close encounters.

The next morning, they did more of the same, and after breakfast, Cinderella said to Dan,

"Unless you have some immediately more pressing stuff, for us to work on, I think that it would be appropriate for us to devote some time to at least giving you an introduction to the kinds of stuff that you will need to know about, in the way of basic training, and how we do some of the stuff that Orla and Maeve, for example, have done, to enhance their abilities in certain areas. You will, as you are probably well aware, likely never achieve any of the high levels of competence that they have worked all of their lives to achieve and maintain, but you might learn just enough of the basics, in certain important areas, to enhance your chances of survival, in a bad situation. I waited until now to start this stuff, because we needed to be much more physically 'In Tune' to each other. We will now be even more aware of what each other does, which makes it easier for me to assist you, and guide you through the learning process. I do not know if you will remember it, but one of the forms that you had to sign was a 'Loyalty Oath', whereby you pledged to protect Sir Percival, and defend him with your very life, if need be."

Dan answered, "Yes, now that you mention it, I DO seem to vaguely remember something like that!"

Cinderella said, "Well, today we begin your rudimentary training, so that you will be better able to fulfill your pledge, should it become necessary to do so."

"Okay," Dan said, "Where do we begin, on my journey toward the Enlightenment?"

"Come with me!", Cinderella replied, "We will return to the acoustics chamber."

After they returned to the acoustics chamber, Cinderella had Dan sit down in a revolving office chair, with wheels on it.

"I will now program the chamber for the easiest starting lessons", she said, as she stepped over to the control panel,   "And you are now ready to begin."

She sat down in a similar style of chair, and as the machine began to execute its programmed instruction set, she began to point at the various speakers, identifying the LEDs that were flashing on, when the speaker that was attached to the LED played a note.

Cinderella said, "This is done so that you will gradually come to make a faster, and more accurate, determination of where a particular sound is coming from. Eventually, we will be mixing up the sounds, and moving speakers around, and so on, as I was explaining to you a while back, but for right now, this is enough to attempt to grasp."

After about an hour or so of this, she could see that Dan's eyes were starting to glaze over, so she stopped the program, and said, "Well, that seems to be about enough of this lesson, for today!"

Dan agreed, and said, "What is the next thing that you can show me?"

"Well, the next thing that I want to show you, is what it is like, to carry jars of pennies around, all day long. Of course, we won't do it ALL day, at first, and you will be very unlikely to achieve the mastery that Orla, for example, has arrived at, but it is still a useful exercise, nonetheless."

She brought out some 2-Liter mayonnaise jars, partly filled with pennies, without lids, and placed them on a table, and showed Dan how to grasp the jar, by the open mouth.

"First", she said, "Practice just lifting the jar, by the top, just like you might do if the lid were on there. There are not enough pennies in there to matter, yet. Just hold it up in the air, for a few seconds, and then gently set it back down again. Then do so with the other hand."

Dan did as he was told, and she then had him repeat the operation several more times, alternating hands, every few minutes. Again, after about an hour, they stopped, and then she led Dan to another area.

Cinderella said, "In this room, I will introduce you to some of the very basics of knife throwing. We are going to start with some small knives, at close range, with fairly large targets. After quite a while, I will gradually make the targets smaller, and move them farther away, and then make it more challenging, in other ways, too."

She showed him that the knives are well balanced, and how to hold them, and how to best throw them, and then said, "While I am nowhere near as good as Orla, I will show you an example of what I can do!" Then, she reached behind her neck, and whipped out a knife, and threw it, all in the same motion, and hit a stationary bull's eye, about three inches across, at 100 feet away!

This startled, and impressed, Dan, and he said, "Wow. I had no idea that you could do any of this stuff, too!"

"Yes", said Cinderella, "I most humbly hope that you will find me to be of a satisfactory skill level, to serve you in these, and other areas."

Dan said, "You are superb!" Cinderella replied, "I am most honored, and flattered!" She walked over to the target, to retrieve her knife, and replaced it in the sheath on her neck, and walked back to Dan.

"Now," she said, "That is enough of those things, for the moment," as she took his hand, and kissed him, "I would like to serve you, again, as I did last night!" She then led him back to the extra bedroom.

Well, after a whole night of sex, and sleeping together, with small meals in between, Dan woke up first, and rolled over on top of Cinderella, and entered her. She had been pretending to be asleep, hoping that this would happen, and immediately went back into orgasm, and after a couple of hours of that going on, including her having an orgasm that lasted 105 minutes, they were both satisfied, for the moment.

"You know something?", said Cinderella, "If you keep that up, I believe that I will just simply HAVE to keep you!"

Dan said, "Why, thank you! I am most flattered!"

"How," asked Cinderella, "do you last so long?!"

"Well," Dan replied, "In the end, it is all about mind control. Without that, I would not last for very long at all, because you are so very enticing, and exciting, to me!"

"Whatever it is that you are doing", said Cinderella, with a very dreamy, and satisfied, tone of voice, "I most thoroughly approve! Keep it up!" She gave him a hug, and a long kiss. "What would you like for breakfast? I am going to call upstairs, and have it delivered! We can just stay right down here, and after we get cleaned up, and eat, I want to tell you a story about a very old and dear friend of mine. We talk about physics a lot, as well as many other subjects!"

So, after a shower, and getting dressed, there was a knock at her door, and Cinderella answered. She looked over the delivery, and seeing that it was fully correct, signed for it. Dan and Cinderella set up the food on the table, and had a nice meal together. Rice-flour waffles, with bacon, sausage, and sliced ham. Blueberries, and strawberries, were in a bowl, on the side, for the waffles. Frozen yogurt, and orange juice, as well as warm tea, rounded out their plan.

Dan asked, "I noticed that you never eat wheat. Do you have an allergy to it?"

"No," answered Cinderella, "but I have a friend who does, and I have learned how much better foods can be, without wheat, from the time that I have spent with her. Her allergy is not just a gluten intolerance. It is a true allergy to wheat! The kind that runs borderline on anaphylaxis! I have also learned that it would appear, from some limited amount of research that I have attempted to do, whenever I remembered to do it, and it was convenient, that humans really should not be eating wheat, anyway. I have no doubt that there are those who would say something to the effect of, 'What? Of course humans can eat wheat! Look at how long we have been doing it!' Well, I am sorry, but the fact that humans CAN eat wheat does not, in any way, imply that we

SHOULD be eating wheat! A similar thing applies to corn. Besides, I have also discovered how satisfying non-wheat foods are. They take a little bit of extra work, initially, to discover substitutes for certain properties, such as Xanthan Gum, to replace the stickiness needed to hold stuff together. The kitchen staff knows that I prefer to not have wheat, and Percy has made sure that they accommodate this, when I have food delivered. In this way, when Mary Ann comes to visit, the staff is already set up, and well trained on what to do, and how to fix things, and we do not have to worry very much about her having any problems from the food."

Dan said, "Well, I have found all of this stuff that you have ordered to be perfectly, and wonderfully, tasty", as he dove into the food, "If the food is this good, without wheat, I would not miss the wheat, either!"

After they had a nice leisurely breakfast, and while they were settling down on the nice, comfortable couch, Cinderella, said,

"Well, now that we have had a nice meal, and a very satisfying night, and morning, of being in bed together, I think that this is as good of a time as any, for me to tell you of some ideas I learned about from a physicist, who is a personal friend of mine. We have shared ideas that pretty much amount to an alternative hypothesis of the origin of the Universe, which does not really contradict the current models, but rather expands them, and relieves certain inherent problems, such as 'What was there before the Big Bang?'

"The short version of this set of ideas begins with the acceptance of the notion that the Universe, proper, is infinite, and never ending, in all directions. If there is no end, then there is no center, and to attempt to talk about a center is inherently meaningless. Notice that if there is no end, then we also avoid the problem of, 'What is beyond the boundary of the universe?' Further, we postulate that the Microwave Background Radiation, which is assumed in the conventional thinking to have just 'conveniently' cooled to the temperature of 4 Kelvin, always was, and always is, at this temperature, on the average, in our model of the universe. Now, this does not mean that there are not going to be places that might happen to be much hotter, for a 'short' amount of time, in the universal time scale, but on the average, the temperature is postulated to be that of 4K, or about the temperature of liquid helium. Notice, further, from this, that since the volume of the universe is infinite, and it has an average background radiation of about 4K, then the energy store in the universe must also be infinite.

"Now, you will recall, from math and physics, that waves can be stacked, or superimposed, on top of each other, and depending on how closely the phases, and frequencies line up, they sort of add together. If the waves of energy mostly cancel each other out, then nothing happens, most of the time. But every now and then, depending on the factors that I just mentioned, they will suddenly line up, and there would be a peak, of a very much higher amplitude than its surroundings. So, that would be a wave of just two components.

"If, on the other hand, we have many waves, (as in an infinite number of them!), traveling around the universe, going from one nowhere, to another nowhere, eventually some of them are going to happen, sooner or later, to be in the same place, at the same time, and all line up in just the right way, so that this zone of space will become significantly warmer than its surroundings. It will also happen that, every once in a while, given that the universe is infinitely large, and has infinite time, and infinite patience, enough of these waves will coincide at the same place, and same instant of time, that the energy released exceeds the carrying capacity of the surroundings to dissipate. At which point, a colossal explosion occurs! Our common parlance for this, is what we currently call 'The Big Bang.'

"This explosion releases so much energy, in so small of a space, and so rapidly, that it destroys, locally, for a short while, the very fabric of space-time, in its general vicinity, which coincides with why they cannot, at least at present, run the mathematical models, at the point of the Singularity. The very concepts which we would use to model the

Singularity, space, and time, do not even exist at the point of the Singularity. Further, it appears, from Bekenstein's limit, on the smallest possible meaningful distance, of approximately 10 to the minus 35 meters, that the smallest possible meaningful volume would be on the order of 10 to the minus 105 cubic meters. Therefore, the 'Singularity', as it is described in physics, could not occupy a space that would be smaller than this volume. To this, we can then add that, if the smallest possible distance is on the order of 10 to the minus 35 meters, and light travels at 3 times ten to the eighth meters per second, then the smallest, physically meaningful, amount of time would be on the order of 10 to the minus 43 seconds.

"If we now further assume that it is very possible that this event could occur more than a few times, and that other occurrences happened at some fairly great distance away, we might be able to have the situation where there is more than one 'Universe' at the same time, to the extent that we can only see out about 13.7 billion light-years, because that is all of the light that we have sufficiently nearby, which we could detect at all. Notice that the term 'Universe', here, is an improper usage : By definition, there is only one Universe. It is the set of all things.

"However, this does not mean that this is all that there is! Indeed, far from it! Suppose that a similar event happened at 10 to the power 300 light-years away. We would never see anything from it, because of the inverse-square laws of light. Such a signal would be hopelessly drowned out, by the microwave background radiation. In fact, this distance is so far away that, if we were to attempt to plot it on a fairly standard logarithmic graph paper of 2 inches per cycle, it would be 600 inches, or 50 feet, away, and that is on log paper!

"Now, depending on how much starting energy is available, at the point of the 'Initiation', or birth, of a sub-universe, as long as there is sufficient energy for the process to start, each sub-universe will activate with a very different set of initial conditions, and may therefore have entirely different forms of matter which would dominate that sub-universe, including, possibly, whether such a sub-universe could be dominated by a form of anti-matter, which could be hostile to our own.

"Also, depending on how much initial energy is available, a sub-universe could expand, but fall short of being able to completely blow itself entirely to bits, and then collapse in on itself, after perhaps losing part of its 'Original' energy, and then oscillate and dissipate itself, over one or more additional cycles of expansion and collapse. If it happened that this sub-universe dropped below the energy level needed to blow itself apart, then it would just collapse into what would be a truly super-massive black hole, and would gradually evaporate over a very long time, or else it would eventually acquire sufficient energy from the background radiation to blow itself apart again.

"So, what we think of as our 'Universe' could just be another one of the sub-universes, in much the same way that we used to think of the Milky Way galaxy as being the only one that there was, and then, with better telescopes, we began to discover that there were other galaxies. It seems that 'Sub-Universe' is a better terminology than 'Parallel Universe', which, in science fiction, at least, has somewhat acquired the notion that events that occur here, are being duplicated in another universe, in lock-step.

"Notice, further, that in this way, the 'Universe' can be both young and finite, and at the same time, infinite and eternal!"

"Boy!", said Dan, "With all of that stuff that you just threw out there, you REALLY muddied the water, on the little bit that I thought that I had understood!"

"Yes", said Cinderella, "That is another one of the areas of thought which I have to be very careful about, anymore. In a sense, my mind leaves my body behind, and I become 'Locked Out' of reality, as all of my mental faculties start to 'run away' in a sort of a human equivalent of an 'infinite loop', in computer parlance!"

Dan said, "I remember that you had mentioned something about this, before. So, if I follow your story correctly, you are saying that you would have no other connection left, to an external, or an internal, reality, once your mind becomes 'Locked In', so to speak, like a computer might do, on a mainframe, rather than swapping jobs, back and forth. It would then just run that job, to its completion. Thus, you would literally leave a mess in your underwear, and die of thirst, and have no notion that you were 'On the way out the exit door', so to speak!?"

"Yes", replied Cinderella, "And that is why Percy has made it a priority to work with me on achieving the Enlightenment. He says that I may be able to eventually return to some of my more mental pursuits, once I have become a 'Grandmaster Of The Enlightenment', and during this training, I might be able to rewire my brain, in such a way as to prevent the runaway-train-wreck from taking hold.

"In the interim period, between now and the time that I learn how to reliably break this cycle, I need to have a live-in supervisor, so to speak, just to make sure that I do not become trapped. Since that is the case, it might as well be someone that I have come to love very much, with bedroom privileges! The closer, and more tuned-in to me this person is, the better are the chances that this problem will be caught in time, to stop me from going on a disastrous 'Brain Trip'. I can make this NEW trip, WITHOUT drugs!"

Dan asked, "Is there any chance that an extended sexual orgasm will cause you to leave your body?"

Cinderella answered, "Apparently not. If anything, it seems to make me want to stay IN my body! There are so many wonderful pleasures going through me, all at once, that I just want to focus on all of them. This has been a GREAT opportunity for me to start to rewire my brain, so that I am more attuned to what is going on, 'Down There', so to speak!"

"So", said Cinderella, blushing, "I am looking forward to your next lesson, in helping me to stay in my body! Kiss me, you fool!"

Dan did as he was told, and they returned to her bedroom. A few hours later, she was floating on air, as they took a shower together.

Cinderella said that it was almost time for lunch, and she was hungry, so she swallowed up Dan, to let him know what she was hungry for! "I hope you don't mind! This is all a part of my therapy!" She said, with a giggle.

They skipped on finishing the shower, for now, and had each other for a pre-lunch snack, and then got cleaned up, and managed to finish the shower, this time.

After a nice lunch, Dan said, "Boy, I sure am glad that Percy had his ravens dive-bomb me, and send me on a wonderful adventure, beginning with a totally unexpected balloon ride! If I had ever heard of an adventure like this, I would have just dismissed it as a fantasy, including the part of ending up living in a very different place, in a castle, in Wales, and finding someone as wonderful as you, and having all of this come to happen because of a truly super-intelligent cat, who learned how to communicate through a computerized voice-synthesizer."

"Well", said Cinderella, "There will be more of that later, but for right now, we need to do some work. This morning I learned that Percy has accepted a request for me to manufacture a set of molds that can be used to make some ceramic castings of extraordinary detail. So, we can start work on this, when the plans arrive here, which will be in just the next few minutes. So, it is off to clear a work-table in my ceramics lab, we go!"

Just then, there was a knock on the door, and Cinderella answered it, and said, "Oh, good! Thank you!" She then took delivery of the plans, and proceeded to her ceramics lab, with Dan following close behind.

Cinderella spread out the plans, and concept drawings, and specifications, on her work table, and her eyes lit up brightly, as she began to study what was wanted. Dan noted that a wonderful glow took over her face, indicating that she was quite pleased with the project, and the commission.

"YES!", She said, "I can do this! It will be wonderful!"

After a few minutes of study time, to make sure that nothing had been overlooked, she picked up the plans and they went to the milling room, and spread out the plans again. The computer on the automated miller's Computerized Numerical Control system was activated, and she began to load in her programmed instruction set. After this was done, with Dan watching, and assisting as best as he could, she said to Dan, "Okay, let's load a slab of plate aluminum onto the worktable. I want the 25 millimeter stock."

Once the aluminum plate was loaded, and locked onto the worktable, she told the Miller control to execute the programmed instruction set. Once the Miller completed its checklist of starting requirements, the machine asked, "Program verification complete! Clear to SEND?" Cinderella typed in "LGO", for "Load and Go!" and hit return.

"Okay," Cinderella said to Dan, "Would you bring me a glass of iced tea, with lemon, and an apple, and get whatever you want for yourself? I need to keep an eye on the work for a while, to make sure that the Miller does what it is supposed to do."

Dan nodded, and left to fulfill her request, and got himself some iced tea, as well. Upon returning, he saw her dancing, just a little bit, which showed him just how happy she was, to have this commission. He noted that she was again seemingly floating on air. He entered the room, and after a few seconds, she saw him, and said, "Oh, Thank you!", and took the tea and apple, and said, "Pull up a chair!"

So, for the next several hours, they supervised the job, together, so that she could make sure that nothing weird happened. This was also a good opportunity for her to explain to Dan some of the operational features of her "Home-Built" machine. They watched, and Dan asked questions as he thought of them, and she also explained additional things that were not necessarily immediately apparent. The machine would switch cutting tools automatically, from end-mills to drill bits, to square reamers of various sizes, etc , all as required by the program, moving from one wall plan to the next one. Seven hours, and several potty breaks later, the miller announced, on its screen, "Assignment Complete. Idle."

Cinderella said, "It is finished! How about some dinner?!"

Dan said, "Yes, I am in the mood for some more of that wonderful wheat-free stuff that you have prepared, if that is okay with you?"

"What would you like?" She asked.

"Well," said Dan, "How about some cod-fish, battered, and chips, along with a nice salad, and some blueberry scones, and some more iced tea?"

"Okay", said Cinderella, "That sounds good, and I will add to that some sliced ham, and strawberry shortcake!"

She phoned upstairs, to the cafeteria, and they took her request, for delivery. The order-taker said that it would be about an hour.

Feeling temporarily refreshed, by knowing that dinner was on its way, they returned to the work on the milling table.

"As I was watching this machine at work", Dan said, "I could not help but to notice that it hummed a tune, just like it was trying to sing!"

Cinderella replied, "Yes, and depending on just exactly what the job is, I have heard it doing just what you described! If certain actions are repeated, over and over again, in sequence, it almost sounds like it is a refrain, in a song. I once wondered if it might be possible to have the miller play some kind of mechanical tune, but that was just an idle thought, as I quickly realized that it would just become an enormously expensive noise-maker!" She said, laughing!

"So," asked Dan, "What would a machine like this cost to buy, if you were to accept an order for one, that you would make?"

"I have duplicated this machine, already," said Cinderella, "and Percy sold it for 185,000 Euros, plus delivery and setup charges! The amount of metal and work, and other materials that go into having me, and my staff, build such a monster as this, requires a couple of months of work. But even at that price, it is still a fair bargain. We make a significant profit, but this machine is so good, that it is 'State-Of-The-Art', and a company that runs it continuously will recover its investment in less than a year, and there has been very little wear, and only minimal maintenance required."

"Yes", said Dan, "I can see that it is a NICE machine! So, how long did it take for you to design, and build, the first one?"

"Well, that is a tricky question to really answer, because, in a sense, I spent many years learning how to build, and evolve, my way through to this point, from self-made metal lathe, to shaper, and a crude miller, and gradually becoming more sophisticated, so in that respect, in took me about 11 years. But, once I had put in the required time as an apprentice, to myself, and started to work on the making of this particular machine prototype, it took about six months, to design, and make patterns, and get the parts, and do the castings, and let the larger castings 'season' for a while, to help to relieve any internal stresses hidden in the casting. Of course, there were the parts that had to be re-cast, due to various defects, and there were a couple of times that we screwed up, and had to re-melt our mistakes, and try again. So, the real answer to your question is, 'about three months', after I edit out all of the various interfering factors, over the course of the job."

So, he let her examine the project pieces, from the current job, without further distracting her. The pieces looked quite good, to Dan, but he kept it to himself. Cinderella became very intently focused on the work, and had compared these sections to the specs, and measured several locations. At the end, she looked pleased, and announced that all was well, just before the knock on the door signaled that dinner had arrived.

"Oh, good!", Cinderella said, "I was just starting to lose my concentration, and fade away!"

She answered the door, and looked over the delivery, to make sure that it was right, and signed for it, and wheeled it to their dinner table.

"Boy," said Dan, laughing, "It is a good thing that it is time to eat! About another hour, and I would have been gnawing on the furniture!"

So, after dinner, and a nice relaxing evening, watching a little TV, waiting for the food to settle, they both started to feel quite a bit better. Cinderella, who had been just sitting beside Dan, on the couch, suddenly got up, and straddled Dan, facing him. She started kissing him, and unbuttoned his shirt, as she said, "Take me, you fool!", with a teasing laugh!

So, they got up, and went to her bedroom, and undressed each other. She settled down on top of him, for a few minutes of a teasing introductory variety, and then hopped off, and flopped onto her back, pulling him over, on top of, and into, her. Cinderella went immediately into orgasm, and stayed that way, for just under two hours. Finally, Dan came, and she kissed him.

"I just love how long you can last for! However, after a couple of hours like this, I need to try to get up, and move around some."

Dan said, "Yeah, me too! I think that we are both getting better at lasting longer, which is good, because I want to make sure that your mind never leaves your body, and as you told me, the longer we can last, and the more time we can spend on doing this, the better your chances of avoiding becoming trapped in an infinite loop."

So, they took a shower together, and settled down, for a nap.

When Dan woke up, at dawn, he noticed that she seemed to be asleep, with her legs up, and spread, so he rolled over on top of her, and slid into home plate. She opened her eyes, and smiled, and said,

"Hello, darling! I woke up about 20 minutes ago, and was hoping that you would wake up soon, and accept my invitation!"

Sometime later, they had been at it for so long, that Cinderella was just about ready to beg for mercy, when Dan came, at the end of another long orgasm on her part.

"After breakfast", she said, "I have to go spend a few hours, with Percy. He has an opening this morning, and we need to have me in another session of the Feline Mind Meld, so that he can evaluate how I am progressing. If you would like, you can just go back to your nap, either now, or after we eat. Either way is fine, but I need to get a shower, and eat, and then go see my wonderful friend, Percy!"

Dan said something about how this sounded like a good morning for a nap, and rolled over, and closed his eyes, and checked out.

Cinderella got into the shower, and later ate upstairs, in the cafeteria, where she ran into Orla and Maeve, who were having a quick breakfast, before heading out on another job.

"So", asked Orla, first, before Maeve could, "How are you and Dan getting along? Rumor has it that you must be doing quite well!"

"Yes!", answered Cinderella, "Have either of you ever had an orgasm that goes on for two hours, and sometimes more, while having sex, with a man, who has incredible staying power?"

Maeve, said "What? I did not even know such a thing was possible! How do you, and he, do it?"

"Well, I do not know for sure how he does it, but he said something about extreme mind control, which allows him to hold on, and do the 'Energizer Bunny' thing! As for myself, I guess that he is just such a 'turn-on' for me, so that all that he has to do is just to slide into me, and I am immediately in orgasm, sometimes for hours. If he comes earlier, we just keep going, and he stays hard. After he comes again, we will sometimes stop to take a break, but I swear that there are days where we have sex several times a day."

Orla said, "That is wonderful!", and Maeve said, "Honey, if it ever happens that you decide that you don't want him, tell me, first! I would like to have a shot at someone like that! Well, Orla, is it time for us to go?"

Orla answered very quietly, to Cinderella, "Yes, unfortunately, we were just getting a quick snack, before we have to board a plane for our next little 'Fix-it' mission, to the Middle East."

"Oh, okay!", Cinderella said, "Good luck on your latest impossible mission!" And she gave both of them a hug, and said, "Thank you", for bringing Dan to her.

Realizing that it was getting close to the time of her appointment with Percy, Cinderella scurried along a little bit, to make sure that she would be there, with plenty of time to spare.

Well, Percy was running a few minutes late, as he said, once she got called into his office, because he was, "Having to snort a little bit of fire, and whip some tail!", while explaining to some moron of a government official, in the British Virgin Islands, why it was that this official was not going to hold up the paperwork on real estate that Percy was trying to buy there!

"But, never mind about such things, dear! All of that is easily fixed. If necessary, I will send Der Sniper, to explain to this man all about the error of his ways. Then there will be no more problems from a certain snooty government official, one way or the other! What I am most interested in, is how you are doing, and how you and Dan are getting along?"

"Dan is wonderful!", said Cinderella, to start with. "He is probably perfect for me. Thanks to his phenomenal staying power, I am becoming connected with my body, possibly for the first time ever, as far as staying in my body. We are more compatible, on all levels, than I could have ever dreamed of. Thank you so much for the wonderful gifts that you have given to me, not just now, but over all of the years!"

Percy responded, through his voice synthesizer, "You are very welcome, my child, and dear friend. I am very limited in how much I can express my deep, and loving, feelings for you, in this form of communication. Please lay down, so that our thoughts can be shared directly."

Cinderella did as she was told, and Percy hopped up on top of her, and began to stare into her eyes, as he placed his forehead on top of hers.

After several minutes, Percy was deep into her mind. About 20 minutes later, he was done, and rubbed his nose all over hers, to wake her up.

Percy gave her a kiss, and went back to his chair, and spoke through his voice machine: "You are doing MUCH better, Cinderella! My diagnostic scan showed me that your brain is rewiring itself, so that you may someday, before too long, be able to carry on with a more normal life, possibly without too much fear of being trapped within your own mind, and locked into that infinite loop problem. Please carry on with Dan, as you have been doing. It seems that he really is good for you. Oh, and also, that project that you are working on, for me: there is plenty of time for that job. Just concentrate on becoming connected with your body, and with Dan. When you have some spare time, and you are feeling good enough, then you can devote that time to the project. Please lie there, and rest, for as long as you need to. I must tend to another issue. I am not too far from being annoyed enough with some of the bureaucrats, in some of these places, to simply buy the country that they are in, and have them deported to Pitcairn's Island, or, worse still, French Guiana!"

So, Cinderella left, to return to her studio. She took a quick shower, and crawled quietly into bed, naked, and swallowed Dan into her mouth, and began licking him. He woke up pretty quickly, and she giggled. She flopped onto her back, and pulled him on top of her.

About two hours later, she was worn out from the activities of the moment, as Dan came for the second time. Her eyes looked a little jaded, as she came out of an orgasm of about 100 minutes.

Cinderella said to Dan, "I wanted to tell you that I had a meeting with Percy, while you were asleep. We talked for a few minutes, and then had a Feline Mind Meld. Percy went deep into my mind, to examine how my recovery is coming along. He is most pleased with the progress that is being made. He said that we are good for each other, and for us to keep up our current activities, as it is working, for helping to repair the brain damage. A true, and very deep, love can cure many things! After lunch, I would like to have you love me deeply, again!"

Dan said, "Oh, well, then! I should be most honored to do so! The deeper, the better! Yes, it is time for some food!"

Cinderella then said, "After that, and a shower, we will return to the training areas, so that we can evaluate your abilities, in the use of certain weapons."

So, after lunch, and a "Quickie" of only 70 minutes, they got into the shower, and then went to the rifle range. Dan was able to hit a bulls-eye, of three inches across, at 100 meters, after making a few minor adjustments to his technique.

Cinderella said, "Well, you meet the basic requirements for being able to start your real training. Now, watch this!"

She took the rifle, and stepped over a few feet to the right, and focused her sights on a different target, and rapidly fired off five consecutive rounds, from a distance of 400 meters, and put all five of them into a space the size of a quarter.

Dan said, "WOW! I figured that you must know how to shoot a gun, but I had no idea that you could do this. How long did it take for you to get this good?"

Cinderella said, "I have been learning about this stuff, for almost my whole life. I made my first trip to the firing range, with my parents, at about age six. While I did not do any more than just watch, at first, I eventually was strong enough, at about age eight or nine, so that Dad felt that I was ready to start my firearms training. It seems that there is an advantage, if you are a CIA official, in particular, to having your young children be able, and willing, to kill any potential kidnappers, when needed! So, let's just say that there are a few, unaccounted for, bodies lying around!

"So, the direct answer to your question is, 'about six years!' I might have just been happy, to be a Sniper, except that I had a very good set of career prospects, thanks to my academic successes. While being a girl sniper would have a certain set of inherent drawbacks, I have learned, from Orla, that it can also have a huge advantage, as well. Most people simply dismiss the notion of a woman being a Sniper, often to their own peril!"

Dan said, "Well, I, for one, admit that I am not used to thinking in those terms. It simply would not have seriously occurred to me, before I got here!"

Cinderella said, "Well, that is enough shooting, for right now. I just wanted to get a sense of what you could do with a gun. We will work on this some more, but not today. Your basic skill level is minimally adequate, for most of the situations you are likely to run into. I have some books for you to read, on basic ballistics, and then, once you have grasped them, we will return here.

"So, I assume that you have also not fired a Bazooka, either, right?!" She said, laughing.

Dan said, "You do a bazooka, too?!"

"Oh, yes!", Cinderella replied, with a smile, "It is great fun! I also have used a homemade rocket, to drop a warhead on a target, from ten kilometers away! A good knowledge of chemistry, and other relevant fields, such as ballistic mechanics, and the mechanics, and thermodynamics, of rocket propulsion, can be quite useful, when you have to improvise."

Dan asked , "How big of a warhead was this?"

Cinderella replied, laughing, "Oh, not much! Just 20 kilos of homemade TNT!"

Dan laughed, and said, "You dropped 45 pounds of TNT on a target, at over six miles away? How big was the target?"

"About the same size as a large garbage can would be: it landed inside of an open-topped, 55 gallon drum, that we had cut away the lid on, and blew the can totally to shit!", said Cinderella, laughing, "I neglected to mention that I had the ability to steer my payload onto its intended point of delivery, by radio control! There was also a TV camera on board.

"Let me show you some photos, in this book. Here, this is me, with the rocket, just before I launched it. And this one is my target area, so you can see that it was literally a steel drum. Percy bought a small island, north of here, where I placed the drum on the island, and then we had a small, floating, launch platform, which is what you can see, right here, in this picture. In the next picture, the rocket is clearing the pad, right after liftoff, (notice that there are seven shock diamonds, in the exhaust), and then there is an air shot, just before the rocket ran out of fuel. The next one shows what was left of the steel drum, or, more precisely, what we could find of what was left!

"All of this is made possible, by a knowledge of chemistry, and the willingness to try, and to learn what we can, and do what we can, having not much more than scrap materials, a few hand tools, some imagination, and the real desire to be able to make something useful from the junk that is lying around, or easily acquired. One of my favorite TV shows was 'Junkyard Wars'. It captured the basic idea of what I used to do a lot of, but they usually just had a day to do a job. If you are very good at what you do, and really know what you are doing, you do not need to buy chemicals. That is how the FBI is able to catch people, in the United States. A most interesting case study, not only for the FBI, but for others, as well, was the Unabomber. This was a most fascinating fellow. He avoided being caught, for a long time, about two decades, because he improvised on everything. He made stuff from junk! Probably the only reason that they ever caught him, was because he had more or less insisted that they catch him! If he had just quietly disappeared, and stayed in hiding, it is unlikely that they would have ever caught him, in spite of one of the longest, and most expensive, and extensive, manhunts in US history! They studied him for a long time, after that.

"One time, I built a single-stage, solid propellant rocket, which I placed on a platform, and my crew and I towed this platform far out to sea, about 200 miles from the nearest land. We cast the platform adrift, and sailed away. When we were about six miles away, far enough away so that any nosy satellites would be less likely to associate us with the launch, and the airways were verified to be clear by the RADAR on our boat, the rocket was launched. Once the rocket cleared the pad, the platform was automatically scuttled, and sank to the bottom of the ocean. (At that place, the bottom of the ocean was more than two miles down!) The rocket was of a style similar to a United States rocket, called the ASP, or Atmospheric Sounding Projectile. My rocket was a little bit bigger. The ASP reportedly could achieve a five-second burn, and when the fuel was exhausted, it was at an altitude of about three miles, and traveling at over one mile per second, and it then coasted to an altitude of about 40 miles. My version of it was also a single-stage, solid propellant, fin stabilized, free-ballistic, atmospheric sounding projectile, but I added on two really cool features! In order to help ensure that the rocket behaved itself, I built into the nose cone a sensor system, to make the rocket be 'Solar Homing', so that if the winds, or other problems, attempted to drive the rocket off course, during the ascending portion of its flight, the guidance system had an auto-correct feature. The other feature was that if the rocket turned upside-down during the powered portion of the flight, it would automatically destroy itself! My rocket had a nine-second burn time, and it achieved a velocity of 1.8 miles per second, and a peak altitude of 65 miles. It might have gone higher, except that it was set up to be a solar-homing rocket. I sacrificed some altitude for safety, but it was a really FUN project!

"After we got back, I learned, from Percy, that he had been monitoring the satellite activity, and it seems that we had created quite a stir! Percy told me to NEVER do that again, even though it was in international waters! So, I guess that you could say that I have been 'grounded', ever since! This was really too bad, because my next little experiment would have been to build a rocket similar to the US rocket, called the 'Aerobee'. I was even almost set up, to make my own Furfuryl Alcohol, and RFNA. All of the stuff that I needed would have been made from recycled junk, and the chemicals and propellants would have been homemade. It is easy, if you know how, and are willing to work a little bit harder! There was a time that I used to blow my own glassware, from homemade borosilicate glass, just so that I would know how, and so that I could make certain highly specialized pieces.

"Well, I am about done here, for the moment, in more ways than one! So, Dan, I am ready for some dinner. What would you like? I am thinking about fish and chips, unless you have a better idea, with a vegetable salad, and a fruit salad."

"Sounds good!", said Dan, "And throw in iced tea, with lemon!"

They walked back to Cinderella's home, and she phoned in the order.

"Dan", she said, "It looks like about 45 minutes before dinner will get here. I just noticed that Mary Ann called. She said that she could come to dinner, tomorrow night."

"Right!", said Dan, "Okay, can do!"

So, they set the dinner table, and since there was still a while before the food was supposed to be there, Dan asked, "What can you tell me about Mary Ann?"

"Well", answered Cinderella, "Her father owns several square miles of farm land, and he runs his own Rye Farm, with his own stone miller. Her father grows specialty grains, and does not grow wheat. My father has known her father for over 40 years. They went to college together. They have to meet secretly, and seldom, to reduce the risk of an enemy agent learning that dad is alive, but they are still good friends.

"Originally, Mary Ann's father grew wheat, but at about age six, Mary Ann developed a severe wheat allergy, and she now carries the 'Epi-pens' with her, everywhere she goes. When that happened to her, Mary Ann's dad literally burned the wheat crop and flour that he had on hand, and had the place thoroughly cleaned out of any possible traces of wheat, and then he replanted with rye seed."

"Wow", said Dan, "He must have lost a lot of money, that time!"

"Well, not really", answered Cinderella, "It turned out that the rye sold for more than the wheat, so he still came out okay, that year, and has done much better, since then."

"Mary Ann also has an interesting set of talents. Her father needed extra help around his farm, but could not really quite afford to hire the help that he required, so he took some time, and started teaching Mary Ann how to do some of the work. She discovered that she had a knack for creative machine repair, a sort of natural born, almost self-taught, ingenuity for mechanical engineering. She could capture the essence of what the situation required, and improvise a repair, usually with just the junk that was lying around, if needed. She graduated early from high school, and then did 20 years with the United States Navy, where they, very grudgingly, let her show them that she could do the work as well as any man that they were likely to find, and then she did that while attending college, for her BSME. It can make a hilarious story, when she decides to tell it, about how she was eventually promoted to being an Ensign, after she completed her Bachelor's, and the Chiefs, and Master Chiefs, were all quaking in their boots, afraid that they were going to get some of the same chicken-shit stuff, that they had been giving her for all of those years! She let them stew, for a long time, wondering about what she would do, and when. Then she just quietly went about doing her job, just being the very sweet person that she really is, and later on, when they all saw that they really could get along, they became very loyal to her, and she was rewarded, when they fixed something that a higher officer thought that she had missed, before the officer could confront her about it. When he dragged her over to where the problem was, the problem was no longer there. It had been fixed. A Master Chief happened to be nearby, and had his crew fix the problem, before the officer could flip her any shit over it! So, it could be said that 20 years, and nine days, in the Navy, did not ruin the very sweet person that she was, and still is.

"So, now that she has retired from the Navy, she works for a company in Swansea, as a Consulting Mechanical Engineer. Mary Ann takes some time off, now and then, to visit her family, and usually comes by to see us, too.

"Mary Ann also has sometimes provided me with ideas for projects, or help with solving specific problems. Most of the time, I would have gotten there, myself, eventually, but it is nice to have another brain to help, now and then.

"After dinner, I need to go to visit my mainframe computer, to run a mathematical simulation of an idea that came to me, just as I was coming out of that last delicious orgasm!"

"Gee," said Dan, "You did not say anything about getting any thoughts, from that one!"

"Yes, that is true!" She said, "I needed to think about it, for a while longer, to study the mathematical plausibility, before I said anything about it. There was no point in my saying anything about my idea, if I could show myself that it was mathematically untenable, before I even went to the computer to run a simulation. You deliver such nice orgasms to me, that my mind is completely cleared out of ANY thoughts about anything else! I just relax, and breathe, and enjoy! It just happened that this possible solution popped up, as I was floating back down to earth."

Just then, there was a knock at the door, and Cinderella said, "Oh, good! That must be dinner!" So, she went over and opened it, and had the server roll it on in. She looked it over, and decided that it was all correct, and signed for it, and the delivery person left.

So, they had dinner, and then watched the news, on TV, and afterward, Cinderella was ready to work on the computer, using her FORTRAN compiler. The food must have agreed with Dan, quite well, as she saw that he was sound asleep on the couch. So, she quietly snuck off to her computer.

Since she lived, breathed, and thought, in FORTRAN, it was always something of a mystery to her, as for why anybody wanted to go to the trouble of creating any other languages, for any reason other than money. Sure, some languages could do a few things a little bit better, but not enough, in her mind, to justify the dozens, or even hundreds of computer languages that have been created since FORTRAN. However, she did consider FORTH to have some interesting possibilities.

So, Cinderella sat at the keyboard, and very serenely typed in the instruction set, that she had already compiled, in her mind. It took about five hours to type in the 2000+ lines of simulation code. The program compiled correctly, and ran perfectly, on the first pass, with her test case. It was a variation of a Fourier Analysis routine, and she then turned the computer loose on the real problem, and went back to where Dan was, knowing that the computer would likely run all night.

Dan must have stirred enough to crawl off to bed, while she was working, as he was no longer on the couch. So, she looked, and he was sound asleep. Cinderella undressed, and quietly, and carefully, slipped into bed, with a very contented smile on her face, as she contemplated the possibilities of a wonderful future with this man. Soon, she was off to sleep.

Early in the morning, she was awakened, by Dan spreading her legs, and sliding inside of her. She kissed him, and managed to say, "Hello, Darling!", before she slipped away, into the land of Orgasm, for a full hour and a quarter, before he finally came, and then he asked her if she wanted any more.

Cinderella seriously contemplated whether she'd had enough, for the moment. She then said, "Well, maybe a little bit later. Right now, I have to go take a pee, and I might also want to take a peek at the results of the computer simulation, that I created last night. If it worked out right, the results just might be interesting. I had a vision last night, and decided to see if I could make it work, at least in a simulation."

Dan said, "I guess I must have really been out of it. I do not remember anything about you going off to the computer."

"Yes," said Cinderella, "The fish must have been good for you. It was also good for me, too. In my case, it provided the extra amino acids, or whatever, that got my brain really going, and the tea stimulated my thoughts. This all contributed to a vision, and I was able to capitalize on it. When we go back to the computer room, we will see whether the vast resources of our CDC 6500, was able to turn my vision into something useful!"

Dan said, "Sounds good! Do you want to have a look at your printout, before or after breakfast?"

Cinderella answered, "I think that what I would like to do, is get a shower, and order breakfast, and then we can go take a preliminary look at the results. After the food, then I would want to really analyze my results, if it looks good at all!"

So, Dan got up, and they got cleaned up, then took a quick look at the results, and then had breakfast. After which, they returned to the computer room.

Cinderella picked up the pile of printout, and started wading through it. Her eyes lit up, and she started nodding and smiling, as she waded through the hundreds of pages of the report. She said to Dan, "Yes! This just might work. The mathematical simulations look promising."

Dan asked, "So, just what did you do, last night, after I conked out?"

Cinderella explained, "Well, you helped me with it, in a way. As I was coming down from my wonderful orgasm, last night, I had a vision of a way to turn a Unit Impulse Point Function, into a Unit Impulse Cylinder Function. I then stacked a whole mess of the cylinders, one inside of the other, with a finite spacing, and integrated to obtain the limit, with the end result being a stacked cosine, square wave, that would have a very high energy density, with an adjustable, uniform, amplitude. The end result of this, if I can turn the model into a reality, will be an ideal milling cutter. It will plane material from a work surface, but this cutter will never need to be sharpened! It works by vaporizing the material that falls inside of its zone of action, but does nothing anywhere else. The only immediately obvious disadvantage, is that any body parts that enter the beam will be gone! If my simulation holds up, the way that I have written it, my model shows an energy density of 5000 watts per square centimeter, which I would eyeball to be about 6000 Kelvin, or roughly the temperature of the surface of the Sun!"

Dan said, "Wow! So how do you keep the conduction of the material bordering the workface from simply being vaporized, too?"

"By moving the work along so fast, that the heat does not have time to penetrate the material that we wish to keep, and perhaps, by cooling with liquid nitrogen. That issue will have to be examined, and possibly addressed, but the cutting tool will be able to work so fast, that it might be possible, depending on the material, to plane several square meters, per minute, which would totally blow away anything that we have now, and this process would be patentable, which would easily make millions for Percy, and a good chunk of money for us, too!"

Dan asked, "So, now what do you need to do?"

"Well," answered Cinderella, "I think that the first thing that I need to do, is to ask Percy if he has a few minutes, so that I can show him my results, and ask him if I can work with you, on seeing if we can turn this into a reality. It should not take too long to verify whether there is any hope of this working."

"Okay", said Dan, "That sounds reasonable."

So, Cinderella picked up the phone, and called, on her private, direct line to Percy.

Percy answered, which automatically put her voice on his speaker phone, and he spoke through his voice synthesizer, "Yes, my dear Cinderella, what can I do for you?!"

Cinderella answered, through the speaker, "Percy, do you have a few minutes? I had a vision last night, and ran a simulation of it, which looks promising, for a new milling cutter. Would it be alright if I came up there?"

Percy answered, "Yes, of course. For you, I can almost always make time. If you want to come up, right now, that would be good. Katrina is here, but that will not be an issue, as the two of you have always gotten along well. Our children are running around, in the room, too, but they usually behave well enough."

"Okay", said Cinderella, "I will be up there, in just about fifteen or so minutes."

Percy said, "Okay. Sounds good! Bye."

Cinderella turned to Dan, and said, "Well, I am going to go see my wonderful friend, Percy, and his wife, Katrina, and their children may be there, too!"

"What?!", said Dan, "I did not know anything about his having a wife! I would have figured that he was too busy for such a thing, even if the thought had occurred to me!"

"Yes", answered Cinderella, "I can certainly see why one would think that. He is quite busy! Well, I must get going. I would not want to be late, for this might be a very important date!"

So, Cinderella rounded up all of the material she wished to show Percy, and went upstairs, to his office. His secretary had been told to show her right on in. Upon entering, Cinderella immediately sat down, so that Katrina, and her children, could all come over and say "Hi!" She hugged Katrina, who gave her a kiss right back, and purred up a storm.

Their babies were now a couple of months old, and Cinderella made very sure to say "Hi", and hug and pet, each of the five of them, in turn. This made everyone feel quite good.

Percy said, "Well, now, what wonderful ideas do you have to show me, today? Katrina said that she, and the children, will stick around, until after we are done."

So, Cinderella explained what she came up with, last night, and asked Percy if he thought it could be worth a little bit more time devoted to the work, to see if it could pay off.

Percy said, "Yes, this could be good. The mathematical simulation looks plausible, so it is just a matter of whether the physics works out right. You might even be able to modify the pattern created by the wave generator, so as to allow some specialty cuts, such as variations of a V-groove."

Cinderella said, "Yes! That could work. That is a good idea, and a logical extension of the basic method. Thank You!"

Percy replied, "Thank you too, dear. It is always nice to see you."

"Okay", said Cinderella, "Time to go back to work! Mary Ann is going to try to come to dinner, tonight."

Cinderella petted, and hugged Katrina, and each of their children, and then left.

Percy purred, to Katrina, in cat-speak, that he sure liked Cinderella, and then they all went back to whatever they were doing, before Cinderella arrived, which was probably just visiting, and enjoying each other.

Cinderella returned to her studio, and said to Dan, "Well, that went over well! We got the green light, to explore this a little bit further."

Dan said, "Okay, I was thinking about this, and it just might work. Can you tell me anything about Katrina, and their children?"

Cinderella replied, "Well, Katrina is also a Nebelung, a beautiful variation of the Russian Blue, and their children are quite darling little kittens, and one of the males seems to perhaps be taking a little bit more after Percy. He just might be a smart one, too! But, we will have to see if Percy can nurture him in the right directions. They have not named any of their children, yet. It is too early for that."

"Okay", said Dan, "What do we do, now, to develop your idea?"

Cinderella said, "Well, the first thing, is to remember that Mary Ann is still coming to dinner, tonight, so we have to make sure to keep an eye on the clock, to leave us enough time to get cleaned up, before she gets here. Then we go over this simulation with a fine-toothed comb, to look for any possible errors in the math, or my programming, or in the physics."

So, they messed around for a while, looking for, and discussing, any possible errors. They made a list of various ideas, for ways to test the simulation. After they finished with this, and related stuff, it was time to hit the shower, and then set the table for dinner.

Not much later, Mary Ann arrived. Cinderella introduced her to Dan, and they all sat down, and had a few drinks, and chatted, while waiting for dinner to show up.

Mary Ann was a very beautiful girl, when she was younger, and even now, at roughly 50-something, by Dan's estimate, she would still be considered quite attractive. After dinner, they were playing various card games, and chatting, and Mary Ann asked Cinderella if she had told Dan about Katrina, yet? Cinderella replied that, no, she had not, and said that Mary Ann could do so, if she would like, but it was only just this afternoon, that Dan even learned of Katrina.

"Well, to avoid spending quite some time on the whole story, and all of the details, about just exactly what happened," Mary Ann said,

"Katrina and I were traveling in the Southern United States, and along the way, we went through New Orleans. I was walking along, carrying her to the house where her sister, and my sister, lived. It was just from the car to the house, across the sidewalk, and some dogs surrounded us, and one of them jumped at me, which caused Katrina to jump, and run. We were minding our own business. Well, I broke that dog's neck, right there on the spot, and crippled a couple of the others. Katrina was chased by a bunch of dogs, and narrowly managed to escape. After I caught up with her, I learned how close of a call it was. She told her sister about what had happened, and I told my sister, whom I was also there to visit, and I said that we all need to get out of there, as I had a strong sense of foreboding that Katrina was pissed. I could not get her to calm down. So, we all got packed, and left the town. A few days later, Katrina came back to New Orleans, and wrecked the place! The city has still not recovered."

Dan was left speechless by this story, wondering if this could possibly be real, but considering what he had seen up to this point, he had no real reason to doubt this story. He had seen many strange things in the last couple of years, things which he had previously considered to be impossible, or at the very least, extremely improbable, yet they were happening all around him now, almost on a daily basis.

Cinderella then said, to Dan, "By now, you have probably guessed that Katrina is a 'Black Belt.' She is a Grandmaster of the highest levels of the Enlightenment, at Feline Level Nine. She is a true Ninja warrior."

"But how", asked Dan, "Is this even possible?"

Mary Ann replied, "Well, I am a Mechanical Engineer, and I can't entirely explain it. We are all about the laws of Thermodynamics. Yet, all I know, is that Katrina channeled up the energy, from one of her dark and destructive moods. She got away from me, for a half a day, and when I found her, it was at a chemical plant, and I saw her launch a balloon, just before I caught up with her. It was a rather large balloon, like for high altitude weather research. The balloon rose quickly, and drifted ESE, until it was lost from sight. I picked her up, and said,

'You naughty little girl! What were you doing, just now?'

"Well, it was a strange thing: She was a whole mess of different emotions, all at once. Katrina both purred up a storm, and smiled, and at the same time, would whip her tail in rage. She refused to tell me what she did, until a couple of days later. She kept watching the Weather Channel, on the TV. Any time I was on another channel, and left the room for a minute, I would come back, and find that Katrina had pushed the button on the remote, to restore the previous channel. She would watch the TV contentedly, from a comfy pillow, as long as it was on the Weather Channel. Eventually, I took the hint, and just left it on the Weather Channel, except for a half-hour in the evenings, when I sat through the National News. After a few days of this, she began to purr up a storm, even during the National News, which began to have increasing coverage of a tropical storm, and later Hurricane, that they had, oddly enough, or maybe not so oddly, now that I think about it, named Katrina. Well, after a few years of having lived with a cat, it is possible to learn, sometimes, to understand what they are saying. As Cinderella can probably tell you from sessions of the Feline Mind Meld, with Percy, Katrina told me what she had done. That balloon that I had seen her launch, just before I caught up with her, was loaded with chemicals, to seed hurricanes! She was most pleased to report that she had been entirely successful. Even more so, was that she was almost 99% certain that this storm was going to go exactly where she wanted it to, and that it was going to make one Hell of a mess!

"Well, by this time, it was too late, and nobody would have believed me, even if I had told them about it. So, all I could do was just to tell my sister that the four of us needed to take a trip, to be far away from the South, and that I could not tell her why, exactly. All I said was that it was just a sense of something bad that was about to happen. So, we ended up, in northern Maine, just as Tropical Storm Katrina was upgraded to Category 1 Hurricane status! A few days later, and Katrina's prophecy had been fulfilled. New Orleans laid before us, on the Weather Channel, and the National News, on all stations, in shambles! My sister asked me how I knew, and all that I could say was that I had received this overwhelming sense that we needed to leave!"

Dan had flopped back, on the couch, stunned! After a short time, he realized that he needed another drink, and got up and poured himself a double, and got refills for the girls, too.

So, they continued to play cards, and talk, while Dan mostly listened, and thought about what Mary Ann had told him about Katrina. Cinderella decided to tell Mary Ann about her idea for a new milling cutter. Mary Ann was very receptive to, and interested, in her idea. Cinderella sort of asked if Mary Ann thought there was any hope for the project. Mary Ann said that it might work out well, but she just did not know enough, to know for sure.

"However, even if you run into some small difficulties, try to hang in there. One thing that I learned, for very sure, from Katrina : 'All things are possible, IF you are crazy enough!'

"Katrina really showed me what could be done, if you have the dedication, and the talents, and are pissed off enough, to not give a damn!

"Well, I am about done in, for tonight. If I stay around for very much longer, I am likely to have a nap attack. As I have gotten a little bit older, I have found that I do not have as much warning as I used to get, so I think I will need to say, 'Good Night!'

"It was nice to meet you, Dan. I think that I will see you again. You and Cinderella seem to be very good for each other!"

Dan replied, "Thank You! I enjoyed meeting you, too! I hope to see you again, soon. Your little story about Katrina, in particular, has given me quite a bit to think about!"

Mary Ann and Cinderella hugged each other, and Dan shook Mary Ann's hand. Mary Ann then said something about maybe being able to come back, in a few weeks, since she had some vacation time that she had to use up, to avoid losing it. Cinderella said that it would be wonderful, as she is always welcome, and Mary Ann then said, "Good Night!", and left.

After Cinderella locked the door, and turned around, Dan said, "Well that went fairly well, and I thought she was quite charming. I am glad to have met her."

"Yes," said Cinderella, "She has always been very wonderful to me! I have received much inspiration from many of her ideas, and suggestions."

Dan replied, "Yes, I particularly appreciated the part where she said, 'All things are possible, IF you are crazy enough!', as it just might be enough, to open up some avenues that I have only vaguely considered, before now. They were only sort of dream-like notions, and I will need to give them more time to percolate, now that Mary Ann has turned up the gas under them."

Cinderella said, "I am starting to realize that I am tired, too, so let's clean up enough, and go crash!"

They cleaned up the various things which needed to be put away, and got into the shower, and went to bed.

8

In the morning, they ate breakfast and then Cinderella said to Dan, while they were still seated at their breakfast table, "Our dinner with Mary Ann, last night, indirectly reminded me of another one of my project rooms, which I usually keep locked. It is hidden behind a closet. Would you like to go there, now?"

Dan said, "Certainly! I have found all of your projects to be quite profound!"

Cinderella said, laughing, "Then come with me, as we take a stroll on the 'Yellow Brick Road!'" She took his hand, and interlaced his fingers with hers, and led him on a merry walk, with many twists and turns, going down stairs, and up, as well.

Dan said, "I STILL do not understand how it is, that you know where you are going!?"

Cinderella answered, "Well, it is easy enough, when you are the one who designed it, and lived here for quite a few years, and added new rooms, a little bit at a time. It also follows the basic tenets of the Feline Mind Maze, for general design guidelines."

So, Dan walked along quietly for a while, as Cinderella escorted him on a confusing trek, which seemed, indeed, to be designed so as to cause the uninitiated to get totally, and hopelessly, lost!

Eventually, they got to where Cinderella wanted to go, and she applied a little bit of pressure, high up on the wall, and the wall panel automatically slid away, and they stepped into what, at first glance, appeared to be a storage room. Cinderella stepped to the back wall, and pushed against another, small, and seemingly invisible panel, and a small hatch opened, and she pushed a couple of buttons. The door opened, and the room lights came on, and there before Dan was a Yellow Brick pathway, leading toward a large machine, or another similar apparatus.

"Well", said Cinderella, "Follow the 'Yellow Brick Road', to my 'Tornado Machine!'"

Dan said, "What?!"

Cinderella laughed, and said, "You heard me, silly! This is my Tornado Machine. This is where I simulate tornadoes!"

She took him by the hand, and had him stroll on the yellow brick pathway, to the giant beast of a machine. It seemed to be 20 Feet, or so, square, and perhaps 100 Feet high.

Once Dan had gotten over his initial shock, at not only what it was supposed to be, but also how big it was, he said, "Okay, now, you are simply going to have to do a whole lot of background explaining, here! For instance, how does it work, and why did you build it, as well as how?!"

"Well", answered Cinderella, as she led Dan to a nearby table and chairs, and they sat down, while Cinderella reached into a refrigerator, and got out some iced tea, and lemon wedges, "it was designed, and built, by me, with assistance from some tradesmen, who did most of the construction and welding, and the heavy work. Percy had heard about a contract, for some atmospheric research, and he got the contract. He named me the project supervisor, and I got the job done for well under the bid amount, and Percy made over a million Euros on the deal, which included construction of the machine, and being able to simulate certain aspects of how tornadoes form, and behave, and how they die.

"A tornado is basically just a heat engine, much like the gasoline engine in a car. The tornado uses a difference in temperature, from one zone to another one, to extract a portion of the energy, and convert it into 'useful' work. We call it 'useful' work, even though, in this particular case, we, as humans, usually only see the results of this machine as being destructive. Up at the top of the machine is an apparatus that takes Carbon Dioxide gas, and compresses it, while using electricity to run the compressor. The Carbon Dioxide gas is cooled down, by a refrigeration system, to being a compressed liquid, at well below room temperature. The, now liquefied, Carbon Dioxide is then allowed to escape suddenly into a sealed chamber, which causes the Carbon Dioxide to vaporize, and condense as dry ice, at below -100F. This dry ice condenses in the cooling tubes of the next step in my refrigeration cycle, which is to repeat the process, using Ethylene gas, to cascade down to -202F. So, that provides my cold reservoir, at about minus 200F. This is what you see, way up on top of the machine, or rather do not see, because it is enclosed behind aluminum walls. Down here, at ground level, is the combination heating system, using large electrical heating elements, and propane burners. The heat comes up from below, and the cold air falls from above. I can vary the temperature at the bottom, much easier than I can from the top. This, plus the various air injectors, which can be controlled from computerized, and programmable, air flow control valves, allow me to simulate a wide range of weather, and mixing conditions. Up above is a precipitation system, and I can control the rate of flow, and the temperature, of the moisture down-flow. There is also a series of injectors, to allow me to somewhat mimic dust in the air, and control size, and distribution, as well as the quantity, of incoming dirt, into the tornado. I can simulate rain, as well as hail, and super-cooled water droplets. There are also several other little features that are much more subtle, but the net result is that I can model some aspects of tornadoes. We have completed several study contracts for various agencies, and Percy, as well as myself, have made a fair chunk of change off of this machine. I normally would not fire it up, since it costs some money to do so, but I need to run it occasionally, to keep it certified, and ensure that all of the seals, and other important pieces, are in good working order. Today is your lucky day! This is probably the biggest heat engine that you will be likely to ever see, aside from the real thing and, of course, jet engines, and rocket engines, etc. Of course, a hurricane is bigger, but hopefully, you will not have to see one of those, up close and personal!

"So, are you 'game' enough, to assist me with my Tornado Machine Certification?!", she said, laughing.

"Yeah, sure!", Dan said, rather dubiously. "What do I have to do?"

"Well, mostly not very much. You may have to turn some valves, or push some buttons, or, if things were to go really bad, to hit the 'Master Kill Switch', to turn the whole thing off!"

Cinderella showed Dan where the necessary controls were at, and provided basic instructions about what to do, and when to do it.

She then said, "If you think that you might need to go to the bathroom anytime soon, I suggest that you do it now! They are over in that corner. Once we initiate the start-up cycle, we need to be here, for a while."

So, Dan took the hint, and then Cinderella hit the bathroom, too. She started turning on the computers, and throwing switches, and opening valves. Things began to whir, and stir, and come to life. Lights came on, and motors started spinning, and the compressors started pumping. Then, Cinderella told the computers to initiate their test routines. Other parts, responding to computer commands, began to open, and close, and the computers eventually completed their self-diagnostic routines. The whole 'Start-up' process took almost an hour.

Eventually, things quieted down a little bit, and Dan then said,

"WOW! This has to be one of the most complex pieces of machinery that I have ever watched, as well as one of the biggest!"

"Yes", said Cinderella, "It does remind me somewhat of a jet engine! I was able to make all of this stuff, just starting from very simple home-made tools, and then evolve from there to larger tools, and so on, just as I have already shown, and described to, you."

The Master Control Computer then responded, on screen, "System Verification Complete! All operations report as ready!"

"Okay, this is your last chance to cut and run! Once I push the 'GO' button, you are committed! As the door to the 'Inferno' said, 'Woe to ye, who enters here! Abandon all Hope!'" Cinderella said, laughing.

Dan said, "Let's do it! You have captured all of my attention, in more ways than one, and you have clearly lived through other firings of this machine, and survived in one beautiful piece, so I hope that it should not be all that bad!"

"Okay", Cinderella said, "You were warned! Put on these ear protectors! The noise is one of the reasons, for why this machine is underground!"

She then pushed the "GO" button. Most of the escape doors then went into "Auto Lock" mode. The CO2 pumps began to stir, and valves began to open. Then the heating elements began to pre-warm, on the bottom of the machine. After a while, the system got even louder, as the Ethylene pumps began to run. About 20 minutes later, the compressed air pumps kicked in, and then the noise was nearing the 'Normal Tolerance Limit', without ear protection. The propane burners activated, from near the 'Ground Level', as simulated by the artificial terrain model. Air valves opened, and the air began to swirl around in the chamber, carrying the heat from below, up toward the descending cold air, falling from above. Dan could see the boundary layer, and watched the swirling and mixing of the components of warm, moisture - laden air rising, as well as the condensed moisture attempting to fall down. The swirling was initially a horizontal mixing, and then the wind injectors forced the issue, and the mixing turned toward the vertical, and the funnel cloud began to form and lengthen, soon descending toward the bottom of the chamber. The noise kept increasing. The computers, and their sensors, began spitting out data on the screen, and on the printers, which added even more racket. Then Cinderella ignited the propane burner under the tornado's funnel, where it touched down, and the burner threw up a flame, which was sucked upward, into the funnel, for several feet, thus simulating a small 'Fire Tornado'. At about this time, she wrote a note on a piece of paper, and handed it to Dan. The note read, "Welcome To Hell! I hope that you never have to get any closer!" She then turned off the fire, and opened another lever, which sprayed in tiny dust particles, which helped Dan to visualize the boundaries of the updraft. She later pushed a button, to open a sliding door, at the 'Ground Level' of the machine. This released a couple of dozen small balloons, which were then sucked upward, into the funnel cloud. This served to help with visualizing the air movement. When the balloons reached the top, they popped, when they ran into various metal components.

A little while later, Cinderella told the machine to begin the slowdown, and shutdown cycles.

Gradually, the Tornado Machine turned itself off, and returned to its napping phase. The Giant went back to sleep, ready to literally roar back to life, the next time it was commanded to do so. Finally, it was safe to take off the ear protection. Cinderella removed hers, and Dan took the hint, and followed suit, just in time to hear the 'Auto-Locks' release on the doors.

Dan was stunned, but he did manage to say, "Boy that is one Hell of a machine!", as he made his way over to the table, to sit down, and pour the both of them a refill on the ice tea, just as Cinderella sat down with him.

Cinderella laughed, and said, "Yes, it is one of my more interesting creations! Today was just a 'Dry Run'. Sometimes, I will also put miniature building simulators in there, and install a 'Guard Screen', and then have the vortex suck them up, and destroy the test building design. The model building is designed so as to scale, not only the size, but also the strength of a proposed, prototype building design. This results in something which can produce useful data, for building codes. Well, I do not know about you, but that stimulated my appetite. I think that it is time for lunch. What about you?"

"Okay", said Dan, "I am ready for some food, and after having witnessed THAT, I think that I am also ready for a drink, too!"

So, Cinderella made sure that all of the components had shut down, and then turned off the lights, and locked up the room, and closed the camoflauged outer door.

As they began to walk back toward Cinderella's home, Dan thought again about what Mary Ann had said: "All things are possible, IF you are crazy enough!"

"So, Doctor Frankenstein", Dan said, laughing, "What other creatures, and surprises, do you have, to show me?!"

Cinderella replied, laughing, "Wouldn't you like to know?! Perhaps I will show you, when it is the right time!"

So, they walked back to Cinderella's "Studio", and she then asked him if he had figured out what he would like for lunch. He replied, "Yes, how about a slab of baked salmon, with a Brown Rice concoction, and a vegetable salad, and a fruit salad, with chopped walnuts, and pecans, added?"

Cinderella asked, "Oh? Are we hungry today?"

Dan nodded, "Yes, I seem to be", as he was walking toward the bar. He mixed up the ingredients for a Mai Tai, and asked Cinderella if she would like anything, as long as he was at it. She said that a Mai Tai was fine, and to throw in some extra maraschino cherries.

Cinderella phoned in the order, and then told Dan that they said that it would probably take about an hour.

They flopped on the couch, together, and sipped on their Mai Tai's. After a while, Dan said, "After lunch, and maybe a nap, I think that I may be ready to tackle your computer simulation printout, for that cutting head, which you told me about. Most likely the nap will be needed, though."

Cinderella said, "Yes, I think that a nap would be an excellent idea, especially after a good batch of fish! In the meantime, if it is okay with you, I think that I shall be lost in thought, for a while. I do not think that it will be really deep thought, though."

Dan replied, "Right! Good enough.", and he fell asleep, on the couch, right after finishing his drink.

Cinderella went and got the printout from the cutting head simulation, and came back to sit on the couch. She spread out parts of the report, and wrote some notes on it, while just so very slowly sipping on her Mai Tai.

She grabbed her calculator, and started crunching numbers, using estimated rates of heat transfer, heat capacity, melting points, etc, to make rough calculations of various aspects of the proposed procedure. The computer's cutting head simulation was still standing, after her crude estimates, and thus she was encouraged to take the next step, and grab some of her manuals, and turn on her desktop, personal computer. By the time that the knock on the door came, she was magnificently involved in the checking process.

She answered the door, and looked over the food, and signed for the delivery. The server helped with placing the trays on the dining room table, and rolled the cart away.

Cinderella locked the door, and went over and sat down next to Dan, and woke him up, with a very sweet kiss. She then said, "Dinner is here!"

Dan woke up enough to eat, and once the food reached his brain, he began to feel better. He woke up enough more, after a while, so that he could be helpful in the checking process. After they had made their way through the entire simulation report, they were both satisfied that there was still hope for the proposed method.

Cinderella then said, "Well, I shall be several hours making the corrections, and other changes that we have identified, and you look like a nap that is waiting for a place to happen, so, how about if you go to bed, and get some sleep, while I fire up the simulator, and complete the editing, and turn the CDC 6500 loose on the job?"

Dan said that he hated to duck out on the job, but a good long rest would be about what he could use, right about now.

So, Cinderella shooed him off to bed, and then went to the mainframe computer, and got to work.

About seven hours later, she was satisfied, and ready. Cinderella then told the computer, "LGO", and stuck around, for the start-up process. After which, she went to bed, knowing that it was likely that the computer would run the job all night, and maybe even a wee bit more. She then took a shower, and quietly sneaked into bed, so as to not disturb Dan. He seemed to not budge, and she very contentedly went off to sleep.

In the morning, she went to the bathroom, and then came back to bed, and pretended to be asleep. Dan woke up a little bit later, and also went to the can. When he came back, he noticed that Cinderella had her legs up, and that she seemed to have scooted over, more toward the middle of the bed. So, he crawled into bed, with her, and slid into her waiting loveliness, and her eyes popped wide open, teasingly, and she managed to moan, "OHHH!", as she slipped away, into the land of Orgasm.

135 minutes later, Dan came, and then slowed down a little bit. As Cinderella began to come down, he asked her if she needed any more, for the moment. Her eyes looked a little jaded, as she answered,

"Oh, that was LOVELY! However, I am afraid that if I have you go on, any more, right about now, I shall be too stiff to move!"

So, Dan brought her down, slowly, and then stopped. He rolled over, to flop on his back, and restore the range of motion to his body. Eventually, they were able to get out of bed, and she came over to him, and placed her arms around his waist, and gave him a very deep kiss.

Cinderella then said, "Well, off to the shower, and then, while breakfast is on its way, we shall see what kind of presents the CDC 6500 has for us, today!"

Almost as an after-thought, she added, "Oh, by the way, it seems that my therapy just may be starting to work, Doctor! I was able to work, and monitor myself, and there was only the very slightest hint of any problems, and I knew enough to be able to manage them, and to know when to quit!"

"Excellent!", Dan replied, "I am happy to be able to provide your treatments, whenever you may want them!"

Just as they were about to get into the shower, Cinderella made an observation : "You know, it is a very curious thing for us. I was just realizing that I am always hot, because you are always hard, because I am always hot, because you are always hard......!"

So, they got into the shower, and because they were both sort of satisfied for the moment, and were curious about the computer results, they had actually managed to finish the shower. They got dressed, and Cinderella phoned in for breakfast, and they then went to the computer, retrieved the printout, and went back to the table that they had done the analysis on, last night.

As they went through the results, Dan had an opportunity to glance at Cinderella. Her eyes were lit up, and she was happy, but more than just merely happy. She was seemingly close to being supremely content. This is what she was meant to do. It was who she is, and he also realized that he was able to help to provide her with the ability to reach her full fulfillment. It also was very satisfying to him, too. This was a style of life that he would have never even believed to be possible, let alone to be a part of, and the nice thing about it was that "Fulfillment" was only as far away as the nearest bedroom. He was quite content, too!

"Okay!", said Cinderella, "I think that we are close. The latest run just needs to have a few minor tweaks, and a few changes to some parameters. I think, this time, I will let the computer calculate the values of the heat transfer that is needed, to optimize the performance, and then estimate the temperature needed, for me, rather than me making another guess. The equations are simply too complicated for me to solve exactly. This reminds me of one time that I had derived an equation, and as it turned out, for this particular equation, the only way to arrive at the answer was to already know what the answer was. Otherwise, it was essentially impossible to answer the question. But if you already knew what the answer was, there was no point in solving the equation, in the first place! It is computers that make this possible. I will be adding approximately another 500 lines of code, and the program will take much longer to run, as in all night, starting when I get done with the changes. It may take several iterations for the program to obtain the optimized results, but we just might get there, tomorrow!"

So, she began to scribble notes all over the printout, and outline the changes needed. She had just finished making her notes, when the food arrived.

After they ate, and relaxed for a little while, Cinderella decided that it was time for another refresher course, in staying in touch with her body, and grabbed Dan by the hand, and led him back to the bedroom.

She said, "Well, time to make sure that I do not float away, while I am concentrating on my computer, for the next several hours!", and she started undressing him. He took the hint, and started to undress her, as well. Pretty soon, she was on her way, to visit the land of "OHHHH!", where she stayed for the next 95 minutes. When Dan also came, she was aroused just enough, for him to ask her if she wanted any more. Cinderella slipped back into orgasm, and Dan took this as a hint that she did, indeed, need more Fulfillment. So, 45 minutes later, Dan came, for a second time, and slowed down enough, to gently bring Cinderella down to Earth.

"Oh, God!", she said, "I hate to stop this thing, but physics, and biology, really get into the way. I guess that we have to at least occasionally deal with such things! How long was I out?"

Dan replied, "About 140 minutes."

Cinderella said, "Oh, thank you! I love you so much!", and she planted a deep, and hungry, kiss on his mouth.

When they came up for air, Dan said, "I love you, too, very much!"

"Well," She said, "I guess that I need to move around some, and then go back to work, on my simulation."

So, they got up, and got cleaned up, and then Cinderella went to her computer, and spent several hours working on her program changes. At around midnight, she realized that she had been working on the changes for much longer than expected, but she was finding that she was not in any real danger, for now, so she finished the programming, and started up the program. Due to the extensive changes, which lengthened the "Source-Code" considerably, plus the complicated iteration formulas which were needed, the new estimate for the run time was about 32 hours. It would take more than a whole day, on a CDC 6500! She then realized that what she was going to attempt to build would not even be possible, without a computer having at least this much capability, and even if the simulation works, the reality may still not work, much like the inherently unstable airplane designs that are now only possible to fly, because they are controlled by a computer! The airplanes receive greatly improved performance characteristics, but the price was that they would crash, if the computer systems failed.

The computer completed the preliminary checkout, and she then typed in LGO, and hit the return key, and yawned, and went off to bed, knowing full well that she would probably not receive any answers, tomorrow, unless the program bombed, or the simulation totally failed.

Cinderella felt good, though. This was a very satisfying project, for her. She was doing the kind of work that she loved, and was well qualified for. She was helping to push the boundaries of what was known, and what was possible. If this worked, she realized, it might only be just barely possible, but it might also represent the highest pinnacle that a milling machine could reach, anytime soon. Soon, she was off to visit, and count, the reindeer, in Napland, while visions of delicious Brownies, loaded with walnuts, and dark chocolate chips, danced in her head.

The next morning, Cinderella woke up early. She saw that Dan was still sleeping soundly, so she carefully slipped out of bed, and quietly got dressed. Curiosity had the better of her, at the moment, and she wanted to know if there was any information that she could glean, from what was already printed out. She walked down the hall, slowly, while contemplating whether she was really prepared for what she might find, good or bad. Eventually, she decided that she was as ready as she was ever likely to be. After all, it WAS just a computer simulation, and at this point in time, nothing more would be lost, if it were to have hopelessly failed! All that would be lost is a few days of computer time, and some of her time, and a little bit of Dan's time.

She opened the door to the room, and turned on the light. The CDC 6500 was still running. No real surprise there. She checked the page count, on the printout. It was well past 700, which was also no surprise. When she tore off the part of the printout that had finished, and placed on a nearby work table, and started flipping through selected portions of the report, her eyes lit up. The simulation was working, but in a different way than she had expected. The program had been written to run an iterative sequence, which it was doing, but with a twist: The very large, and quite complex, program also simulated a simple form of artificial intelligence, as well! The program had access to information, stored in digitized form, from reference books, and it was automatically accessing these files, and other sources that were available to it, with the result that it was now doing, in hours, what would have taken her years of looking up, plus time spent on making program adjustments. It seemed that the program was also writing parts of its own code, as it was going along!

Cinderella grabbed the nearest chair, and sat down, stunned! Even if she eventually verified, and accepted for herself, what the program was doing, could she tell anyone else, without absolute, and irrefutable evidence, that this was the case? At the very least, she had to keep it to herself, for probably quite some time, while she attempted to understand just what had happened. Dan would likely not attempt to concern himself with what she had put into her program, unless she asked him to.

Then another thought hit her, square in the face: Were the orgasms that she needed, to help to keep her in her body, also rewiring her brain into a new, and much higher level of intelligence than what she already possessed? Or was that intelligence already there, but merely inaccessible to her? In either case, she could not tell anyone about it, at least for long enough to attempt to understand the consequences of what such a revelation might be. If it was her own intelligence, it might be that it had found a subtle way of emerging from her subconscious, through a computer code. Regardless of which way it went, this would be an extraordinary claim, and, therefore, it would, correspondingly, require extraordinary evidence!

Cinderella then attempted to focus on what else she could learn from the printout. As she waded through the report, now with a very different viewpoint, than what she had started with, she found that the energy density of the beam was much higher than she had estimated, due to the heat transfer efficiency of the lasing material, and that the amount of energy needed for the input was adjusted by the program, to avoid burning up the simulated beam source. The beam was running at 7400 watts per square centimeter, which would completely, and hopelessly, burn up any known material, and the computer program compensated for this, reducing the beam to the proposed test target of 5kW per square centimeter, or about the temperature of the surface of the sun, which, while admittedly still a scorcher, she MIGHT be able to transfer enough energy away from the interface zone, so that the lasing medium, and the finished surface of the work piece, might survive. If necessary, it might be possible to lower the input energy, as well, but that would slow the work speed, by some amount, as well. Even so, this method could still run at a speed that would completely blow away anything currently available.

As Cinderella continued on through the report, she realized that a micro-jet of liquid nitrogen could provide enough cooling, for steel, if the work piece was thick enough, and the amount of liquid nitrogen was computer controlled. A human could not be involved. Humans could not react fast enough. This whole project was turning into another thing that would only be possible, because of computers.

She then realized that the objective here, at this stage of development, should be to show that it was possible, at all! If she could get it to work, the idea could be patented, and then other researchers, with different ideas, and experience, might be able to improve it, under license from, and contract agreements with, Sir Percival.

Cinderella had been lost, for quite some time, in thought, about this whole project, and all of the various ramifications and consequences of it, including the unexpected discoveries about the program and, perhaps, about herself, as well. After a while, she realized that, by now, there must be considerably more printout available, for her to start sifting through. She went back to get more, and was startled to realize that, not only was it still running, with another 300 pages printed out, but the program had further optimized itself, and had continued to rewrite its own code, apparently adding another 2850 lines, and it had activated the DISSPLA pen plotter, and was making drawings of the optimized design for the milling cutter, and the milling machine, and all of the supporting hardware and equipment, as well! This was not even included in her conscious programming instructions, which had only been told to make a few modest estimates of some parameters.

She then was starting to wonder if all of this must be a hallucination of one form or other? But there was too much detail, here, and too much going on, so she proceeded on the assumption, for now, that this must be real. All of the material specifications, and dimensions, and assembly instructions, were on the drawings. Everything that was needed to build this project was there! But what the Hell happened?

About a half an hour later, everything quieted down, and then Cinderella ran to the computer, to make sure that the modified code had saved itself, and then loaded a couple of back-up reels, to make some "Safe Copies" of the, now apparently precious, modified code, and she then made sure that they were labeled, and stored them in a safe. After loading another box of printer paper, she also instructed the computer to print out the source code that it finally completed the job with.

Once this was done, she locked this printout in a cabinet, and left the computer room, and went to the meditation room, with the speakers and LEDs, that she had recently shown Dan, so that he could begin his sound identification training. She activated a special program, and sat down, cross-legged, on the floor, back up straight, and then the room lights dimmed, and she closed her eyes, and began to concentrate on this exercise.

About two hours later, she had completed this phase of her self-diagnostic run, and stopped the exercise. A sense of calm and serenity had been partially restored, but the mystery remained : What the Hell happened?

Cinderella returned to her home, and found that Dan was in the shower. She stuck her head in, for long enough to ask him if he had eaten, yet?

"No", Dan replied, "I only woke up about a half an hour ago. You were not around, so I figured that you went down to make sure that your computer simulation was still running."

"Yes, I did, and it was. What would you like for me to phone in, for breakfast?"

"How does some blueberry scones sound, with French toast, and sliced ham, and a fruit salad sound?"

"That sounds good, to me! You got it!"

Cinderella then phoned in the order, and asked if they could make a small chocolate milkshake, to go with it. They said yes, and that it would be about 45 minutes, before it was delivered there.

Cinderella poured herself a glass of iced tea, with lemon, and grabbed a straw, and settled down on the couch, to contemplate her next move.

Dan emerged, dressed, and Cinderella set the table, just as the knock on the door came, to signal that the brunch had arrived. She answered the door, and the server wheeled the cart on in. Cinderella looked it over, and signed for the delivery. The food was placed on the table, and the cart was taken away.

Cinderella gave Dan a big hug and kiss, and they sat down, for the food. Dan asked about how the program run was looking, and Cinderella answered,

"Well, it did much better than I expected. It may have done so good, that this thing just might be a real possibility. I will probably have to spend a couple of days down there, just by myself, as I attempt to truly understand just exactly what did happen. If this thing is what it looks like it just might be, I think that we could be on to something. So, unless you have some objection, or something more pressing, I believe that this project, at the moment, should take a fairly high priority, at least until I can figure out what had happened."

Dan said that he had no objection, and could use a few days of rest, in any case.

"However", he said, "I believe that I like the idea of something more pressing!"

Cinderella replied, dreamily, "Yes, I could use a little bit more pressing, too, after breakfast!"

So, after breakfast, they went off to bed. Cinderella, just before she slipped away, into an orgasm of over two hours, had acquired an even deeper vision of the role of the Enlightenment.

About 145 minutes after she slipped away, into the land of Orgasm, coming closer to the Enlightenment, Dan had, by this time, already came, twice, and gradually slowed down, just enough, to bring Cinderella back to close to fully conscious, and asked her if she wanted anymore, right now.

Cinderella replied, "Well, I would really like to never stop this, but I think that it is about all that my body can handle, for a while. If I stay here any longer, I shall soon be unable to move. So I guess that yes, I need to stop, for now. Once I fully float back down to Earth, and we get a shower, I must go see about earning my money."

So they stopped, and took a shower. Cinderella returned to the computer room, with some refreshments, and a snack, in hand. She put up a sign on the door, saying, "Do Not Disturb!" and signed it. This was just a minor formality, since very few people knew how to get there, in the first place, but she knew that this could be an important time, so she wanted to emphasize the point. She locked, and bolted, the outer doors, and the inner doors, too, and turned the phone ringer off, so as to not be disturbed. She knew that Sir Percival had a way to gain entrance to the room, even though it was locked, and that the room had security cameras, so that she would be safe enough, for working there, all by herself.

Cinderella first retrieved the drawings, and all of the code printouts, that she had locked away. She started reviewing the drawings, which were something of a mystery as to where they had come from, since she thought that she had not inserted any instructions for drawings to be made.

Gradually, as she waded through the drawings, she began to build a mental visualization of what her computer program had created, detail, by detail. There were several hundred drawings and specification sheets, and she needed to study, and absorb, them all. Several hours later, she felt satisfied that she now possessed a grasp of the machine that she was proposing to build. One crucial thing that she had not yet considered, when she was first thinking of the project, but which she now fully understood, was the role that liquid helium would have to play in this project : The Lasing transfer medium would absolutely have to be kept fully cooled, almost to absolute zero, to the point of becoming a superconductor. With the rate of energy flow through the cutter being so high, even the smallest amount of real resistance would almost certainly cause the cutting head to vaporize instantly. This is why there was so much additional paraphernalia added to the design and drawings, stuff that she had not really thought that she was ready to even begin to consider.

She next turned her attention to the question of how all of this was created. Where did this additional code come from?

To even begin to answer this question, she would have to dissect the original source code, first line by line, and then module by module, and subroutine by subroutine. Eventually, it began to emerge that she had created an oscillating, almost Bi-stable, code in her program. Between the original source code, and the Job Control Language, she had built in an ability for the program to call the JCL, so that the program, which had the ability to write and edit code externally, would then be able to interrupt itself, and compile the newly minted changes to the code, and then resume its operation. If it happened that the changes were not fully satisfactory, it could interrupt itself again, and either modify, or discard, the changes, as needed. The computer would then resume its operations, while seeking to optimize the project. The "Intelligent Code", which had apparently emerged, as an expression of a subconscious part of her brain, would be able to shave many years off of the project time, perhaps being what made this project possible, at all.

It finally began to dawn on her, that she now commanded an even higher form, and level, of intelligence than she had previously possessed. She now understood, for the first time, the true meaning of the teachings that Percy had been attempting to bring to her, for several years. She recalled, thinking to herself,

"Percy once told me that when one achieves the full and complete Enlightenment of Feline Level Nine, a Transformation occurs, and you will then possess an intelligence, and an understanding, which seems to fully transcend your own. It is as if a door has opened into a new room, or almost an entirely new dimension. Your brain, or rather your grasp of reality, begins to grow in size exponentially. Another part of your understanding of a larger reality begins to emerge, and it may take over."

This computer code thus became the first tangible, and direct, evidence that a new form of consciousness had come upon her. She had opened the door to another aspect of the subconscious, and new stuff just came spilling out.

Cinderella now elected, after several more minutes of thought, to retrieve a copy of the last program code, as modified by the computer, and then see if she could turn it loose, and watch what it did, just to see if the source code could tell her anymore about itself, and also about herself. She opened access to more of the computerized reference books, and other files that were available to her, as canned data storage, and re-compiled the code, and turned the computer loose, after checking the printer's paper stock, to see where the program went, and thus took her along for the journey. Just as she issued the command, "LGO", she was realizing that the computer had become an extension of her own brain. She now just might have access to the speed that human brains lacked, if she could figure out exactly what she had done. Her brain might be able to transcend the normal human limitations, in a great many areas.

Several hours later, as she continued to think about, and follow, the evolution of the computer's run, the program again reached a pinnacle in the optimization of the design of the new milling machine, and the precious new cutting head design, and then began to print out a new set of several hundred drawings, and specification sheets.

At this point, once the various aspects of the program had finished running, she made several back-up copies, and locked up the, now even more precious, output material, so that she could store it until tomorrow, when she was ready to tackle it all again. Having done so, she returned to the meditation chamber, to seek to achieve an even greater understanding of what she had done, in just these last couple of days.

After spending a couple of hours in the dark of the meditation chamber, with the speakers randomly moving around, and emitting musical notes of varying frequencies, and lengths of time, she had further enhanced her serenity, and was ready to return to the light. She got up, and stopped the program, and returned to her home.

Dan was awake, and had been resting, and reading various books.

Cinderella asked if he was ready for dinner, yet, since she had been gone for several hours. Dan said that he was, indeed, just starting to think about dinner.

So, they made dinner plans, and Cinderella phoned them in. Dan asked about how things were going on her little project. She then explained that the progress had been phenomenal, even almost exponential.

"If it continues like this, it is possible that we may soon have a fully finished, and optimized project, and perhaps even just a wee bit more!" She said, adding, "If this current trend continues, I may even soon be able to do other things, as well. I have, possibly, arrived at a new place of understanding! By the way, after our food has settled down some, I am hoping that you can send me on another very long, and quite deep, journey, on my pathway toward the 'True Enlightenment!'"

"Dear Lady", Dan replied, "I shall be most happy, to be your tour guide!"

She then grabbed him, and they spent quite a few minutes in a long embrace, and very deep kiss.

Right after this, there was a knock at the door, signaling that the food had arrived. After dinner, and a little bit of relaxing conversation, and some playful hugging and kissing, Cinderella reached down, and grabbed Dan in the crotch. She said, "Oh, good, you are ready!"

So, they went off to the bed, and undressed each other. Cinderella laid down on the bed, and Dan entered her. She managed to kiss him, one more time, before sliding away, on her journey to the Land of Orgasm.

This time, she was gone for 195 minutes, during which time Dan had also come three times, but was still able to keep going, because she was such an exciting creature, for him to be able to explore the depths of her personality. By this time, however, they would soon need to take a break, so he began to slow down, and slowly returned her to Earth, so to speak.

Cinderella's eyes began to open, looking a little bit jaded, and then she awakened enough to lock her arms around Dan, and said, "I think that I really, and simply, MUST keep you! You are doing things for me, that I am not even sure that I fully grasp, as of yet!"

Dan said that he would be most honored to be a part of her, forever, if she would like that.

So, they got up and moved around a little bit. They were both a little bit numb and stiff, but they knew that such minor discomforts would soon pass. The rewards that they were gaining were more than fair compensation for any temporary discomfort. Off to the shower, they went. She kissed him, while they were soaping each other up, and asked, "How long was I out for?"

Dan replied, "About three and a quarter hours!"

Cinderella dreamily said, "Thank you for being such a wonderful tour guide!"

After this, they went to bed, and both slept very well, feeling that they were quite secure in each other.

Not long after dawn, Dan was aroused just enough to reach over and gently begin stroking one of her inner thighs. Soon, she pulled up her legs, and Dan moved into position, and entered her. She seemed to be only a little bit awake, at first, but soon slipped away, for a 45 minute trip. Afterwards, Dan slowly brought her back down to Earth, and kissed her. She woke up enough to say, "That was nice, but I am going to need to move around for a little bit, and after breakfast, I must return to my study, of my latest computer run, but I will really need more of this, very soon!"

So, they got cleaned up, and ate breakfast, and Cinderella returned to her work at not only understanding the drawings that the program had generated, but also the seemingly magical qualities of the program, and also, perhaps, to greater insights about herself.

She retrieved the output from yesterday's run, and began, again, with the study of the latest set of drawings. While they were similar to the previous set, they were also more refined. There were very subtle changes in some places, but the main lines of the design were starting to become clear. Adding another day of reiteration, with even more source material, added from various stored tapes, having immense quantities of physical knowledge, gleaned over the last century or so, after really good, and reliable, data became generally available, might be just enough to close out the iteration process. The computer, she loosely estimated to herself, could do more work in a day, than what she could manage to do in thousands of years, even if she managed to remember all of that stuff.

Next, she began to study the changes in the code, as compared to yesterday's run, hoping to tease out the magical secrets of the source code. Slowly, over several hours, she gleaned a few more of the secrets, not only from the code, but from her own mind, as well. She set up a test program, so that she could try out a few hypotheses, to see if she was at all on the right track. After a few hours, and a few false starts, she began to get someplace. She found a few thousand lines that appeared to capture the essence of the simulation. A few more cycles, and minor changes, which she edited into the program, and it began to work, on its own. Cinderella then suddenly realized that she had created a Genetic Algorithm, and not just a genetic algorithm, but one which was able to substantially duplicate her own thought processes and personality! It was almost a computerized version of herself. She stored several copies of this precious gift, in various files on the mainframe, and also made copies of this on magnetic tapes, as well, and locked them in various scattered cabinets, and drawers and other secure places.

By now, she could turn the mainframe loose on the latest revelations, and additional data. Cinderella watched the drama unfolding before her eyes, before realizing that she had done just about everything that she would be able to do, for at least the next several hours. It was now up to the computer, to do more work, in a short time, than she could hope to do, probably ever.

After verifying that the computer run was apparently going well, she realized that it was time for a break. She went upstairs to eat lunch, in the cafeteria, and felt good enough after this, to go get her rifle, and go to the rifle range, to be re-certified as a Fully Qualified Marksman. After she got set up, at the range, she went to the ammunition stores person, and got a box of Match Grade Ammunition. When she returned to the assigned booth, she found Orla, setting up in the booth next to hers.

They hugged, and said "Hi."

Orla asked how Cinderella was doing, and Cinderella replied, "I am really doing quite well! I hate to use the word, 'Phenomenal', because it has been so overused, as to be rendered almost ordinary, but I would say that I am pretty close to where this would be an appropriate word. In just the last few days, I have moved forward years in my understanding and progress, in many fields. In fact, the reason that I came up here, today, was to test a hunch about the evolution of my own abilities. Let us see what there is, that I can do here. The best that I have usually done, before, consistently, was to put five shots into a space about the size of a quarter, at 400 yards."

So they had the Field Range Supervisor move two, side by side, targets to 200 yards. Both Cinderella and Orla qualified well. There was no surprise here. Next, new targets were moved to 400 yards, and again, this was to be expected. Orla then shot first, and scored nicely, at 600 yards. This is where Cinderella's previous scores began to not be quite as good as she would have hoped for.

However, she now seemed to be possessed by a higher ability and confidence. There was a sense of a finer muscle, and nerve, control and coordination. Cinderella placed all five shots into a space of about the size of a nickel.

After this, Cinderella shot first, at 800 yards, and she and Orla produced similar results. A supreme confidence now possessed her, and Cinderella had the Range Master move the targets to one kilometer. Her newly discovered mental algorithm carried her to victory, placing all five of the shots into a space the size of a quarter. She was able to 'read' the wind drift, and air density, and track variations in temperature of the air, as each shot traveled down range. Cinderella was also now able to sense smaller divisions of time, as well. She seemed to have developed a sort of "Hyper-Awareness", which reached far beyond her previously, already quite high, abilities. Orla was only just able to match this, and they agreed to call it a fair draw. Having both re-qualified, they hugged again. Orla asked about how Cinderella and Dan were doing, and Cinderella explained,

"Well, things are going splendidly well. Dan is teaching me about things that I would not have even dreamed that I could have achieved. Right now, I have a program running, on the CDC 6500, that may allow us to reach the very summit of what a milling machine, and particularly the cutting tool, may be able to achieve any time soon. This work is only possible, because we have really great computer capabilities, and because Dan is teaching me how to stay in control of my mind. I would tell you more, and in more details, but right now this is all just still a work in progress, and I am not really sure as to exactly what is going on, just yet."

Orla said, "Well it is just as well that you are still learning about what is going on, because I am supposed to be someplace else, in just a few minutes, so I have to leave."

Cinderella smiled, and said, "Oh, okay, I understand. I am quite curious about how my computer simulations are doing, anyway." So, Orla left, and Cinderella cleaned and stored her rifle, and carried it back to her own locker.

Cinderella went up to the cafeteria, and ordered a Ham Sandwich, on rye, with a Dark Chocolate milkshake, plus Dark Chocolate Morsels on top of the milkshake. She knew that she was likely to be many more hours, reviewing the printouts, and correcting any errors, or making any other changes to whatever needed to have additional editing. She might also be quite some time, on just trying to grasp what was going on.

She ate the ham sandwich, while walking back to her workroom, and sipped on the milkshake, also. Once she arrived there, she took off the lid, and spooned out the chocolate chips, and devoured those, as well. A short time later, she was back to reviewing the gifts that the computer had given her.

The computer had finished the drawings, and the run, already. This was something of a surprise, and she thought that something had gone wrong. A detailed inspection revealed that the program had run even faster, as it continued to self-generate an increasingly optimized code. The drawings now only contained minor changes from the last batch. Even the main program only had limited changes, so that she was satisfied that it was nearing the optimum limit of what the physics could achieve. The real surprise was that the Genetic Algorithm, which loosely modeled her personality, had better than doubled in size! She carefully stored away copies of everything, and then began to make a last, and thorough, review of the drawings.

About three hours later, she felt that she had a fully adequate understanding of what had been accomplished, and would soon be ready to show Dan what she had done, with the help of a massive mainframe computer! But first, she realized, it was time for a reward: Another journey, in search of the land of the Enlightenment!

Cinderella returned to her home, and Dan asked, "Well, how did it go?"

Cinderella said, "Oh, it went marvelously! In fact, it went so well that the project is probably done! You and I will need to review it, together, looking for any of the obvious little screw-ups that I, and the computer, might have missed, in several different simulation runs, but aside from some glaringly obvious mistakes that might have totally gotten past me, plus any subtle ones, as well, we are done! If it survives our review, I can send it on to Percy, to look over. After that, he sends it on to our engineers, and Patent Examiners, to determine which parts, and processes, can be patented.

"But first, I need to have you take me on another journey, toward the land of the Enlightenment!"

So, Dan very willingly did as she asked, and about 110 minutes later, she was coasting back down to Earth. A shower, and a quick snack of Strawberry Shortcake, and then they were ready for Cinderella to escort Dan back to the computer room.

Cinderella set up the stack of documents, and Dan looked at the immense size of the results. While he was certainly willing to try to wade through, and understand, the full contents of the work that she had produced, he was somewhat dubious about his ability to really grasp what had been achieved. There were over 200 pages of drawings, alone, and many hundreds of pages of relevant computer printout, as well.

About four hours later, after making a valiant stab at trying to even begin to grasp what Cinderella had accomplished, Dan was ready to acknowledge that her work was fully and completely beyond his feeble ability to comprehend! He suggested that, if she was ready, it would be time to send it on, to Sir Percy.

Cinderella agreed that it was time to show Percy what she had apparently managed to achieve. She thought of it this way, because there was still a possibility that something was overlooked in the physics, because this was still a totally new process, and had only been simulated, and not actually tested, but it was also something that she could not reasonably hope to test, on her own. There was still a real enough chance that it would not work. But for the mere investment of a few days of her time, plus a little bit of Dan's time, and some computer time, and computer paper, this could make many millions of dollars. This was the type of stuff that Percy routinely approved of, and it was part of why he was so rich.

Upon returning to her home, Cinderella sent an e-mail to Percy, explaining what she had accomplished, with some help from Dan, and the fact that she was able to run simulations on a very large mainframe computer, which led to the apparently optimized results.

They then went to bed, for the night, and Dan took her on an extended journey, toward the land of the Enlightenment.

In the morning, they awoke to find a reply from Percy, saying to come on up, anytime, but about 1:00, right after lunch, would probably be about the best time. So she sent back a reply that they would be there, just before 1:00.

So, then they ate breakfast, and arrived with the full stack of documents, at the appointed time.

Percy's secretary then showed Cinderella and Dan into Percy's office, and after a few minutes of chit-chat, they got right down to business, with Cinderella doing almost all of the talking, explaining what had happened, including her having accidentally created a piece of seemingly intelligent code, perhaps a form of a genetic, self-evolving computer program, which is how all of this happened so fast.

Percy said that he would forward the drawings to their Patent Staff, but that absolutely not one word is to be said about the intelligent code, to anyone, including for Cinderella and Dan to not discuss it with each other!

"That must remain secret, for now! However, I would like to have Cinderella continue to try to understand just what it is, that was created. When you have some confidence that you can explain it, let me know. It is just possible that you have created a new, and perhaps very valuable, life form! But, that is what we must now seek to understand."

So, Dan and Cinderella left Percy the drawings, and then they went off to get some lunch. Because of the "gag order", Dan could not say much, and Cinderella was both curious, and quite excited, about the assignment to understand the mysterious piece of computer code, that she had accidentally created.

So, after they ate lunch, Dan went off to whatever he was working on, and Cinderella went off to the computer room, to study the Evolutionary Algorithm, and attempt to learn some of its secrets, and thereby, possibly, some of her own secrets, as well. She locked herself into the computer room, as much to protect her secrets, as to not be disturbed.

As Cinderella continued to investigate the code, carefully and painstakingly teasing out vital clues about what had happened, she kept notes, and made changes to a copy of the mysterious file. Every now and then, she would edit the copy, adding new refinements to her model, and compile and run the simulation. A few of the changes went nowhere, and those were removed. However, most of the changes resulted in improvements, either directly in the efficiency of the program, or in its ability to further optimize itself, perhaps on the next pass, as well as in aiding Cinderella in understanding either the function of the program and/or herself. Each time a significant leap forward occurred, she would save a copy of it, so that she would have the ability to recover the program, in the event of a catastrophic failure.

Cinderella also frequently allowed the program to modify a copy of itself, and each time she turned the program loose upon itself, so to speak, the length of the program grew, sometimes just a little, and occasionally, quite a bit more. The new copy was then "backed up" on tape, as well.

The process of understanding the new program then began again, and new insights would emerge, some of them subtle, and others profound. It was then that Cinderella realized, even more, that the program, and herself, were starting to co-evolve. Each was now moving forward, in leaps and bounds. She, and the computer program, were starting to approach what she thought of as the "Singularity", where she came to exist, in both the physical world, and now also in "Cyber Space".

At the end of each day, she would carefully ensure that backup copies were labeled, and stored on magnetic tape, in several widely scattered, locked cabinets, to minimize the risk of a total loss. Each evening, she would return to her home, and order dinner, for both herself, and Dan. After dinner, and some time relaxing together, Dan would take Cinderella on another extended Journey toward the Enlightenment, often for hours at a time. Sometimes, in the morning, there would be a long Journey, as well. But most of the time, because of the apparently critical work that was now being done, they would settle for about an hour and a half, unless Cinderella felt that a longer Orgasm was needed.

Cinderella would retrieve a paper copy of the latest file, and study it, painstakingly and exhaustively, making a few notes for changes, as she gleaned new insights. A copy of the latest file would then be edited, and another simulation would be compiled and run, where the new program would work on a copy of itself. Each time she did this, the program would continue to grow significantly, in both size, and complexity.

Each evening, she returned to her home, and moved closer to the Enlightenment. The next day, Cinderella would return to her studies. In the morning, she would refresh her understanding of what transpired on the previous day, and night, and then turn the Evolutionary Algorithm loose on a copy of itself. Eventually, after several weeks of this pattern, the Evolutionary Algorithm was allowed to access some of the on-site data files, and then gradually more files followed. Whole reference books, and textbooks, some of them previously digitized and stored on tape, as well as some newly digitized ones, were made available to the Evolutionary Algorithm which represented the Proto-Essence of herself, in Cyberspace. Eventually, almost every single textbook, treatise, research paper, etc, that she had ever read, was digitized, and then digested by the Proto-Essence. Soon, all of this information was stored in the code of the Evolutionary Algorithm, having also been reduced to its essential components, and stored in its most compact forms.

The program continued to evolve, by analyzing copies of itself, and, now only sometimes, by further insights from Cinderella herself. The Evolutionary Algorithm was now approaching the point where

Cinderella's personal ability to contribute directly to its further evolution was approaching her own limits. All she could really do to further enhance it, was to feed it new textbooks, particularly in mathematics, physics, chemistry, and engineering, and also serve as its custodian, providing direct care to it, by making daily backup copies of it. In a sense, she was feeding herself the knowledge that she craved, and now the program craved, for her.

A few days after having reached this point, she took a day off, and spent it in bed, with Dan. After a very satisfying breakfast of fish, and blueberries, and other "Brain Food", Cinderella, and Dan, were ready for an even more extended journey, toward the Enlightenment. They had both been preparing for this journey, for quite some time, with stretches, and very physical exercises, of various forms, as they had found that there were certain physical inhibitors, and other resistance, that needed to be overcome. Mind control was also sometimes an important factor, as well. They were now much better prepared to climb the mountain to the very top, at the limits of what was likely their own human endurance, at least at the present time.

Dan entered Cinderella, and she soon slipped away, into orgasm. They kept going and going. Finally, after just over four hours, she reached the point where a brilliant flash of white light occurred inside of her brain, and she then had crossed into the "Understanding!" Her body, and her brain, shuddered, and then relaxed, and Dan could see, from the physical changes, that something must have happened. So, after a while, he began to very slowly bring her back down. She said that she felt like she had transcended her own body.

"Dan", she slowly began to reply, as she drifted back down to Earth, "That was just the loveliest, and most phenomenal, and incredibly deep experience that I have ever had! I believe that I reached 'The Enlightenment', just now!"

Dan replied, "I thought that SOMETHING must have happened, just now, as your whole body felt like it had suddenly changed!"

So, they spent some time, with Dan still inside of her, as they stroked and kissed, and cuddled each other, while Cinderella slowly floated back down to Earth.

"How long", asked Cinderella, "Was I out for?"

Dan answered, "From the time you entered the Orgasm, to the time that your body suddenly relaxed, near the end, was 247 minutes! Over four hours!"

"WOW", replied Cinderella, "I sure am glad that you can last for that long! Otherwise, I would have almost certainly never gotten to where I am now!

"In a sense", she continued, "It felt like I had reached the Orgasm that awaited me, at the end of the Extended Sexual Orgasm! It completely blew me away!"

So, they got cleaned up, and ate a late lunch. Cinderella, now feeling fully energized, had a little bit more of a "Bounce" in her step than usual, decided to go to the computer room, after all!

During the night, Cinderella had left the Evolutionary Algorithm running, to see what would happen. When she got there, she had printed out a copy of the file, and found that the code had better than tripled in size! Startled by this, she made a new backup copy of the file, and locked it in a cabinet. The main changes that she could see, beyond how much the Algorithm had grown, was how many new branches there were, connecting various places to each other, as functions and subroutines. She gradually came to realize that the program, before she allowed it access to a great number of references and textbooks, represented HER, in some ways, just before she discovered chemistry, and mathematics, and began that sudden growth spurt of knowledge, which led her to this point in time and space, and now to the Understanding.

Cinderella decided that she was now prepared to explain to Percy about just what it was that she had created, at least as far as it could be known at this time, and sent an e-mail up to Percy, to this effect.

Percy shot an e-mail right back, saying that NOW would be a most excellent time! So she replied that she would be up there, just as quick as she could walk.

Cinderella arrived at Percy's office, and the secretary said, "Go right on in! He is most anxious to see you!"

"Please sit down", Percy began, through his voice synthesizer, "Your e-mail was most excellently timed, as I was just about to send one to you. The Patents Review staff have found that there are a great number of processes in your Milling Cutter plans that are fully patentable! Some of them are even revolutionary! They have also established methods of manufacture for all of the various components. The full file was escorted to the Patents Offices, just this morning.

"So, what can I do for you, right about now?"

Cinderella explained what it was that she had discovered about the mysterious program that she created, which had led to the whole process, up to this point.

"It seems", she said, "that this mysterious Evolutionary Algorithm is a Cyber-Space copy of the Essence of me! If such turns out to be the case, and this is starting to strongly appear to be true, I may be able to evolve, even beyond myself, and my own physical limitations, and now accomplish feats that would not be directly humanly possible for one person to achieve alone. I have been feeding it textbooks and manuals in various subjects and, if it has not already done so, this program will soon exceed my own knowledge and understanding, and my own ability to understand it.

"I also have another interesting piece of news: It was just this morning, near the end of an orgasm of just over four hours, that Dan had taken me to what appears to be the 'Enlightenment', and the 'Understanding!'"

"Marvelous!", replied Percy, "It now appears, if you are ready, that this would be the optimum moment, for another Feline Mind Meld!"

So, Cinderella laid down on the couch, face up, and Percy hopped up on the arm of the couch, and massaged her forehead, and began to stare deep into her eyes. Soon, their minds were connected, and Percy began to run a deep diagnostic scan. This took about an hour, and when he was done, he gave her a kiss, to start to wake her up.

When she was fully conscious, Percy said, through his voice synthesizer, that he no longer found any evidence of the brain damage that she had previously had. It was gone!

"It appears that you may now proceed with whatever reasonable pursuits that may appeal to you, including a Ph.D. , cautiously, if you would wish to do so! As long as you will, at least for a while, allow me to scan your brain for you, if you start to feel even the least bit stressed, I believe that you are cleared, for probably just about anything that you may wish to pursue.

"If you do elect to pursue a Ph.D., in mathematics, for example, it appears that you, combined, with your cyber essence, will make a formidable team. Have you attempted to ask your 'Evolutionary Algorithm' copy of yourself if it can prove any theorems, yet? You, and the Algorithm, may be able to advance the study of mathematics, in many different branches, by many years."

Cinderella replied, "Well, no, I have not really begun to examine what a 'Cyber Copy' of me could do, yet! It was only just this morning that I arrived at the Enlightenment, and the Understanding! However, this looks like it could be a most excellent idea that you had, just now. I believe, if it is okay with you, that I will look into this. Thank you. Oh, by the way, Dan and I have not actually discussed it yet, but I believe that we are nearing the point of Marriage! I wanted you to be the first to know! If he does not ask me, soon, I am likely to ask him!"

Percy replied, "Marvelous! Let me offer you my full blessing! If things work out right, with your new inventions, you may well end up being fully, and financially, secure, for the rest of your lives!"

Cinderella said, "Oh, thank you so much, Percy, for everything!", and she hugged him.

Percy answered, "You are, as always, very welcome! Thank you, too, my dear. Well, I see that there is a blinking light, on my phone, so I think that this is a call that I am supposed to take. See you again soon!"

Cinderella then left, floating on air! She stopped by the cafeteria, and had some more "Brain Foods", and then went down to the computer, and started to feed the Evolutionary Algorithm more and more books on mathematics, including increasingly difficult, and more advanced subject matter.

After Cinderella loaded absolutely all of the mathematics textbooks that she had from her college years, plus many more that she had acquired later, some of which she had found to be even beyond her own comprehension. She then started to test the program by asking it to prove various simple theorems. She was able to watch the thought processes of the Evolutionary Algorithm, as suggested by the lines in the program, which began to appear on her monitor, to glean some notion of what it was doing. The program began to search for clues, and was writing additional instructions to itself, as it was going along, to eventually arrive at the right answer. She repeated this, hundreds of times, with different theorems, and eventually it appeared that the program began to solve the questions faster, even though the theorems and problems she presented were increasingly difficult ones. By following the display on the monitor, Cinderella also eventually began to understand some of the theorems that she, herself, had failed to prove.

By this time, it was getting close to dinner, so she made another backup copy of the latest state of the Evolutionary Algorithm, and locked it in the safe. She then told it to attempt to solve all of the problems presented in the various mathematical texts that she had provided to the program, and left for the evening, after having recharged the printer's paper stock.

Cinderella arrived back at her home, with a profound sense of joy, and hopped into the shower. After she got out of the shower, and dried off, she went out to the living room, and took Dan by the hand, and led him back into the bedroom, while explaining, as she was undressing him:

"I had a session of the Feline Mind Meld, with Percy, today. He says that the brain damage, that I previously had, is now apparently all gone. He believes that the last of it disappeared, when you guided me to the Enlightenment, today! The Orgasm which came at the end of the 247 minute orgasm, that you guided me to, was a fully new dimension of orgasm! Thank You!"

So, Dan took her on another peaceful journey, and while it did not quite reach what had been achieved that morning, both found the experience to be very satisfying. After she came down, they got cleaned up, and Cinderella phoned in for dinner, and they watched TV for a while, as she pondered what she would find waiting for her in the morning, once the computer had run the Evolutionary Algorithm for the whole night.

After dinner, and a while spent staring at a movie on DVD, they were ready to return to bed. Dan slid on in to home plate, and Cinderella immediately went into orgasm, and stayed there for about two hours. Eventually, Dan came, and started to bring Cinderella back down to Earth. They got cleaned up, and went to sleep for the night.

In the morning, they picked up from where they had left off, last night, and Cinderella made another journey. After breakfast, she went down to visit what she had begun to think of as a cyberspace copy of herself, except that this "Person" could now do much more than she could have ever hoped to do, and far more efficiently than she would have ever dreamed of.

As the weeks went by, she spent almost every day with her cyber-self, providing ever more mathematics texts, borrowed from various libraries. Most of the texts were kept only for just long enough to scan them into her knowledge-hungry computer, and then packaged up for a return trip, to the lending library. As she followed the computer's thought processes, it eventually occurred to Cinderella that her own were evolving, in both speed and understanding, as well. Finally, one day, she realized that she had been transformed, in another way. She now felt ready to attempt to tackle a Ph.D. in mathematics, the very one that had previously eluded her, and could have killed her, now many years ago.

She told Dan that she now felt ready to attempt to pursue her Doctorate in Mathematics, but she wanted him to know that she now believed that she understood what had gone wrong for her, when she was finishing up her master's, way back then. She also believed that she could complete the work, much faster and easier than would normally be expected, as she had gone through the "Transformation!"

She also then asked him about what he thought about the idea of them getting married, anytime soon?

Dan said, "Wait for just one moment", and he got up, and went to a drawer, and got out a little box, and returned, handing it to her, "I believe that the answer to that question is in here! Open it!"

Cinderella unwrapped the little box, and opened it, and squealed in joy! It was a $7500.00 sapphire and diamond ring, and inside was a little note, which said, "Will You Marry Me?"

She squealed, "Yes!", right there on the spot, and they hugged and kissed for quite a while. Then she asked, "So, when did you decide to ask me?"

Dan replied, "Well, do you remember that day that you reached the Enlightenment? After you were in orgasm for more than four hours, and then had a Transcendental Orgasm, that was when I decided that I was going to do it! I left the ring in the box, in a drawer, hoping that you might stumble across it, before too long. But that dragged on for just a little bit longer than I had figured on, since you were busy with your computer research, and I was just about to move it to an even more obvious place, like the front of the top shelf of the refrigerator. However, the rest is now history."

Cinderella asked, "So, how soon were you figuring on?"

Dan answered, "Well, I was going to leave that up to you! What level of ceremonies, and how many guests, and where, and when, were all going to be things that I was going to let you decide upon. Make it the wedding that you had always dreamed of, and as long as it does not become ridiculously expensive, it does not matter to me. As long as I get to have you, pretty much when I want to, there is not that much else that matters to me!"

"So", said Cinderella, taking the clue, "Would you like to have me, right now?"

Dan took her by the hand, and led her to the bedroom, and they undressed, and Dan entered her, and they kissed, and then Cinderella slipped away, to revisit the land of Orgasm, for more than two hours.

9

Cinderella spent the next several weeks alone, during the day, with her CDC 6500, learning more about the Evolutionary Algorithm, watching it evolve, and solve mathematics problems, and do proofs. Her understanding of mathematics grew profoundly, and with a speed that would not have been possible, had it not been for the resources that she had access to. Because the program mimicked, and enhanced, her own thought processes, it was just like she was the one who was personally solving the problems. The computer would sometimes start down a blind alley, or into a box canyon, on a problem, and as she was following the steps, she realized that this is just exactly the same pathway that she would have taken, before realizing that the pathway was a dead end. The advantage that she gained from this, is that the computer could discover that it was a bad choice of direction, in a tiny fraction of a second, or perhaps after several seconds, and discard the tactic, whereas she would have wasted perhaps several hours on what would have been a road to nowhere. In this way, she acquired decades of experience, wisdom, and maturity, in mathematics, and related fields, in just a few weeks. It was all easy enough to learn, because it was HER that was doing the learning, just at a greatly accelerated level. Her confidence, in both herself, and her mathematical abilities, became supreme. It was SHE who possessed this knowledge, and she could immediately recall how to prove anything, and solve any problem that she presented to herself. As she grew in knowledge, she also grew in maturity and confidence, which further accelerated the growth of her knowledge.

Cinderella would frequently test herself, weeks later, with the same problems that she had previously absorbed the understanding of, and found that she could easily recall, precisely, what had been done, because it was a part of her. She was the one who did it! The pathway to the solution was presented, with all of the blunders and false starts, and she could show it that way, or as the final, elegant, solution sequence. There was no great pressure on her brain.

Eventually, she felt that she was ready, and purchased some of the texts that would likely be used in her proposed Doctoral program, according to the current syllabi. She fed the textbooks to the Evolutionary Algorithm, and watched the changes in the code of the program occur, as new branches were reaching out to, and connecting with other parts of the program, writing new code, and creating new functions and subroutines, as parts of the solution process. Books, and subject matter, that would have previously been either impossible for her, in the condition that she was, until fairly recently, still in, were now easily within her grasp. Having passed through the Enlightenment, and into the Understanding, she had also now become one with the Singularity, and the Proto-Essence of her Self. All of the knowledge that she craved, she might now come to possess. She was also able to study the code generated by the Evolutionary Algorithm, and over time, could start to anticipate some of the changes and refinements which would occur within the program. She was watching a model of herself grow, and she, then, also would grow, as well. She now existed in both the physical world, and also in cyber-space, and had thus transcended the three-dimensional physical world.

The contents of the Doctoral texts were easily absorbed, and digested, by the Algorithm, and the results began spilling out, with Cinderella also quickly absorbing them all. At the end of each day, a back-up copy of her updated Essence was carefully stored away, and she would go back upstairs, and resume her Wedding plans.

Cinderella also continued with her investigation of which school she would like to do her Doctoral studies at, and she eventually elected to apply for admission to The University of Wales, at Swansea. Since she and Dan would likely have to live near there, for the duration, it would also have the benefit of being near Mary Ann, as well.

After some additional months spent on the various parts of both of her current goals, of planning a wedding, and pursuing a possible Doctoral program, she learned that she was accepted into the Ph.D. program, at Swansea, to start the following fall. The Wedding plans also came together nicely, after a few minor glitches, mostly related to scheduling. Dan helped where he could with this, but mostly it was going to be her show, the way that she wanted it to be. As he said, he did not really care all that much about the details, as long as he got to have her, which he did, pretty much every evening, and often in the morning, too, until they were both satisfied enough, for the moment.

One day, while all of this was going on, she received an E-mail from Percy, in which he requested to see her in his office, briefly. Cinderella sent back a reply, saying that she could be there, in just a few minutes, about as fast as she could walk up the stairs. Percy said that this would be just fine, and she went to Percy's office, to learn that the milling machine, and especially the revolutionary cutter, were now covered under several patents, and because of the detailed plans that she had created, have gone into production, and that she and Dan were going to be receiving a lot of money, over the next several years, as their share of what Percy's company would be earning, from sales and royalties.

Percy also wanted to do a Feline Mind Meld, with Cinderella, to examine her brain, and make sure that things were still doing okay.

So, Cinderella laid down on the couch, and Percy scanned her mind. After he was done, and she woke up, he said,

"Well, Cinderella, not only does there continue to be no signs of the brain damage that was previously there, but your brain now shows extensive evidence of synaptic growth, and other signs of an extensive, and apparently profound, amount of rewiring, with new connections having popped up everywhere! You must be doing quite well, on the Doctoral preparations!"

"Yes, Percy,", she replied, "I have been making very great progress in this area. Thanks to my Evolutionary Algorithm, I have covered more material, in just a few weeks, than I could have hoped to learn in decades. I think that I will soon be ready for my Doctoral studies."

"Then you have my full blessings, and we will cover your costs, and Dan's, too, so that he could be there to assist you, in whatever ways you may need such assistance."

Cinderella said, "Oh, thank you so much, Percy! I simply cannot find appropriate words, to tell you how much I love you!"

Percy replied, "Thank you, dear. You just did!"

Cinderella gave Percy a hug, and left his office.

Cinderella got some lunch, and returned to her work on preparing herself for the Doctoral program, and finalizing the wedding plans.

That evening, she told Dan about what Percy had told her, regarding the Milling Machine patents, and how they were going to be receiving a lot of money, over the next several years. She also told Dan that Percy had done a Feline Mind Meld, and saw great evidence of brain synaptic growth, which would appear to indicate that her mind was storing and recalling, with understanding, the immense amounts of knowledge that she was gaining, with the assistance of her Proto-Essence, the Evolutionary Algorithm, computer modeling, of her Self.

Eventually, the day came for the wedding. Cinderella's Father was there, as was Orla, and Maeve, and Mary Ann. Several members of Percy's organization were there, including all of the people that Dan worked with, such as John Griffin. Percy made sure that they all had free schedules for this event, and Percy and Katrina brought their children, as well.

Afterward, Dan and Cinderella learned that Percy wanted to see them, in his office, for just a very brief couple of minutes. So, they dropped by his office, and Percy said, through his voice synthesizer,

"When you two get back from your planned honeymoon, I am sending you on your REAL honeymoon! Cinderella, do you remember that one day that you were in my office, and I had said something about how I was pissed-off enough to have that government official that was interfering with my purchase of that piece of property in the British Virgin Islands, deported to French Guiana?"

Cinderella replied, "Well, yes, now that you mention it, I DO recall that! Why?"

Percy responded, "I was anticipating this day, and the wedding, even back then, and I am sending you two, to the British Virgin Islands, for a full month, and I will cover your costs!"

Dan was dumbstruck, and Cinderella was elated. Dan was, too, once he recovered some of his senses. They both thanked, and hugged, Percy, who then said,

"As soon as you get back from your trip, you will be flying there, on my own private jet, for a full month! It will also be a good opportunity for Cinderella to test whether her mathematical learning, of the relatively recent past is real, and profound enough to carry her safely through the Doctoral studies. I have full confidence that they will, and that she is now ready, but we should still test this, to be a little bit more confident that you are ready. So, I would like for you to leave your math texts, and notes, and all of your thoughts about math, or pretty much anything else, behind, until after you get back from the British Virgin Islands, and then you can continue with your Evolutionary Algorithm. If your knowledge and comprehension are real, then you are ready. Only time away from it can really tell."

Cinderella and Dan agreed that Percy was right, and they thanked him again for everything, and left.

While the trip that they took around Wales was spectacular, and Dan learned much more about the rich history of Wales, and they saw the remains of many of the castles, and Dan had the opportunities to learn about the culture, and acquire further knowledge of the language and geography of this fascinating place, they did agree, at the end, that it was just a bit too hectic of a schedule. They were both looking forward to a very nice, quiet, relaxing month at the home that Percy had purchased in the British Virgin Islands, and plenty of time, just to themselves, so that Dan and Cinderella could just spend time, fully alone. Percy was right about that one, too!

The very next day, they were on their own private ride, going for their real honeymoon, and after they got there, they had the options of what they wanted to do, and see. Mostly, they just relaxed, and tried to play each day by ear. If they felt like doing something, great, then they looked to see what they could find to do, that looked like it might be interesting, and easy enough. Otherwise, they just stayed out of sight, and Dan got to have Cinderella, pretty much whenever he wanted, just like she had promised!

After they returned to Wales, it was time for Cinderella to test the robustness of her knowledge, and also, to prepare for her Doctoral studies. They traveled to Swansea, and found an apartment sufficiently near the college.

Dan and Cinderella also had some opportunities to visit Mary Ann, as well, while they were living there. Cinderella found that her mathematical knowledge was fully and sufficiently sound preparation, and her professors were very impressed with her. She was able to take extra coursework each term, and thus finish faster than normal, and her Doctoral Thesis and Dissertation presented no difficulties, and she graduated with highest honors, at the top of her class. She finally had the Ph.D., in Mathematics, that had eluded her for a great many years, and they packed up, to return to their home, with Sir Percy.

After several years of a great many, further, spectacular mathematical achievements, Cinderella was awarded several honorary degrees, and titles, including Doctor Of Science, and the rank of Dame, the female equivalent of knight.

The day after being promoted to the rank of Dame, Sir Percival was satisfied that Cinderella was now fully ready, and is one of the select few who possessed the qualities of the "Fully Enlightened", and she was declared to be one of those who were now a Grandmaster of the Full Enlightenment of "Feline, Level Nine!"

They had two children, and one of Sir Percival's boys did, indeed, learn to communicate, using the digital keyboard translator.

Remember: "To Err is human, but to PURRRRRR is Feline!"

INTERLUDE..........?

45901866R00121

Made in the USA
Middletown, DE
17 July 2017